TULIPS *of* FATE

TULIPS

of

FATE

ILYA ROCKWELL

ISBN Paperback: 978-1-948375-01-6
ISBN Hardcover: 978-1-948375-02-3

Interior Design: Ghislain Viau

To Humanity and all the Humans
who Do Good Things

"Every man is guilty
of all the good he did not do."
—VOLTAIRE

CHAPTER 1

This was a regular village, with not much to differentiate it from the thousands of other villages and little towns around the world. There were all kinds of people that lived here, as in most places, but the majority were the kind, good citizens that lived mostly stagnant and simple, although not empty lives. These people, like everyone else in this world, however, didn't see their stagnation; they didn't look at themselves as being any less than anyone else. Like most people, they didn't want to know the disconcerting truth about their existence. They were completely satisfied with their routines. Happy even with the mendacious stories they grew up telling themselves about their lives. Maybe this was exactly why they were happy.

Granvill was the last person on Earth who would tell them the truth. Not because he wasn't an honest man, quite the opposite actually. But he never felt that he knew the truth better than anyone else. After all, he was just a human. One of them, living in this village, though in a different way than the most.

And it's not like people in this village didn't have the capacity to know anything they truly wanted to know, it was that they were more focused on the things that were important to them. And the truth was not one of those things. Families came first. Then they worried about local mayor elections, on trying the new pastry at the local coffee shop, or getting the newest haircuts, although the last one didn't provide them with many options to choose from. There was only one hairstylist in the whole village. The two other places called themselves barber shops instead; they could cut your hair slightly better than someone's mom could in their house, but anyone who wanted a fancy hairdo for a wedding, or some other big occasion had only one place to go – the salon.

Generally, people in the village were proud to be residents of this small place in the middle of nowhere. They were proud of their local newspaper, and any news that was good enough to be published in it. They were proud of their beautiful landscape; the village was surrounded by the woods in the west, green mountains a bit further on the same side past the woods, and it wasn't too far from the large lake a little towards the south where people went fishing, swimming, boating and could enjoy other recreational activities.

Although, there was a sort of dilemma with the lake. Another village was located just right of the shore, and any resident of that village could just walk to it anytime they desired. People of that village, Fish Haven, were proud of *their* lake and the fishing they did in it, as you could probably tell from the name of their village. They called the lake their own, without longing to share it with anyone else.

About half of Granvill's village was proud to be in the approximate vicinity of the lake and counted the lake as one of the attractions of visiting their home place. It was an easy fifteen-minute drive to the lake after all. But the other half of the village didn't want to associate themselves with the lake and looked down on the people of Fish Haven in the way that a housekeeper, who is smarter than everyone else, can look down on the local royalty who did nothing to achieve the status they have in the society, but were just lucky enough to be born into it. They thought the residents of Fish Haven were snobs and that they had nothing else going for them, besides that lucky shorter distance to the beautiful and tourist-desired lake.

But the people in Granvill's village did have some things that people in big cities didn't have. They had freedom from corporate bosses because they worked for smaller companies in which one of their neighbors who they knew as well as one of their own family members was most likely running it; they had kindness which showed in such a way that when one person was in trouble, the whole village would come to the rescue and figure out together how to help the unfortunate one; and they had more free time, not abused by brutal work hours, urgent appointments and endless meetings. They spent that time with the people they loved, sharing it in between their comfortable houses and the magnificent outdoors of the surrounding area.

Although the people in the village were not protected from envy, jealousy, frustration, anger, or even stress, they had a more peaceful and tranquil lifestyle that allowed them to celebrate more days and lose less sleep because of their overwhelming problems.

This was the main reason why Granvill ended up here. That's exactly what he wanted, what he was looking for. He had lived through enough extraordinary experiences in his previous life, but in this one he wanted peace and quiet.

Despite Granvill living in the village for the past seven years, no one knew exactly how old he was or what exactly had brought him here, just that he showed up one day and stayed. When the man decided to shave or trim his hair at all, he could look like he is in his early fifties, but on a regular unshaven day, people probably would give him a lot closer to seventy. His gray beard and gray uncombed hair spreading everywhere around his head was giving off the impression that he was too old to care about his appearance. He walked almost straight, in a healthy and confident kind of way, but slow, almost as if he was in meditation mode, which also added to his image of being an old grandpa.

Granvill was quiet and lived his life mostly isolated. He spent a lot of time in the woods or the mountains. He would fish once in a while, and he was well-mannered and gracious any time he would interact with the locals, like when buying the local newspaper or groceries in one of small village shops, but he almost never talked about himself. People in the village knew that Granvill lived alone and didn't have any family, but they didn't know why. He was alone for such a long time, people just assumed that he never married or had any kids. No one knew his story, and, regardless, he wasn't about to tell anyone.

It wasn't like the villagers really cared though. He was just another alone old man slowly transporting his body from one spot in the village to another. They would greet him politely when they saw him, and get the same polite greeting back from him, and usually that would be the end of it. Sometimes they would have a minute-long conversation about the weather, or how his last fishing trip was.

Granvill had something to say on almost any occasion when he was asked about something in particular. There was enough life experience and knowledge in the fiber of that old body to give any kind of information or advice. But he had nothing at all to say when he wasn't asked it probably was the biggest disconnect from him to the youth of the village. While millennials were eager to share their life events either on social media or in person with anyone who wanted to hear them, and not just life events – everything. They would indulge themselves in conversations about what they had for breakfast, what they think of the latest local newspaper issue, what they think about painting the fence around the city hall a different color, or how many more fish they are going to catch next week when the weather will be better suited for fishing.

Again, the old man wasn't volunteering any information about anything. Though quite often, he would still ask people around if they needed any help, and many would gladly accept it. After that, they would extend their gratitude, and Granvill would politely accept it and quietly move on about his own day, like nothing even happened.

This fall, Granvill was doing something else that he hadn't done before. He had cleared space in his garden to plant something new. No one in the village knew if Granvill had any money at all or if he was barely surviving on government help, but he was known to pull off some big transactions every once in a while. This time, the big transaction happened to be connected to a large pickup truck that came in to the village.

The village outsider, who happened to be the delivery guy named Keith, pulled up near Granvill's modern, wooden, country-style two-story house. Keith looked at the number on the mailbox on the front lawn and confirmed that this was the right place. He didn't notice the house owner just yet. Granvill was sitting outside on the ground amongst green grass that was at least a foot tall. The old man was enjoying the sunny warm day while waiting for the delivery. He looked like his usual self, his hair sticking out in different directions and his beard, while trimmed, still covered his whole chin. He was wearing a red and black flannel shirt, jeans, and ordinary black boots on his feet. The old man slowly stood up from the ground and, with a smile on his face, approached the outsider, who had noticed him as soon as he started to move. They exchanged some common pleasantries, and then Granvill gave Keith directions on where to unload the delivery.

The delivery was quite unusual in its nature; it was not often Keith had to bring such a big order, and have it not be a place of business. The whole bed of the truck was filled with large blue crates. Keith started to unload them, following Granvill's instructions on where to place them. He walked into the very clean and well-organized house and saw a glass floral cooler installed on the first floor on the opposite side of a large open kitchen. Keith had noticed that all the kitchen appliances were brand new and modern. Most of the things inside the house looked better than the house from the outside, which could use newer materials and the fixing of a few wood panels, although even his first look was pleasant as well.

"Should I stick them up here on shelves or leave them on the ground?" asked Keith.

"Either way works, but if you can get them on the shelves, that would be great. Thank you," responded Granvill.

Keith nodded in agreement and started arranging the crates around the shelves, which were custom ordered by the owner and built inside of the walk-in glass cooler. While he was doing that, Granvill went back to the truck and picked up two crates of his own. He was quite strong for his age. Although, if he was only in his fifties, it made even more sense. All of his actions were almost in slow motion, slowly moving his body through the universe, but yet smooth and direct, getting the job done in an efficient manner. There were about twenty-five crates in total, and Keith unloaded most of them, with Granvill making two trips to help out the delivery man. Once the job was done, the old man looked at the floral cooler, full of crates now, with a smile on his face. Granvill thanked the driver, shook his hand, gave him a ten-dollar tip, and wished him a great day. Keith got inside of his truck and continued on his with his deliveries.

The next morning Granvill got up as usual, without his alarm clock, which he used only in emergencies. He liked to let his body rest and wake up on its own most days. That was one of the reasons why he came to the village, to get away from appointments and alarm clocks who kept humans as prisoners of their will.

Today he woke up at 8:14am. Per his morning routine, he took a shower first, then he got dressed and slowly moved his body to the kitchen. He put a cast iron tea pot filled with water on the stove and turned the gas on. Granvill didn't have a TV in his house, or internet or a phone. The only way to reach him was by mail, but no one was trying to reach him, so it didn't matter anyways. Once in a while, he would receive a credit card application invitation, or another coupon for one of the big chain stores which he could only find outside of the village. The closest big city with any of those stores was two and a half hours away. He left that life behind and mostly everything that went with it. Granvill would go there three or four times a year at the most. He was happy with his life away from it, and it never crossed his mind to go back to the city life.

He liked music in the morning, as it helped him to establish the good mood for the rest of the day. He listened to old CDs and played them in his older model of a laptop, the only real technology in his house. He put a CD of one of his favorites, who was dear to his heart, into the laptop while waiting for the water to boil. The typical, yet unmistakable, Italian light baritone of Frank Sinatra filled the room with the right equlibrium.

Granvill rarely had guests in his house, although if anyone in his village asked to be one, the doors would always be open. But he knew no one was waiting for his invitation, and no one was in any hurry to invite themselves either. There was a closed circle of association between Granvill and the rest of the village. There were villagers who were curious in their neighborly spirit who may have asked for it at some point, but that bridge was never built between them and the old man. Probably half of the village doesn't even know where he lives, thought the old man at this moment. His house was located on the outskirts, and even the mailman complained when he had to deliver mail to this address, as he had to adjust his regular route. It's not like it was far. Even walking, it was maybe fifteen minutes at the most from Granvill's house to the rest of the village and twenty-five minutes to downtown with all the stores and markets. Driving distance was even less of course, so the mailman really didn't have a good reason to complain about it but complaining was probably a requirement to the federal job, so he did follow that rule to the letter and complained to Granvill every time he delivered a piece of mail to him.

The teapot started to whistle, while Sinatra was singing:

"The way you wear your hat.

The way you sip your tea.

The memory of all of that —

No, no — they can't take that away from me."

The old man slowly came over to the stove and turned it off. He then took his black ceramic cup, poured a spoon of instant coffee into it, added the water from the pot, and then added two ice cubes from the freezer to make the coffee the right room temperature so he could drink it right away. He wasn't in a particular hurry, and he definitely could wait for the coffee to cool down on its own, but this was one of the old habits he kept from the times when he was living as busy of a life as everybody else around him. Instant coffee was also one of those habits. It seemed he had at least two habits still left over. He had in mind the idea of switching to a nice espresso machine, which he always wanted when he was younger, but it got less relevant with time, so he never bought one. So, instant coffee it is then.

He took the coffee cup in his hand and slowly proceeded out of the kitchen. He walked through the dining room, then to the front door, and when he was outside, he walked over to the long green bench that seemed even older than the house, probably even older than he was. Maybe one of the old landowners had built it, and it survived all the changes of the property throughout the years. He sat down on the bench, sipped his coffee and looked up into the sky, relaxed yet focused, like he was trying to send his hidden powers into the universe.

CHAPTER 2

Today wasn't like yesterday or the day before that. While the morning routine didn't change at all, the plan for the rest of the day was going to be different than usual. Granvill went to check on his delivery inside of the custom built, walk-in cooler, and looked over at the blue plastic crates. It made him more excited than he had been about anything for a while. He was a typical happy man, and he enjoyed his quiet life at the village, but this newly found idea gave him a new sense of purpose. A feeling he loved most of his life, and that feeling wasn't as easy to stumble upon in his retirement.

He walked over to peer inside the blue crates. Inside were beautiful tulip bulbs of all different colors: red, purple, pink, white, yellow, and some rainbow variations as well. He had high expectations for the tulips. He never had them before. He had a small garden on the east side of his house, where he grew some vegetables, and some simple plants, mostly sunflowers and hardy geraniums, that didn't require a lot of day to day care. He had cucumbers, but not tomatoes, although he loved to use both in his cooking, tomatoes even more so, but as it turned out the fruit required more care, so Granvill would rather buy them at the local market.

Local farmers knew what they were doing, and he was totally fine with supporting them. After all, he didn't retire from a successful corporate life negotiating real estate deals to turn around and work long hours in the ground. Like most things in his life today, he enjoyed gardening as a hobby, investing his time on his terms, and not because it was a must to do on certain days, or even worse, every day. These tulips were a one-time project that he could commit himself to. After he was done with it, he could go back to his routine.

The tulips were not going inside of his garden though. He had a nice patio on the south side of the house facing the mountains, away from the rest of the village, and a lot of space in between the woods and his house that was perfect for planting the tulips. The open stretch of land between the woods and his house reached all the way to the last half mile just before the wood line. He didn't have a fence on that side, but there was unpaved road and a couple of trails leading to the woods going parallel to the mountains, connecting the village downtown to the outdoor adventures for the locals. And then, just a bit further from the unpaved road on his side of the land, there was a stick hammered into the ground, about three feet tall, and half a foot was planted, the rest visible enough for the villagers to know where Granvill's land started. At the top of the stick Granvill hung a large, dark red flag that was visible from the road, especially on days when the wind would swirl the piece of fabric around, doing its best to give the napkin freedom. To no avail, the napkin was there as long as Granvill was in this house, almost seven years. It really was the perfect place for planting tulips.

He started working in the chosen spot soon after his lunch, digging holes, planting bulbs deep in the ground, making sure there was enough distance in between them. While tulips didn't need to be watered regularly, they needed water in the beginning to start the process of growing. But he was glad it hadn't been raining in a while, and while generally a dry fall like this was common for the beginning of the season around here, it was not guaranteed. There would be some heavy rains coming eventually. There was no doubt about that. They come every year. Granvill wasn't even sure the tulips would grow here, but he was hoping they would.

When he finished the first patch, he was pleased with the work that had been done. He could see the future so clearly, it's as if he was psychic, – a field filled with colorful tulips. Every person walking or driving into the woods for picnics, hiking, or any other purpose would see the field from the unpaved road, and it was the perfect spot for Granvill too. He would be able to see the flowers from the kitchen window every morning when he was making his coffee, and he could also see the spot from the backside patio where he usually devoured his late-night drink in silence. Granvill smiled just thinking about it.

He worked hard for the next three days as well. Every morning he would wake up even earlier than the previous one, his excitement uncontainable, and worked for as long as he could. The last two days, he worked all the way to the sunset. He loved those beautiful sun self-demonstrations. It was like a personal fashion runway, showing itself in the best light possible. They were scheduled, inevitable, and amazingly stunning. It was one of the things that Granvill could count on to make his life precious. This was why he came to this village. A peaceful life, freedom, and a sunset any day he wanted. There was no day he could miss one unless he decided so on his own. Sometimes he was busy with other things. He didn't catch the sunrise as often, but when he did, he was even more grateful for the life he had.

After four days of work, the field was full enough. Granvill spent the morning of the fifth day to finish off the crate he had started. He only used six crates out of his delivery to plant outside, and there was more space in the field, but the old man had other plans for the remaining tulips. He went into the house, grabbed a large sporty duffle bag, and went inside of the cooler, starting to fill it with the tulip bulbs out of the crates. Carefully. Hoping they wouldn't break in the next thirty minutes. When the duffle bag was full, he was satisfied with his work. There was still enough time in the day to do the next step.

Granvill started walking toward the village. It was a peaceful day outside, a bit cloudy, but there was still the sun, constantly reminding of its existence every few minutes, shining brightly for a half a minute and then hiding again in the white fascinating shapes of sky foam barely moving in a light wind. Granvill found joy in any kind of weather, he liked rainy days and snowy days, windy days, and sunny days. He never looked at the weather predictions, even when he was planning his fishing trips, and just accepted the conditions the way they were presented to him that day. Sometimes he would adjust his plans a little based on the moment, but never in advance.

After a short, slowly paced walk, Granvill reached the first building of the village where most people lived. He passed the building of the church, but since it was Saturday, there was no one in there. People that believed in God followed a strict schedule. He had passed the house of the Person with No Imagination, and the house of the Selfish Person. The houses of the deeply Republican Person and deeply Democrat Person as they were right across each other and passed them both.

He then passed the house of Comfort Zone Person and reached a one-story building that looked like most of the houses in the village, not the biggest, the smallest, nor the fanciest either. Almost a regular house. What differentiated it from its neighbors was the fact that it was going through a transition. It used to be the house of the Person with the Deepest Family Values, but that person got old and was sent to one of the retirement homes in Fish Haven by her kids, so now it is occupied by the Person Without Care for Others. He was in his late twenties, and still felt like his life was just starting, and felt that he needed time to build the life he truly wanted. Having no distraction to attend to after his mother was placed in the retirement home, he had the house all to himself to allow him to do things he did care for: random dates with the local and tourist women, playing video games, watching any movie uninterrupted, and drinking beer at any time of the day. Those were the things that made him happy. He was also a construction worker, so he spent some of his valuable time doing that too, but he knew it was just a temporary gig.

One day he will own a business, like the most successful people in the county did, maybe even a construction company, because, God knows, the construction business is good, especially if you serve a whole area, like Fish Haven and the other surrounding towns. He also felt that the company he worked for, which was owned by the Person with Bad Luck, could do so much better than it did currently. The Person with Bad Luck inherited the business from his father, but never really wanted to be a part of it, but since his bad luck followed him everywhere, he didn't search for the one thing that he was meant to do in this universe, and he got stuck instead. Stuck with the company that happened to be providing the bread on his table for the last twenty some years.

But the Person without Care for Others didn't care about that. He just knew that his time would come, and his mother was probably better off in the retirement home anyway. His siblings were of a similar opinion as they lived too far away from the village to take her in. Why would she want, why would anyone want, to spend her last days in the lonely house with no one to serve her? In the house where she grew up and built her life with her husband until his passing? In the house where she raised her only son? In the retirement home she had everything she ever needed. There she had the pleasure of people attending to her, serving her, cooking meals for her, and helping to clean after her. Who wouldn't want that?

When the Person without Care for Others would grow old, he would prefer to be in that kind of retirement home. But hopefully with more money in his pocket. He wasn't planning to have kids though, so most likely this is where he would be anyways. Unless he marries a younger woman, who would be in better health than him in his old age, then she would take care of him in his house. *Yes, that would be even better*, imagined the construction worker.

Granvill knew most of the people in the village, he lived here long enough to meet everyone at some point or another. When the Person without Care for others would cross paths with the old man, he would only see just that: an old man with uncombed hair and no worries in his life. In the same exact moment, the old man would see how the Person without Care for others interacted with another human being at the register of a grocery store, how he wouldn't even look back to see if he should consider holding the door for someone behind him, how he never asked anyone how they were doing, and how he never even looked deep in a stranger's eyes to see if they were having a good day.

Granvill saw everything, and he remembered most of it. His conclusions didn't form his final opinion about one person or another, as his life experiences taught him to not judge people without walking in their shoes, but at the same time, he always made some mental marks in his mind with different scenarios to be able to analyze, correctly more often than not, what kind of behavior people tend to lean to in one situation or another.

Granvill passed a few more houses on the way to the city hall, which was exactly where he was headed to. He stopped right in front of the large building, in the scale of this small village, which was still just a one-story architectural structure with higher ceilings. But this establishment was one of the oldest buildings in this place and had some significant historic value.

Granvill then turned away from the city hall and proceeded crossing the road to the other side of the street. Here, there was a piece of an empty land, that was clear in front of the city hall, in between the local fire station and the hair salon for the fancy, elegant, and expensive hairdos, which was busy most of the time. He proceeded to that piece of land and stopped at the furthest end away from the city hall. The land looked about thirty yards long, and there was some grass growing which was mowed carefully by the local landscapers, but didn't have any flowers, *yet*.

Granvill was going to change that. He sat on the ground without any disregard for his surroundings, took out a small hand shovel which was hidden in a pocket in his duffle bag as well, and proceeded to make a hole big enough to place the first tulip bulb. When the hole was done, he reached out to the duffle bag one more time, and took out a tulip bulb, which he carefully placed into the ground, with the tip of the bulb facing up. He then covered it with soil and moved on a few inches to make another hole.

While he was at work, there were a few people passing by, some busy with their own lives as they weren't retired like Granvill, while others were enjoying the post-work period of their life as well. Granvill could recognize the difference by the pace with which different people moved through life. Some of the locals passing by looked curiously at Granvill, some waved at him, some nodded their heads, but no one had thought to stop and start any kind of conversation with him. It seemed to them that the old man was occupied enough. They were not sure with what exactly, but they assumed the city hall gave him permission to do whatever he was doing. After all, no one in this village really broke any laws. Everyone knew each other, and everyone took care of themselves and their neighbors. The village didn't even have a police department. What for? The worst thing that took place in here last year was the eleven-year-old kid who stole candy from the local grocery store. The kid got caught by one of the customers who saw the whole development, and then all three adults who were in the store at that moment gave him a lecture and then called his parents who gave another lecture, or whichever form of punishment they believed in, at home as well.

When Granvill reached back into the duffle bag, he realized that all the tulip bulbs were already in the ground; he looked up at the sky and saw that he wouldn't be able to come back here tonight, it would be dark in less than an hour for sure, if not sooner.

The freshly self-appointed gardener decided to stop by at the local coffee shop before he went home. The coffee shop was owned by the Person Who Smiled at Everyone, and that's why it was quite a popular place, and loved by most, including Granvill.

The coffee shop was just a block away, past the hair salon, then a local bar, then the insurance office, and the local boutique. The coffee shop was inside of an older building as well, almost as old as the city hall, but the interior was recently renovated. Although, it still had wooden tables and a giant brick fireplace which was used only in the winter time. It had also a patio with a few tables outside, but it was empty at this moment, as the darkness of the night was ready to cover the village. Granvill walked into the coffee shop, and almost right away, he saw the Person who Smiled at Everyone and her helper most days, the Girl Who Knew Everything.

The Girl Who Knew Everything graduated Fish Haven high school just a bit over a year ago, yet she was always the girl who knew more than the next person. She felt like she was always better than everyone else around her, and no one else was up to her standard, and that's why, of course, she was working full-time at this coffee shop. Her bills never cared if she was better than life itself, they were coming after her anyways.

The Person Who Smiled at Everyone was about forty years old, and she was a very beautiful woman, who grew a few wrinkles lately, first after her divorce from the Person without Principles, and then from her teenage son who decided to add a few as well. When she saw Granvill, she let her warm smile take over her whole face and show perfectly arranged white teeth in the process. She greeted The Old Man and asked him what he would like today.

"I am not so sure today, any advice?" The Old Man felt a bit in the crossroads of the only major decision for the day.

"You could always try my special Peruvian tea with a cinnamon infusion," she blurted out with a hopeful voice and a smile.

"You know, that's a great idea, let me try that. I should come more often here to try all the new things you kids drink these days."

"Us "kids"? Haha," Now her smile became a laughter, and it was a beautiful laughter, one that Granvill wished he heard more often. "You know, I am already in my forties, right?"

"Probably barely, but you look ten years younger, and your smile even younger than that," Granvill grinned saying those words and looked deeply into her eyes. He wanted to make sure she understood that the compliment wasn't a regular nice sounding line, but a sincere statement from his old heart.

The Person Who Smiled at Everyone blushed for a second and looked again at the strange man who she saw so many times here, but still knew nothing about, and then thanked him for the compliment. She smiled at him again:

"If you sit down and give me one minute, I will bring you your tea."

Granvill nodded, smiled back, and proceeded to an available table near the left wall, across from the fireplace. The place wasn't too busy right now, about half full. This was a good time of the day to come. In the morning, this place was full of middle-aged people who rushed to work to put more meaningful hours of their life into some project, company, or paycheck. They needed a shot or two of caffeine to help them achieve that. In the evening, there were more young people, high school kids and young adults who graduated not long ago but didn't go to college. There was no local college here, so anyone who wanted to go to one had to leave the county and go to the big city which was about a two-and-a-half-hour drive away from the village. Most of those college graduates would never return here, unless it was for a wedding of their younger sibling or the funeral of their parents.

But there were more than one reason why high school kids loved this place. For one, apparently, nowadays young people were all into coffee, as it was trendy and cool, and they liked to hang out here and sip their cappuccinos and lattes, while gossiping about their classmates or friends, or the next big thing on the social media. But the second reason had nothing to do with the coffee, but rather the proximity of the place to one of the two local bars, which was practically next door. This way, the kids could tell their parents that they had spent all their time that evening at the coffee shop. Sometimes parents themselves would drive them and drop them off at the coffee place, but most of the kids ended up drinking margaritas instead.

But this was a bit early for those kids, so the place wasn't busy yet. While Granvill was sitting at his table and waiting for his tea, he was looking at the people around him. He loved to notice the little things around him. He believed that the little things could tell a lot more about people than the big things.

There was simple reasoning behind it. When people want to lie, deceive or adjust the truth to their liking, they are really focused about big and obvious events that they *know* other people will pay attention to, but sometimes they just don't have mental energy left to care how at the end of a frustrating day they treat a waiter, for example. Those are the little things that Granvill would see and apply to his knowledge database about the residents of the village.

At this moment in the coffee shop, among other people, he saw the Person Who Felt Insecure in Relationships. She was beautiful, gorgeous actually, but she was so insecure in her relationships with men that she was still single, and probably not too happy about her life. She knew about her insecurities but couldn't take over that control in her brain, she just didn't know that the person needs to control their mind, not the other way around. Granvill called it mental self-discipline, and he knew most people in the village didn't have it. That's why there were smokers who wanted to quit smoking. Also, drinkers, gamblers, and cheaters who wanted to kick their vices as well. They, all in a different manner, let their brain tell them how to do things in life, how to react to different situations, and how to be the person they didn't want to be. Very few, if any, were proud of themselves for smoking, drinking, gambling or being insecure, yet they didn't know how to escape their reality.

Granvill was always nice to the Person Who Felt Insecure in Relationships, and she was nice back as well, as she was a nice person really. She tried to hide her insecurities and most of the time, it worked well for her. She was successful at her job, as she was the only financial advisor in the village, and two out of the three rich people. Most of the retirees, and the middle-class people, were her clients. Another rich person used some fancy advisor from the big city, but the fact that the other two didn't follow that example, and stayed with their local advisor, said a lot about the skills and professionalism of the Person Who Felt Insecure in Relationships. She was extremely good at what she did, and in some ways, her insecurities forced her to be more prepared for each client, because her insecurities would spill in other areas of her life if she let them. But the one area she didn't manage to figure out was the intimate relationships, maybe because it was at a deeper, more personal level and she just didn't have enough energy to fight those doubts twenty-four-seven.

The Person Who Felt Insecure in Relationships was sitting alone near the fireplace. There was no fire in the pit, and that's why it was quite an isolated spot in the shop this time of the year: no one wanted to sit beside a fireplace without fire.

Right behind the gorgeous insecure girl, there was a couple, who just recently became a couple and neither one was sure if this is going to work out for them long-term, but they enjoyed each other's company for now and spent a lot of time together. The Night Fun Party Person was thrilled to go out with her boyfriend instead of her girlfriends, not only because it added a new element to the fun time, but also because it felt more intimate with him and waking up together in the morning was more meaningful to her. She was hoping her boyfriend enjoyed all of that as much as she did. Of course, sometimes she was up to a quiet evening of just watching Netflix or playing board games, but Friday night wasn't created for that, and she felt it was almost a crime to not do real fun on Friday nights.

Her boyfriend, the Person Who Wanted to Please Everyone, was not as much into it as his girlfriend, but he did like *her*, and because of *her*, he was doing many things that he had never done before, which on its own excited him in a new exuberating way. He wished sometimes to stay at home certain nights, but he also didn't want his girlfriend to not get what she really wanted, so he followed her lead. Granvill noticed that the couple seemed quite happy together, they held hands often, smiled at each other, kissed in public, and showed affection toward each other when any opportunity presented itself. Only time would tell if this couple meant to be together, either they would continue to evolve and understand each other, and grow respect and commitment on both sides, or they would let their differences dictate their lifestyle which will make one of them feel incomplete and not supported by the other at some point. Most people in the village who knew the couple had little belief that the fling would last. However, Granvill wasn't about making predictions, he only cared about this moment, and it was nice to see happy people sharing time and space in this universe.

There were a few others in the coffee shop, either enjoying their drink, or the company of their confidants, or both; but at this time the Person Who Smiled at Everyone came up to his table with a cup in her hands.

"Your Peruvian tea, Sir," proclaimed the owner of the shop while putting the cup down in front of her guest.

"Thank you so much," Granvill again looked into her eyes, like there was no one else in this place.

"Of course."

The owner blushed for a second again, but then she remembered a question that was on her mind for a while. It seemed like as good a time as any to get the answer.

"May I ask you something?"

"Shoot," agreed the old man without hesitation.

The woman fixed her dark beautiful hair with her hand, putting a strand of hair behind her right ear, and then nervously proceeded with her question:

"Do you have any friends in this village?"

She saw that Granvill looked a bit puzzled, so she decided to explain herself further. She pulled a chair a bit closer to her and then quickly sat down.

"I mean, you know, I am sure you heard about my divorce, of course you have, everyone has heard."

She looked at the old man again, and saw a tiny nod confirming he had heard about it. And she continued, while looking away trying to recollect her experience:

"Just before the divorce, I thought I had many friends, but after, I realized that most of the people were either his friends, or some were couples spending time with us as a couple, or some just turned away for… I am not even sure why exactly, but they did. And I don't have that many friends anymore. And you… I don't see you with friends, and you are always so nice, when you see people, but you never come *with* people, or have a meeting scheduled to see someone here. So, you seem like you don't *want* to have friends? Yet… You still look happy… You look quite happy to me."

Now she was ready for some response, and she looked at the old man again.

Granvill was listening cautiously, and he was glad she asked him that. He wasn't offended by the rash assumption about his friendships at all and was ready to give his idea on that topic.

"My dear. There are never enough of friends in this life, especially real friends. They are like family to us. But time does separate real friends from the people who conveniently spend time with us until it's no longer convenient for them. That's life. I am sorry to hear that you have lost a few people who you counted on, but most likely, you are better off without them in your life."

The Person Who Smiled at Everyone paid close attention to the words of the old man, like they were words from the Bible itself. In this moment, she needed someone with more life experience to tell her what was ok, and what was not. She needed some kind of direction, and she didn't have many options to get that direction from. She was really hoping that this nice old man could give her all the answers that caused a distraught state of her mind, even if for a little while.

"But the good thing about life, it only takes five minutes to meet a new person, or make a new friend, or turn something in your life around. Almost anything can happen in just five minutes. And those five minutes can happen anytime, anywhere.

You should make an effort to make new friends, open new doors, look at old places from new angles, and see what life will bring you. I am sure, when you make new friends, you will look back and will pinpoint those exact five minutes that happened to you so unexpectedly."

He smiled at her and took the cup of the Peruvian tea and slowly brought it to his lips, and then, just as slowly, tilted the cup so the hot liquid would carefully flow into his mouth. The taste of it was pleasant, albeit quite strong, and the old man was happy with the spontaneous choice of his drink.

"It sounds all so easy, but I don't know how to do that. I know most of the people in this village, and I don't know how you can make new friends in a place where you already know everyone. There are no doors *to open*."

The Person Who Smiled at Everyone wasn't smiling; just because that characteristic suited her, at this moment she didn't feel the need to cover her fears and she could let strangers see what she is really feeling for once.

"I understand, it's not as easy as it sounds. And I am not trying to preach or anything here. But you asked my advice, and here it is. One thing I do know, there are always new doors to open out there, no matter how small our village is," persisted the old man.

He thought for a second about something that could make the person across from him to feel better, and then proposed:

"If you don't mind, let me do this for you, and it would mean the world to me, if you agree."

He paused for a mere moment to make sure he wanted to do what he was about to offer.

"I know you live at a lovely white house with a backyard not far from here, and I have a whole bunch of tulip bulbs which I don't know what to do with. I can come tomorrow morning to your house, and plant some of the tulips I have in your backyard, and we will see what life will bring us after that."

The Person Who Smiled at Everyone looked confused for a minute.

"But why?" she asked.

"Wouldn't that be a new door in your life? Something you had never done before?" Calmly and confidently replied the old man.

"Yes, yes, I guess it would be," she mused after a while finally understanding what he meant.

"You have nothing to lose here. At the very worst, the flowers will die, and you will get your backyard back. Nothing will change. And at the best… who knows?"

Granvill was sure of the idea and he felt confident the woman will say yes. But at the end of the day, it was up to her to make that small insignificant decision, and he wasn't planning to pursue the idea beyond his last sentence.

The woman was getting rid of her confusion, and the more she thought about it, the more she liked the idea. This nice old man was right, she had nothing to lose, and it was kind of him to offer something like that.

"How much would I owe you?" she had one last question to ask.

"Nothing at all. You will never owe me anything."

Granvill was looking into her eyes with sincerity and care. "But if you would like to make a cup of tea or coffee for me, I wouldn't say no."

He smiled, and she smiled back at him.

"Yes, I can do that."

"Then I will see you tomorrow morning, about 8 am is that ok?"

"8 am works. What's kind of flowers are they, you said?"

"Tulips."

Granvill suddenly thought of something and followed up his thought with a question:

"What's your favorite color?"

"Pink," the Person Who Smiled at Everyone replied.

"Would you like pink tulips in your backyard then?"

The shop owner was even more excited now. She already could imagine how beautiful the flowers would look in her backyard.

"Yes, please. Pink tulips would be perfect," she gave the old man one of the biggest smiles of all, not the one she would give to every customer because that's who she was, but because she was actually happy, just for this one moment, when she was probably gaining a garden of tulips outside of her home, but also maybe even a new friend.

After they were done with the conversation, the woman left Granvill to himself at his table, not forgetting to thank him for his kindness, and while she felt that the answer she got wasn't exactly what she was looking for, as it didn't bring her confidence that she would make new friends who she can go shopping with, or go to movies with, or talk about coffee and men with, but she had something to look forward to tomorrow morning where she would see her tulips planted.

Granvill really enjoyed his Peruvian tea, not only because it tasted good, but also because he was happy about being able to connect more with the Person Who Smiled at Everyone. She always was nice and polite, and seemed to him like a good person. And, as he realized even before today, that her smile wasn't always totally sincere, because of her divorce and her teenage son, and probably some other problems that she went through, including, as he knew now, the loss of some friendships along the way.

He was in his thoughts quite deeply when he heard a voice right in front of him, not realizing that another person came up to his table. He flinched and then turned his focus towards the Person Who Felt Insecure in Relationships. He didn't notice when she left her table near the fireplace and started approaching him, and he wasn't sure why either. Not many people had initiated conversations with him, but it seemed like he was a magnet today.

"Hi, Mister Granvill," she approached him with the extreme caution. "I don't see you that often, may I use this opportunity to mention something?"

Granvill nodded in agreement.

"I have brought up the topic a couple of times, but never got a real answer to. If you need a financial advisor with local support and personal touch, I am here."

Granvill thought for a second about what to say.

"I am not rich, and I don't have a retirement account like most." responded Granvill.

She thought of the appropriate answer for a minute, the one that would allow her chance to acquire a new client alive.

"May I ask, how do you manage then? Also, you don't have to be rich to be my client, and financial planning goes beyond just managing your money. Have you thought what you are going to do with your house, for example, after your passing? Do you have a family to pass it to? Maybe to your favorite charity? I think it is paid off, correct?"

Granvill thought again for a second, but he knew he didn't want to have this conversation right now.

"You know, to be honest, I do need to sit down with you and talk about all of that, but I have a big project in mind which will occupy me all the way to May of next year, but after that we can sit down and have this conversation, if you don't mind."

"Of course, Sir. Anytime that's good for you is good for me." She couldn't contain her smile.

This was far from any kind of guarantee that they would ever sit down and talk about the man's finances, but this was as close as she ever got with the old man about the topic.

There were some people in the village that thought that Granvill had money, maybe not too much, but more than he would need in however many years he had left on Earth, and since he didn't seem to have any family, people did wonder what would happen to his estate and his bank accounts. But all of that was just speculations and gossips, no one really knew with certainty, and the idea that the Person Who Felt Insecure in the Relationships may find out soon enough, got her excited almost as much as the possibility of gaining a new client.

She reminded Granvill to call her anytime if he needed help or had a question, and she returned to her table near the fireplace. Granvill wasn't going to think about this conversation even one more minute, he meant what he said though, around May, which was still almost six months away, he would take it more seriously, but for now, he had other plans, and he was hoping that life wouldn't feel like interrupting them anytime soon.

When Granvill returned to his house that evening, he felt good about his day. He planted some tulips near the city hall, which was his primary objective for the day, but he also had a lovely conversation with the coffee shop owner, and he was looking forward to planting more tulips tomorrow. He never felt silly about his idea of spreading the tulips around the village without asking anyone, but it was an even better feeling putting them in the ground for someone else with their permission.

He needed to separate pink tulips tomorrow morning before he went to his new acquaintance's house. *Tomorrow will be another good day*, thought Granvill. He decided to go to bed earlier than usual, and while falling asleep didn't come easy to him that night, he still managed to leave the reality of the day behind and put his mind into rest mode, exploring his dreams created by his subconscious.

In his dream he saw the whole village covered in the beautiful tulips he planted, and even people from Fish Haven would come to see them as some kind of special tourist attraction. He also saw two main characters in his dream, the Person Who Smiled at Everyone celebrating her life with her new boyfriend, a nameless unknown man who seemed perfect for her. The couple was sitting outside of her white house, in front of the backyard filled with pink tulips, and they were comfortable with each other, snuggling, and hugging each other, and really enjoying each other's company. Granvill felt that the garden built by his own hands had something to do with her newly found happiness. That kind of dream brought a warm feeling to the old man, and it allowed him to get a good night of sleep.

CHAPTER 3

The next morning Granvill woke up minutes before the alarm was intended to go off. It was a rare occasion on its own, that he set the alarm in first place, and 7am was just an hour or so short of his normal time, but his eyes were open at 6:47am, and he quickly, by his standards, proceeded to the shower. He made himself coffee and walked to the cooler to separate pink tulips from the rest. He ordered most of the popular colors, as he didn't have a favorite color, and he liked the variety. After going through three different crates of tulip bulbs, he had collected a full duffle bag of pink ones.

He left the house and went on enjoying his morning walk. When he arrived at his destination, it was just a couple of minutes before eight, and he knocked on the door with full confidence. Almost immediately, he heard steps behind the door, and soon after that, the door opened, and the Person Who Smiled at Everyone was revealed in front of him. She was wearing a bright yellow sweater, and jeans, not much different from what she would wear any other day.

After greeting each other, she invited the old man in and showed him the backyard. The backyard was quite nice; it wasn't too big but had good space and was big enough to put a pool in if she would want something like that. There were a couple of bushes on each side of the backyard, and one lonely oak tree in the corner between the fences on the northern and eastern sides. There was a small patio with a white roof, a bench to sit on, a little table, a tall bar stool and two resting chairs. The rest of the backyard was not used. Green grass filled in the most of it, though it wasn't that green now. It was more of light brown color since fall started. There were quite a few patches around that were just black dirt, since no one cared for the space in a while, but it happened to be perfect for planting something.

Granvill immediately got to work. He was wearing his garden clothes; brownish old khaki pants and an awfully light gray sweater. It wasn't too warm outside today, but again dry, which was great for the tulips.

He worked for about an hour and a half before he saw the owner of the house again. She was busy with something inside the house until then. When she came outside, she asked Granvill if he wanted something like water, iced tea, or coffee.

"I am sorry I didn't offer it before, I am not really used to guests in my house lately." She wasn't sure how to behave in this situation.

"That's totally all right. I didn't really want anything until now, but a cup of coffee would be nice." Replied the old man.

"No Peruvian tea?"

She smiled, because that's what she did when she didn't know what to do.

"You keep Peruvian tea in your house?" The old man was curious.

"Actually, no, I don't." The Person Who Smiled at Everyone burst into laughter, and Granvill noticed yet again how nice her laugh was and thought that she should do it more often. "But coffee I have. I will get the coffee."

And she disappeared into the comfort of her house again. When she came back, she had two cups of coffee in her hands, and she put both down on the top of the bar stool that was sitting right near the window. Then she went back to the house and returned with a tray of muffins which she carefully placed on the table.

"The coffee is ready." She proclaimed out loud.

"Great!"

The old man stood up from his knees and cleaned his hands on his jeans; he didn't wear usually any gloves when he did garden work. He liked the feeling of the soil and the nature on his bare skin.

"You seem to be in great health but are you sure it's not too much work for you?" She was a bit concerned because she had never seen Granvill at work before and wasn't exactly sure what he was capable of.

"Oh yeah, totally all right." He responded with confidence. "Coffee smells really good."

He took his cup in his hands and took a sip out of it. It was a good cup of coffee. She knew what she was doing, that's why her shop was the most popular spot in the village.

"There are some muffins too, regular ones and blueberry ones. I baked them myself," said the Person Who Smiled at Everyone.

"That's very kind of you," the old man was pleased to be around a nice person.

He never wanted anything back for planting tulips. He wanted to leave a small gift of kindness without any reward. He was even mentally prepared to get negative backlash from people, but it was nice to get some positive emotion back. He thought for a second about the tulips across city hall and wondered how that would go. He considered the possibility that it maybe not as positive. He didn't think that the city hall employees would've brought him coffee and muffins, that's for sure. But he did have a vision of what tulips could do for the people of the village. And he needed to go back there and finish the task at some point.

Granvill and the Person Who Smiled at Everyone started a conversation from afar. They talked about some generic topics at first like flowers and coffee, and eventually switched it to something a bit more personal.

"You know, I regret one thing in my marriage." She was already on her second cup of coffee and more comfortable with the old man listening to her feelings. It was clear that the failed marriage had put a heavy burden on her mind and her heart, and she didn't have enough time to recover her normal self yet.

"I wish I would have communicated better with my husband. We had a very good life, and we had so much in common, we could spend whole weeks together and not get tired of each other. Our friends thought we were perfect together. And he was a great father as well, spent a lot of time with our son, and made a real bond with him, probably even stronger than between me and my and son."

She went into a thinking mode for a moment, realizing that last statement of hers was probably the truest. Then she returned to talking:

"But there was one main thing we always fought on. He could get quite jealous sometimes. I am not sure why, I don't think I gave him any real reasons to be, but that's how he was. And I didn't accept that. Sometimes it was cute, and we moved on over kisses and smiles, but… most of the time…."

"It would upset you?" Granvill tried to help with the words.

"Yeah, I was just slowly getting angry at him. I felt like he spoiled a great day or a great evening by being jealous and bringing up something that wasn't there."

"That seems to be a normal reaction to it."

"But in reality, it was never a great evening, at least not for both of us. He suffered quietly sometimes, and didn't want to tell me about his pain, and when he did, I still rejected it, like an annoyance in my life…."

Granvill listened intensively, yet patiently, not trying to interrupt the moment even with an unnecessary body movement.

"Was it my ego? Because his pain was concerning me? Accusing me of something I felt innocent of? Ego of being insulted by the lack of trust? Because I trusted *him*. Completely. And never questioned him about anything. Why couldn't *he* trust me the same?"

She stopped talking. Thought about it. Felt a bit of pain. Then disappointment. And then realized that it didn't matter.

"But I still should have listened. I didn't have to agree with him, or his reasons. But I should have at least listened. Because he was good to me ninety percent of the time! How I could not give him some slack and be patient with him the other ten percent of our life together?"

She looked at the man across the table like he had some answers for her, like he could solve her life once and forever. He cautiously asked:

"There were probably other problems besides jealousy, no?"

"Yeah, I guess so," reluctantly admitted the woman. "But that was the biggest challenge, I think. Most arguments started with that."

Granvill thought that he was in no position to provide his advice to the Person Who Smiled at Everybody, but he also saw that she was looking for something, so he decided to try:

"Most things in life we only understand in hindsight. That's the true tragedy of life. But I think you are thinking about it in the right direction. Generally, in any relationship, it takes time for both a man and a woman to realize something so important, like how he definitely should've trusted you more, or like how you could have handled it. But mostly by that time, they've hurt each other too much to make a comeback from it and be happy."

The old man had a lot of past life experiences to draw this from, but he also had listened to many people around him to make pretty accurate conclusions.

"The real challenge is to find a person who you can communicate with and who can understand the other sides of you no matter how bad it looks and be there for each other no matter what. Maybe if you would have listened, it would've given him time to build that trust and learn how to deal with it, and maybe that wouldn't have made any real difference and instead he would've always expected you to be the understanding one. A relationship is a two-way street. *Always.* But if there is communication, there is hope that the two people will stay together while they are both making their journey to the understanding and realization of how their life should look. It really takes time. And by communicating well, you can sometimes cut down the time it takes to get to that realization. The sooner people can get there, the sooner they can be happy. But it's a tough road to walk on."

"But why? Why is it so hard? Is it supposed to be so hard?" asked the woman in a desperate attempt to get some answers.

"We, as a human race, make it hard for ourselves. I don't want to bore you with my theories, but I just think that people are not prioritizing their lives very well."

She looked at him, thinking for a moment if she wanted to hear more or not. She didn't know the man at all, really, and his theories could range anywhere between long and dull to just pure crazy, but she decided she really wanted to know.

"No, no, please, I would like to hear your theories."

Granvill looked into her eyes, as he has always done while trying to connect with a person across from him.

"Very well." He started. "I think people spend a whole lot of time to figure out how to make their lives easier and safer, which is important of course, more entertaining and more productive, and most of the technological advances move forward with one of those goals in mind. For every polio vaccine found by scientists, there are hundreds of inventions that just made us either lazier, forced us to do more in less time, or brought more fun in our life. Yet, people spent no time trying to develop social institutions like marriage, or personal relationships with others. Each generation adjusts their way of building personal relationships only from what they have seen from their parents, other members of their family, and society. But no one really learns it. They just wing it, letting their subconscious mind and habits run their lives."

At this moment, Granvill realized he might be talking a bit out of touch and not that much to the personal situation of his listener. He made a turn back closer to the topic in hand:

"The biggest advance in marriage we have had in the last few hundred years is the concept of monogamy, which is pushed by churches, and which was probably a good thing for us, but we also never learned what to do with it. Instead of experiencing the most intimate and pure connection with another person, our love became possessive, as if the other person belongs to you, and you should know their every step, and they shouldn't look at other women or men, and they can't go anywhere without you. Until the day they do. And either they do it behind your back and ruin everything you built on the premise that the life you built has no room for anyone else outside of the relationship, or after they get tired and tell you openly that they are ready to move on, still accomplishing the exact same result at the end, but with a different approach. Jealousy is a powerful venom in a relationship."

"So, what's the solution then? Open relationships?" She was a bit confused.

"Not necessarily. I wish I knew the solution. But as I said, only truly open and tolerant communication between two people can accomplish a genuine understanding between two strangers to become one unbreakable unit in life. And as I mentioned, the real challenge is to find a person who will communicate at the same level as you, with the same goal in mind and with the same level of effort. Communication is also not always words. It's body language, a touch, sometimes just the ability to say "I love you" in the middle of a fight. Or the ability to listen to the other person's side even if one is mad and angry."

Granvill paused for a moment before continuing.

"People do not really think about it, they just get together, get hurt and then move on, cursing out the other person like the plague that one was lucky enough to avoid and erasing the whole history from their life like a bad dream."

He paused again as though for thinking about something personal to him.

"I want to let you know that first of all, every experience in life is a great experience, even if we get hurt in the end. Avoiding pain should never be a reason not to make any decision in life. Most people are afraid of pain, but pain is a part of life, and accepting pain is a blessing. The main question is if the pain is worth the reward, something that is positive in our life and our experience of living, or not. If it was worth it, we are capable of accepting the pain that comes with it. And second, if people would spend time realizing what's truly important to them, and how to be more understanding about obtaining whatever that may be and be more patient…. I have a question for you. Why do you think about it now? If you *would have listened* to your husband, would it change anything?"

"Hmmm. I don't know if it would change anything for sure. But I know it feels wrong knowing I didn't listen. I just remember how I felt, I was annoyed by it, thinking "Not this again", instead of being patient. I was anything *but* patient. Just thinking right now about how I felt, makes me disgusted with myself. That's not the person I want to be. Especially for the one person who I cared about the most."

A lonely tear sprinkled out of her eye and went on its way down a beautiful cheek. She wiped it off quickly with her hand, not wanting to be too vulnerable right now.

"Disgusted is a very strong word. Just the fact that you are thinking about it right now and feel bad about it probably more than you should, shows that you are a good and caring person."

"I just know he didn't deserve my annoyance like that, even if he didn't have reasons to be jealous. I should have tried to figure out how to help him, how to be there for him. I never even bothered to ask if there was anything I could do to make him feel more secure in us…..... I just assumed that by being myself it would've taken care of itself on its own."

"And it didn't," Granvill finished the sentence for her.

She negatively shook her head in despair.

"But also…" she stumbled on her own surprising realization.

"I ask myself, why couldn't *he* feel bad for constantly being jealous, why couldn't *he* make me feel like he trusts me? I have this fight within me, where I feel bad about "feeling bad" if you know what I mean."

Granvill waited a second to see if she would continue, but she didn't.

"I am sorry that it didn't work out, but it's not your fault alone. As I said, it's a two-way street. Two people in the relationship have the power to change and influence each other. If both follow their natural instincts to be mad, upset, disappointed, and give up on each other in that anger and frustration, then it is bound to come to an end eventually. And you seem to be taking more than half of the blame here. You shouldn't be too harsh on yourself. It's good to learn from it and improve, but don't take the whole blame on your shoulders. Maybe you were meant to learn those moments, so when you find someone else, you know what to do. Life is a process of preparation and growth."

She burst into tears now, she couldn't control it anymore, or just didn't care enough to control it.

"But what if that was it!?? What if there is no anyone else? There definitely won't be anyone like him."

He stood up from his chair and slowly came over to the Person Who Smiled at Everyone and offered his chest to cry on. She leaned into it, and he surrounded her gentle body with his arms.

"I couldn't tell you that for sure, one way or another. But I could tell you that life is full of surprises. Remember what I said about open doors, and how it has the same principle as finding friends. You may find something else at the end, something you are not looking for, or something that you didn't even know you needed to find."

She continued to cry for a while until it seemed that there was no liquid left in her eyes. Granvill was just standing peacefully and quietly holding her in his arms; he didn't say anything else while he comforted her. He didn't need to. There were two people frozen in space and time, being there for each other. The old man was there to provide support and guidance, but the woman was there for him to give him her open heart, sincerity, and a sense of purpose for that specific day. He was there today for her because the tulips brought him to her, at the right time and at the right place. That would never have happened if he didn't order flower bulbs or offer to plant them in her backyard. He also knew there were events that took place out of his control, but he was happy to carry them out in the order that they were intended.

"I did love him. I loved him so much. And I did *try* to make him happy," the Person Who Smiled at Everybody summarized her feelings. "My mom always told me that the woman in the house was responsible for the atmosphere of the relationship. I don't know if that's true or not. We want to be equal to men, in every aspect. I wonder if that perceived equality affects marriages and relationships. As a woman, I don't know if I should blame myself for this failed marriage or stand up for my right to get what I want in the relationship and blame him for not giving that to me."

"Blame can be ultimately equal, even if it's really not. We can't possibly walk in another person shoes, so we will always see the situation only from our own perspective. So, there is no possible way of measuring the actual level of blame. Relationships are hard enough already without focusing on who's to blame. If one person is mad at the other, but wants to fix it, then they should go and fix it. One shouldn't think about what men or women should do. It's what *equal partners* should do in a real partnership that really matters."

"Equal partners… That sounds good. I don't know if we ever were equal partners though."

"How come?" asked Granvill, noticing the shift of the conversation.

"He wanted me to take care of our home, raise our son, cook, and clean. He only supported my coffee shop enterprise to avoid any more fights, not because he loved the idea of me running a business. And it was tolerable to him as long as it wasn't affecting our life at home.

"That doesn't sound like an equal partnership to me."

"Do you think that's possible though? To be truly equal? Can women be truly equal to men?"

It felt a bit like a trap question. Granvill learned through his own previous relationships to never answer trap questions asked by women. Nothing good ever came out of that. But he had nothing to lose here. He also learned with age that honesty was a good policy most of the time, as well as the fact that he didn't have that much time left on this Earth to worry if his good intentions would be perceived by someone in the wrong way. And he did have good intentions. Almost always. And in this situation too, standing next to the woman with a crisis of her self-worth.

"This is only my personal opinion. I am not in any way trying to force it on anyone, but since we have started this conversation…."

Granvill took the longest pause before releasing the words into the universe that could – depending on the receiver – explode like a bomb in the middle of a silent night.

"What I really think in the bigger scale of life is: people are *not equal*. But all people deserve *equal respect*. I see a big distinctive difference between the two."

Granvill knew this was a tough topic for everyone. Because this topic can't be politically correct. No matter how you phrase it, it will always leave room for debate. Granvill thought, if he would hear that same phrase from someone else a few years ago, he would not accept it as any kind of logical statement at all. In today's age, one must be ready to say an opinion for the whole uninterrupted and unconditional sentence, "Everyone is equal". Anything besides that would meet a wall of backlash by default. But he also knew that real life doesn't work in oversold clichés that you put as a slogan on demonstration posters. Real life is more complex and not *that fair*.

"I will not treat a twelve-year old boy the same way as thirty-year old man. I will not expect a ninety-year old person to do the same work as a man in his prime age. I will not expect a handicapped person to perform physically the same way as healthy adult. And men and women are different too. They think differently, they act differently, they have different strengths and weaknesses. The important part is that every single person deserves to be treated with *equal* respect. But the "I can" attitude is not for women to have as representatives of their sex. I know where it's coming from. But it should be a *personal manifestation of every single human being*. Every person has a personal struggle of doing their best, either it is because of their nationality, race, sex, religion, social status, mental capacity, IQ, physical strength, talents or lack thereof. But every person should have "I can" attitude no matter what their personal challenges and life obstacles are. And every woman should feel that she *can* do anything, period. Not because she is a woman. Because she is a human. And by the way, there are many things women do better than men, and they should take advantage of that, and not try to be equal."

The Person Who Smiled at Everybody was moving her thoughts and moods between getting irritated with this conversation and admiring the new angle on things that she thought she knew her whole life. She wasn't sure yet where she would land at the end of this dialogue.

"Let me tell you something that I don't think is a secret at all. *Men* do not want to be equal to other *men*, they want to be better, the strive to prove they are the best. No one wants to be equal! No one wants to be just like someone else. Being equal to someone is a mental trap. Women shouldn't want the same thing. They should want to be the best version of themselves, whatever that means to them personally. They should have *equal opportunities*, but that doesn't mean *equal treatment*. Each person is different, and each person should figure out on their own what makes them *Them*.

"I think I understand what you are trying to say." She responded, but without any kind of certainty in her voice.

"If your partner offends you, then you can be offended, but shouldn't be *extra* offended because he is a man. Unless he specifically meant to put you down as a woman. But if he is seeing you as just another human being, then you should stand up to that as a fellow human being."

He paused before continuing.

"In an intimate relationship between two women, they still can offend each other, their relationship doesn't go without fights and disagreements. But they can't include being offended because one of them is a woman. Because the other one is too. Same goes for two men."

The Person Who Smiled at Everybody nodded in agreement.

"I like that," she said quietly, but confidently. "Two-way street, communication, equal respect. I think I got it."

She smiled through the tears that were still present on her face.

"Thank you for being here, and listening, and sharing your opinion. I needed that."

"Listen, I will never pretend to know everything. And I have been wrong so many times in my life. I know better than to ever think I know *anything at all*. But I don't mind sharing my views and experiences, while being ready to listen your views and experiences. And I will always respect them no matter if they match mine or not."

"Same here. I will try to live by your philosophy."

She smiled at him sincerely and warmly.

"Granvill's philosophy."

"Oh God," he pronounced out loud. "That's just what the world needs, *my philosophy*."

They both giggled like little kids and moved on from the tough part of the conversation. They didn't talk much about anything after that. When the Person Who Smiled at Everyone finally took control of her emotions, she smiled at Granvill, thanked him for being here for her, and asked him if he wanted more coffee or muffins or anything else. He didn't. But he did, of course, appreciate the gesture.

A few minutes later, the woman said she had to go to the coffee shop to help her workers and asked her newly found friend if he didn't mind staying in the backyard on his own for a while. He didn't mind at all, he still had a lot of work to be done here.

She left Granvill on his own a bit past noon. She gave him instructions on how to look the door in case he left before she came back. She wasn't planning to be at the shop for too long, but three or four hours could fly by.

Granvill worked for a couple of more hours before he started feeling hungry, a coffee and muffin could only carry him so far. He decided to push for another hour instead of taking a break and then he could go home and eat a meal at his house. Since he didn't own a cell phone, the only way he could tell the exact time was to rely on his old watch, which he got as a present from a woman about thirty years ago. It still worked just fine, and that's all Granvill needed.

At 3:10pm the extra hour was complete, and Granvill planted about four fifths of the bulbs he had in the duffle bag. He dumped the rest near the fence, so he had room in the bag to bring more the next day and was on his way. He walked out of the house, and followed the owner's instructions, but he then realized that they never set a time for tomorrow. She could have had other plans, or she could be sleeping in or, at the very worst, she could be not alone, but Granvill wasn't going to sweat about it for too long. He believed that the Person Who Smiled at Everyone needed the tulips and maybe even his presence as well, now more than anything else. So, he was going to come back tomorrow at 8am again.

The walk home was uneventful. He passed the same houses as he did on the way to the village, and he thought about who else could benefit from the tulips he had stored in his cooler. He still had sixteen full crates with some extra tulips from other boxes when he was separating the pink bulbs, but he wasn't about to go ahead of himself. One day at a time. He knew that life could throw a curveball any minute, and he was enjoying today's day. All he knew was that tomorrow if nothing major happened, he planned to wake up at 7am and go to the same white house where he was today to continue his task of planting more tulips.

CHAPTER 4

The next morning, Granvill arrived at the white house just two minutes after eight. He wasn't in any hurry to come sooner, and as they had never established the time of the meeting; he also wasn't generally counting the minutes the same way that most people in the village did. He looked at each day as a whole day at his disposal to do anything he wished to do, and usually that was enough. He didn't need the clock to tell him *when* he should be doing *what*, although his watch proved to be useful to him in many situations regarding certain interactions with other people, especially doctors, lawyers and bankers. Those people worked strictly on the clock. They wouldn't be able to function if someone would take their precious clock away from them.

He wasn't sure if the Person Who Smiled at Everyone was home, but when the door opened quickly after his knock, he realized that she was waiting for him. She was not confident that he'd come either, but she was hoping to see him at the same time as the day prior.

She was wearing similar jeans as yesterday, but she was wearing a top that was light and summer like, which was white with red and pink flowers with green branches in between. The printed silky top looked alive and energetic, which was probably how she felt today when she decided to put it on.

"Good morning," her clear voice was just as alive. "Sorry, I didn't come back yesterday in time to catch you before you left."

"No worries at all, you gave me good instructions on how to leave everything in place, hope I didn't mess anything up." Responded the old man.

"No, no, everything was fine," assured the host, while taking a step back, to welcome her guest to come in.

Granvill walked in the house. The next hour or so, they chatted about the weather and their favorite movies while the man worked on the tulips. After that, he took a break while they shared a cup of coffee and more freshly baked muffins, as well as more life stories and experiences. Around 9:30am, the woman said she needed to go to the coffee shop for a couple of hours, and she left Granvill again in her house by himself. Today, Granvill worked until 12:30pm before he felt hungry, so he decided to go to get takeout and then come back to finish the work.

He left the house unlocked for a few minutes while he walked to a nearby sandwich shop. The village was small, and there was practically no crime here. It's been years since anyone's house was robbed, so Granvill wasn't worried about leaving the house unattended for a short period of time. Although, of course, he realized it wasn't his house, so he did feel a bit concerned.

He walked a block to the closest sandwich shop, ordered a turkey sandwich with everything on it; lettuce, tomatoes, pickles, onions and peppers. He was heading back to the house when, at the exit, he bumped into a person who he didn't expect to meet, even with all the likeliness of meeting any person in the village of that size. But seeing that specific person brought up some vivid memories.

"Granvill!" exclaimed a man in his fifties, maybe just slightly younger than Granvill himself. He didn't have full gray hair quite yet, but it seemed like it was sprinkling through his natural brunette color, and one could tell that he wasn't getting bald anytime soon. "Long time!'

The old man wasn't too happy to see him, but he still wasn't planning to ignore him. He turned his full body to the caller and exclaimed in return:

"Definitely a long time!" He held his hand out for a handshake and the other man did the same, solidifying the meeting in an official gesture of respect, no matter how real or fake it was.

"What are you up to?"

Granvill had thought for a minute on how to answer that. As this situation was reminding him, he wasn't really the sharing type.

"Got a sandwich," answered Granvill and made a weird hand gesture with the sandwich in it, as this would somehow explain his whole life existence to the outsider.

"Ha-ha, you always have been funny," laughed the man while putting his arm around the old man's shoulder. "How is your life? I don't often come to this village anymore, and I am sure you have done something with your life in the meantime. So, tell me!"

Granvill knew this guy wasn't going to let him get away from his questions too easily.

"Not too much has changed lately," he answered hesitantly.

"But what happened to you? You fell off the face of the Earth for a while! You were a big shot in the city at some point." The outsider wasn't giving up that easily.

It was tough to tell right away if he was ready to take pleasure in Granvill's misery or if he was sincerely curious; if he was friendly, or just waiting for an opportunity to gloat.

"Listen, that was a long time ago. I retired and settled in here," patiently answered Granvill. One thing he had always had plenty of was patience with other people and tolerance of almost any nonsense around him.

"But why here?" the man looked around the shop. "This village is not much bigger than this sandwich spot."

Granvill nodded in agreement.

"It's not. But I like this place. *Usually* it's a peaceful place. One of those places where people would not stop you in the middle of their lunch without consideration."

The outsider ignored the comment completely, although he understood it was intended towards him.

"I enjoy the life in the city, man. I know you did before too. Maybe you did get too old, but I never thought I would see *the* Granvill being just retired."

The outsider had a lot of energy, and right now all that energy was focused on Granvill.

"I thought you would still be doing great things. You did some really great things in the past."

Granvill thanked him, while he started moving towards the door. The man followed him.

Granvill decided to take a bit more control of the conversation, but also, he knew by asking this question, he would only give this man an extra opportunity to talk more about himself.

"So, what you are doing outside of your big city?"

The Person Who Wants to be the Center of the Universe was happy to hear that question. His grin splattered on his face, like a mosquito on the windshield of a race car.

"Oh man, I decided to buy some land here and develop my new resort. I am buying a huge piece here, where the main structure will be located, and then I am buying another piece of land right on the lake across of Fish Haven, where I will have my store for jet skis, boats, and so on. They will be rentals, but also some packages will be included for the visitors of my resort."

His grin really couldn't be any bigger, like it went through an artificial filter on a phone app and didn't belong in real life.

"You know, I maybe could use you, if you need to entertain yourself with something. It's an exciting project and will make a lot of money! Probably would be cool for you to get involved."

Granvill looked at him with the same patience and understanding as before. He knew what kind of human the Person Who Wants to be the Center of the Universe is, and it would be silly to expect him to change his colors. One of the talents Granvill had acquired through his lifetime was to see people for who they were, no matter who or what they pretended to be. Sometimes mistakes had occurred, of course, but generally, it was a helpful asset to him in his life. He also knew that when he could recognize people for who they really were, it's wasn't easy to stay away from making judgments. But his ability to listen people and understand them took him a bit longer to acquire, but that was even more useful asset to him after he finally did.

"I already have a project with tulips," calmly noted Granvill. "And I am planning to see it through."

"Tulips?" The Person Who Wants to be the Center of the Universe was confused for a moment. "Like a tulip plantation? Is it a good business?"

Before Granvill even had a chance to answer, the outsider was already brainstorming the possibilities.

"I mean, people do buy flowers, and I am sure people will come to my resort to celebrate anniversaries and weddings, and they will need to buy flowers. Maybe I can get them from you at the wholesale prices and sell it in my lobby at the convenience of my residents. Hmm," his brain was active and energetic, just like the rest of his body.

Granvill knew that the Person Who Wants to be the Center of the Universe wasn't a bad man. Sometimes labels that were given to people by others could be confusing or misleading, so friends, colleagues, and acquaintances jumped to conclusions and assumptions based on those labels. But Granvill was deeply conscious that humans were more complex than any one label would suggest they were, and were capable to surprise people around them, and even themselves occasionally. People stepped up to situations or circumstances all the time, and sometimes, no matter how rarely that it happened, even changed. But in other times, their inability to step up could also define the owners of those labels and their future.

Granvill also knew how tough it could be to try get rid of existing labels, especially the labels that weren't given by others but the ones that the owners of those labels gave themselves. But labels that were created by others and accepted by the owners as their own were just as bad.

Labels sometimes stayed with the people that they were chosen for forever.

"I like how your mind works, but you would have to find someone else for that." Calmly continued Granvill. "I don't have a plantation, or a wholesale business. Just a project. On the side. For myself and my own satisfaction only."

The Person Who Wants to be the Center of the Universe showed some disappointment for a minute. He felt a certain kinship to Granvill, and they shared some good times a while ago. On the other hand, the extreme need to be competitive was in his blood, in his nature, it ran through each fiber of his body, and that had created a few enemies on his journey. But he enjoyed having worthy opponents to be competitive against, and Granvill was one of them.

"Oh man, it seemed like a good idea, but," the outsider was ready to move on, and his disappointment quickly flowed into more energy. "maybe you can contribute in some other capacity. It would be pretty cool to work with you again, Granvill!"

Granvill thought to himself that they have never worked with each other, only against each other, but his opponent didn't seem to realize the difference.

By this time, they were standing almost a block away from the coffee shop. Granvill tried to leave his adversary so he could go back to the tulips, and this seemed like a good time for that.

"Ok, I think this is the time I get back to my project."

Granvill's announcement sounded confident and firm.

"The tulips project?" Clarified his foe.

"Yes."

"Great! I hope it's worth your time, my friend. Life is too short."

Granvill knew that life was too short, but it was interesting to him, how the same realization could have such different meanings to him and this big entrepreneur from the city.

The Person Who Wants to be the Center of the Universe shook Granvill's hand and asked him if he could reach him by phone. He heard the reply that the old man didn't have a phone, so he gave him his own business card and asked him to contact him at some point so they could further discuss the new resort and any possible involvement. Granvill took the card and put it in his shirt's front pocket.

Granvill went back to the white house to eat his lunch. It took him longer than expected because of the unexpected meeting, but he didn't mind. He generally enjoyed talking to people and listening to their stories, and usually supported them in any way possible. In this instance, though, he knew that the Person Who Wants to be the Center of the Universe didn't need his support. The entrepreneur was comfortable in his skin and was going towards what he wanted like an elite race horse, who was bred its whole life for that one purpose, to get to the finish line.

Granvill remembered old times in the city, and of course, he could easily recall the friendly rivalry as well. In general, he had good memories of all of that, but this was a different chapter in his life, and he had no intention of going back.

Granvill spent the rest of the day doing what he planned to do all along: planting tulips. The task was coming along nicely, and he enjoyed the whole process.

Around 4pm, the Person Who Smiled at Everyone was back. She had a good productive day at the coffee shop. She was looking forward to a nice finish with a homemade dinner. She chatted with Granvill for a bit, and then invited him to stay for dinner.

"It would be my pleasure to join you, but I ate lunch not that long ago."

"Oh, it will be another two hours before I make it." exclaimed the house host.

Granvill hesitated for no more than half a second.

"Sure, then I will accept the invitation."

The Person Who Smiled at Everyone was happy about that. Her good day just got even better.

Granvill continued working in the garden till then. He felt that he would be able to complete the task today, as he was pushing forward with all his might now, laboring in accelerated rhythm. It meant that for once, he was moving at a normal pace, and not his usual slow motion one.

Meanwhile, The Person Who Smiled at Everyone was cooking in the kitchen, occasionally looking out of the kitchen window to see the nice man doing the nice thing for her in her garden. For a minute she thought about how lucky she was to have someone in this world that could do such a nice thing for her. It almost restored her faith in humanity again. Then she wondered if it would go *downhill* after this. If she got to know Granvill better, would she be disappointed in *him, his actions, his motives*? Would she still think of him *as a good man* who extended his kindness to others? What if this old man had dark and awful secrets? After all, she didn't know that much about him.

She disregarded those thoughts from her mind. She preferred if this day went down in the records of her life as the only good day without a blemish. The woman tried not to think about the "what if's" of life, but rather focus on "what is" in this kitchen right now.

Granvill finished the garden just in time for dinner. It was almost surreal how the timing had worked out for them. It seemed that the universe planned it all out for the two mortals to make sure everything went the right way. The Person Who Smiled at Everyone did a great job putting a nice table together with plates, glasses, silverware, and napkins. Everything looked up to par to the proper meal shared between the two souls. When they sat at the table, she asked if she could say a prayer, and Granvill agreed to it. After a short but sweet grace, they proceeded with their meals, savoring each bite as an appropriate metaphor of their new bond and comforting time together.

The Person Who Smiled at Everyone had wanted to know something from yesterday's conversation, and eventually she found a good moment to ask the question that was drilling her mind with curiosity.

"You said yesterday that pain is a blessing. I am still not sure how that can be?"

Granvill thought of how to explain this in a better way, though some questions are better experienced and learned through, than told in words. But he didn't want to ignore the question either. So, he carefully proceeded with the answer.

"Because everything works in balance. Things in life are either in balance or off-balance. Imagine an old school justice scale. Imagine that you have happiness and joy in one weighing pan, suspended from an arm on the left, and pain and bitterness on the other side. If you never put anything on the right side at all, then the left side full of happiness will reach the bottom too quickly. There is very little happiness you can place on that scale. But imagine you put something on the right side, some pain and unhappiness. Then you can continue to fit a lot more joy on the left, equating itself and making your life balanced."

The host listened with much curiosity although she didn't know if she could agree with the new concept just yet. It still seemed quite illogical to her.

"But, wouldn't you be happier with your pan empty on the miserable side, and full of happiness on the opposite side? Even if it fills quickly?"

"Not really. Imagine you get all that happiness by the age of twenty-five, for example. You have a husband and a child, and they make your life complete. But there is never nothing new to add on for the rest of your life! You can't have new adventures, new friendships, new travels around the world, new victories, and new proud moments of the people you care for. Life would stall and would become dull. It would become a routine that would drain all your happiness."

Granvill paused for a moment, and he realized it wasn't a simple concept to agree to for anyone, and after all, he really didn't want to force his opinion on anyone.

"People try to avoid pain like a plague. But I think that they should be worrying about shifting their focus instead. It's ok if there is some pain in existence, but also look at how much time you spend looking at it or paying attention to it?"

He looked at the woman to see if she was following his logic. He got the visual confirmation he was looking for, – the heedful eyes of the listener – and continued:

"People take happiness for granted but get mentally and emotionally overwhelmed by their problems too easily. Instead, they should be taking pain and obstacles for granted! Accept it as unavoidable part of life. And then be *completely and utterly overtaken and overwhelmed* by the luck that's present in their life and all the happy moments the universe gives them.

It made more sense to the Person Who Smiled at Everyone.

"So, it is more about perception then? How we perceive everything good that happens to us, and everything bad that happens to us. Right?"

"Yes. I think that's how life is better."

"But it's always so hard to not be overwhelmed by the pain we feel!!!" Her response was the most natural in this universe.

Granvill stopped taking bites of his food, gave his full attention to the question and placed his fork down.

"That could be happening for many reasons. One of them is that we mistake happiness as some kind of total bliss, that has to be present without negative emotions, negative events, or imperfections. We believe in Heaven which was created by God to be a *pain-free zone*, where we all should strive to get to. And even worse, we believe that we can achieve that same kind of bliss here, on Earth, while managing our everyday lives and all possible aspects of it, including the ones that are completely out of our control. And we think that *our intelligence and the technological advances* have something to do with the control of that creation process."

The Person Who Smiled at Everyone was by now completely fascinated by this conversation.

"So, what is happiness then?"

Granvill took some time to think about that. He didn't really know the exact answer to that, and he didn't want to play the ungrateful role of the All-Knowing. But he wanted to attempt to give the woman the best answer he could muster.

"True happiness is the *satisfaction* that comes from the knowledge of *your place* in the universe. It is also connected to your priorities and expectations of course, whether it is work, family, relationships, or our loved ones. Whatever it is. Our surroundings create a specific imaginary place where we feel we have a carefree home in our lives. If we know we are in a good place, then we are happy. Feeling outside of that sacred place creates anxiety, stress, frustration, anger, and pain. When someone hurts us, we feel cheated. We feel we don't deserve to be hurt. It fails our expectation of the place we created for ourselves in our minds."

The Person Who Smiled at Everyone was paying attention. She could see something that she never realized before. She couldn't point it out yet, but she felt different already.

"When we find the right people in our lives, we can be in a really great place, but the same people can make us feel pain. Small disagreements, fights, and so on. It's not a bad thing, if the pain worth the reward, if you achieve the certain level of happiness you get out of it. Even with our children, with the whole innocence in them! Think about it. Despite their unconditional love to us, they disappoint us sometimes, they anger us sometimes; we are concerned about their safety all the time or worry how to provide them the right options in life, the right education and so on. All of that is *the pain* on the other side of the scale. But we know they are worth all of that and we are happy despite it. We are at a place with them that we know is a good place to be, but only because there is another side of the scale. We can see the difference in comparison. We see we can't be *truly happy* without the other side of the scale."

The Person Who Smiled at Everyone was pleased with the conversation.

"It all sounds so simple."

"It is anything but simple." Granvill agreed, knowing what she had meant. "But it is attainable. But do you know why relationships are so hard?"

She waited for the answer without attempting to answer the question in the air.

"Because it is a hard journey of realization. Imagine two people have to come to the same realization about life and happiness and do it almost at the same time of their lives?!"

She nodded.

"You are right," she agreed with the old man. "I feel like most people never come to that realization at all though. "

Granvill nodded back. There was nothing left to add. Unfortunately, that's how this world worked. Many people chase other things. Almost no one has a goal to come to that realization at any point of their lives. *Maybe* some lucky ones through certain experiences, almost by accident, while others resist knowing it or believing in it, even as it stared right at their face. Stubbornness is a unique quality, that has no limits of geographical location, race, nationality or way of upbringing.

"Did you come to that realization together with anyone?"

The Person Who Smiled at Everyone now wanted to hear the answer to this question, more than to any previous ones. She didn't realize herself yet that she cared, but the level of curiosity that arose from the depth of her soul was a telling sign.

Granvill looked at her with his warm eyes glowing with reminisce.

"Yes, I have."

By the look on the woman's face, he felt compelled to continue.

"She changed my life. We did this journey together, and we came to a point where we were just really, really happy. But not without pain in our lives. We had worries, fears, insecurities, and disagreements, like anyone else. But we were going through everything together, and our scale was full of happiness and great memories. All the best moments in my life are one way or another connected to her. She was incredible… We were even more incredible *together*."

Granvill seemed happy just talking about it. The woman across listened to him like it was a fairy tale about a prince and a princess. It was almost as surreal to her as a fairy tale would be.

"Where is she now? If you don't mind me asking," she asked carefully, hoping she wouldn't get the morale demolishing response.

"Not here. But that's a story for some other time," calmly replied Granvill. "But I am carrying her with me wherever I go."

That wasn't so demoralizing, but also didn't provide any real answers. For now, the Person Who Smiled at Everyone had to be satisfied with that though.

They finished the meal not much longer after that. Granvill thought it was tasty and he expressed that to the cook. He was thankful to have dinner with a nice person, as he usually had to settle eating by himself in his house. Not because he was lonely, it was his choice after all, but it was nice to share a different kind of experience. This dinner with the Person Who Smiled at Everyone felt like that kind of pleasant difference from his usual routine. She felt the same. She didn't have many guests in her house after her divorce, and outside of her teenage son, she also rarely shared a meal with anyone. Having a pleasant conversation about things she didn't know was even more rare and it was a nice bonus sharing it with another person.

After dinner, they went to the backyard for a minute, both realizing that Granvill had no more reason to come back tomorrow as his job was done. She thanked him full heartedly and invited him to stop by anytime he wanted to see the results of his work. He promised that he would do that at some point. It was time for Granvill to go home, and on the way out she thanked him again, and then said something else that seemed important to her at this specific moment:

"You were right about opening new doors. I have seen you so many times in the past years in my coffee shop, but I would have *never imagined* us sharing a magnificent dinner in my house and you planting flowers in my backyard."

She didn't have enough words in her vocabulary to express the pleasure she had received from those couple of days around Granvill, and she could only hope that the words that she chose to say out loud would be heard in the way she intended them. She felt little hope for that though. Most likely, he knew what she felt, but not to the full capacity of how much that meant to her.

The old man looked at her eyes sincerely and with the softest voice proclaimed:

"The pleasure was all mine."

She felt a strong impulse to give him a hug and she followed it without hesitation. She held her arms around his neck for a few seconds longer than even close friends did, but she had to let him go at some point. Granvill walked out of the house and started a slow-motion march towards his own home.

CHAPTER 5

For the next three days, Granvill didn't do any work. He went to a grocery store, picked up some fruits, vegetables, and other groceries and spent a couple of hours on each of those three days cooking dinners. Cooking was a part of his creative personality, and since he retired, there were not many things to express it, and none that was better than cooking. While playing and experimenting with ingredients, he enjoyed listening to music that was loud enough to capture the radiant atmosphere in the room. The first day was Chicken Marengo in white wine with mushrooms and olives while listening to classical music, mostly Vivaldi, Mozart and Liszt. The next day, he created a Monkfish provincial meal, with spinach and tomatoes while playing more modern artists, like Michael Jackson and Prince to entertain his ears, and on the third day he made Mexican Salmon with a green salad and lime, while romantic Latin music accompanied him. Each day he let his creative processes flow freely through the music and cooking, and that gave him the most joy.

Eating those dishes, though while pleasant, and the good taste provided a certain level of gratification, was less important than the process of cooking. But no matter how delicious the meal was, the creation process was always more special to him. Especially when he ate alone, which was the case most nights since he moved to the village. Each evening, right around sunset, he took a plate to his patio chair on the south side of the house facing the mountains. Sitting in this chair was a peaceful endeavor to Granvill; enjoying a home cooked meal while watching the sunset was even better. This was a different kind of joy from cooking, this was the time to reflect, to think, and to live in the moment.

Those three days, so many random things had come and went through Granvill's mind: beautiful creations of nature, memories of his travels, human motivations, tendencies, and characters, his own plans for the near future and many other topics that had nothing to do with each other. He thought about the Person Who Wants to be the Center of the Universe and his business ideas, and he thought with equal interest about the Person Who Smiled at Everyone. He enjoyed being sprawled in his patio chair while thinking and relished in the quietness of those moments when the thoughts stopped. The sunsets were beautiful, the days were warm, the food was delicious, and peace and tranquility were real and natural, not forced.

Granvill didn't have a specific plan to do this for three days, or any other amount of time really; it's just how it happened. He took his time to wake up in the morning and allowed himself to decide how to spend the day ahead of him. Reading books, spending time in his garden, and cooking all were a part of improvisation throughout the day rather than any set plan. The next day, the whole process of making new decisions, from the moment of him waking up in the morning to devouring his meal on the patio late evening, repeated itself. On the third night, he felt that the time to move on to the next step had come, and tomorrow he would be ready to plant more tulips.

So, he did. After waking up at 8:40am the next morning, he filled his duffle bag with more tulip bulbs and started walking toward the village. He passed the church, and this time he turned left instead of continuing on the main street which was leading him to the right. On the left, there were a few houses which were a bit more spread out, and the street had less businesses, but there was one target on his mind today. He passed the house of the Person with Bad Luck, and on the other side of the road, he stood in front of a two-story structure that used to look like sunshine with bright yellow walls and sharp contours. But lately, the house lost some of its color, and now resembled a morning omelet with a lot more whites than yolk. But the owner had big plans for it, and she wasn't reluctant to tell everyone in town all about them. She was deciding between remodeling the house or building a new one somewhere down the road and then renting this one out. That was financially smart, which made a lot of sense since this house belonged to the financial advisor of the town, the Person Who Felt Insecure in Relationships.

Granvill looked at his watch, and as it showed 9:47am, he hoped that since it was a business day, no one would be home.

He came up to the fence, which he knew quite well, just like most of the houses in the village, and looked around. Not much had changed, there was a couple of maple trees in the corners of the property, some bushes in between, green grass in the middle, and the yellowish house. There wasn't too much room here, and Granvill wasn't going to ruin the green grass, but between the maple trees, there was enough free space to spread the seeds around.

Granvill looked around. He didn't see anyone on the street and after a momentary hesitation, he started to climb the fence. He was in pretty good physical shape, so it didn't take him too long; if anything, he looked faster in this moment under pressure than his regular slow-motion walking routine. From the side, it was probably a hilarious thing to see though: an old man with grey hair climbing a fence like a ten-year old boy excited to steal an apple or an orange. But Granvill didn't have any intention of stealing anything. He was going to give, he wanted to give, but it had to be done in a manner that could be taken with some plausible hostility from the house owner.

The old man soon crossed over the fence and was standing firmly on the ground on the other side. He checked to see if anyone saw him. He looked at the house right across, where the Very Jealous Person lived. She either wasn't at home or wasn't too concerned with her neighbor's problems. It didn't seem like anyone was looking out of the windows in that house. On the left of it, there was the house of the Person with Bad Luck. He was usually home, not needing to go to work as his managers were running his construction company, but with all the bad luck, he tended to stay away from the windows, front lawn, and stairs. On the right side, there was the house of the Very Ambitious Person, who was, probably, too busy right now making money somewhere and building his career. There were rumors in the village that he was going to partner up in some way with the Person Who Wants to be the Center of the Universe on the resort project. Granvill didn't see anyone near his house either.

Granvill turned around and disappeared from the outsiders' vision into the depths of the backyard which he became an uninvited guest to. He spent the rest of daylight in this wonderful day doing what he came to do. He found spots in between the maple trees and also in the space parallel to the fence. He used those spaces to plant enough tulips to make an impression. He wasn't totally sure it would be a positive impression. Maybe it wouldn't be appreciated at all. But he believed in his heart that the Person Who Felt Insecure in Relationships needed it. She needed to find some new excitement in her life, and while beautiful flowers were pleasant enough on their own, a gesture from a stranger in her life to remind her of something beautiful could tell her even more. It could tell her that she is important to someone in this world. Granvill hoped for that.

It was getting dark when Granvill was finishing up the task of the day. He knew that the Person Who Felt Insecure in Relationships usually worked long hours; she really was putting her best effort to prove to herself and to the world that she is more than capable of achieving success on a high level, and since she didn't have a husband or kids, she had plenty of time for proving that. So Granvill wasn't worried if she came home anytime soon, although even if she did, what would she do? The old man didn't mind the confrontation, but he was hoping for some level of understanding anyways.

When the task was complete, he was figuring out the next step. Should he leave just as fast and unnoticed as he came, or should he let the owner of the house know what he did here? If he left, wouldn't she notice that the dirt was freshly plowed and have questions of how that could happen? He probably should leave a note or something. Wouldn't it be best to wait until she got home then and explain it to her in person? Granvill realized that he didn't think about any of those details in advance, and now he was forced to consider all the options that crossed his mind. He decided that leaving a note would be the least confrontational way to still accomplish the main goal of letting the property owner know what took place in her backyard without scaring her or letting her think something worse than what had actually happened.

But he needed a pen or pencil and a piece of paper to do that. He didn't find either one in his pockets or the duffle bag. He thought for a second about where he could get what he needed and immediately remembered that there was a local inn just five or six houses down the street. Granvill left his almost empty duffle bag on the ground behind one of the maple trees, and then carefully climbed over the fence back to the proper side of the sidewalk. He looked around to make sure no one was paying direct attention to him, and then started to slowly move his body towards the inn. It didn't take him long, even at his pace, to reach the tallest building in the village, only three stories, but nevertheless, a noticeable achievement.

The building was quite old, from the middle of the nineteenth century even, but it went through some modern renovations a couple of times since then; some new appliances were put in and a side addition of the building with a pool inside was built about seven years ago. The outside was painted in an extremely light blue color, which gave it an appropriate warm and welcoming feeling. The owner of the Inn was The Very Tolerant Person. She was a woman in her fifties, and she has seen people from every part of the world staying in her inn over the years, and she welcomed everyone. With that same mentality, she allowed pets in her inn. She didn't want someone to feel excluded purely because of her policies.

The village wasn't a big tourist attraction, but Fish Haven was. Its surrounding areas, with the nearby lake and woods, were a gorgeous piece of land where many outsiders envisioned to spend their vacation, time for getting away from their ordinary, and sometimes dreary, lives. There were times, especially during the summer season, where of all Fish Haven's hotels were booked weeks in advance, and then people searched for any hotels in the vicinity, including The Very Tolerant Person's home village. The business was pretty good all year round though, either because the prices were a bit cheaper than Fish Haven's, or because of contagious word of mouth about her inn, as well as her returning customers who would visit the inn again for special occasions, wedding anniversaries, the Christmas season, or simply a getaway. So, there was not much to complain about. And the Very Tolerant Person didn't.

The only one thing that she wished was different in her life was to have her husband by her side. Unfortunately, as often it happens to the best people, her husband passed away five years ago from a sudden heart attack. It wasn't completely sudden, to be honest, because he had his first occurrence about fourteen months before that, which was, at the time, completely unexpected. Especially considering how healthy he had felt prior to it, but the second one was fatal. They were hoping that it wouldn't happen for many more years. They were so happy together! But it did happen. One day, her husband, the Person with Almost Unlimited Generosity, was cleaning his fishing rods with soap and water, and before he could finish the task, he collapsed to the abyss from where was no return. The Person with Almost Unlimited Generosity was loved by everyone in the village, and by all the hotel's guests. The Very Tolerant Person wasn't always that tolerant, but her husband influenced her to find a better way to live her life.

When she graduated high school in Fish Haven, she had big plans for her life. She was ready to conquer the world. It was certain to all around her that she would move to the big city and create a new life for herself. But in her first semester at a business school, bad news about her dad interrupted her studying. Her father enjoyed skiing, and he was good at it too, despite his age. But what had transpired this day in the mountains about two hundred miles west of the village had nothing to do with his skills or his age.

A much younger and more athletic skier had lost control at full speed and was flying towards the trees on the side of the skiing slope. Her father, The Person with A Lot Left to Give, had seen that, and he didn't hesitate to act. At the last second, he jumped in front of the airborne human weapon and extended his arms to push him away from the trees. He knew that those upright polls of bark and branches would kill the skier instantly, and he couldn't let it happen. In the process, he was hit by the skier's force and thrown into the trees with his back hitting the still wooden object with too much power for anyone to take on without any serious damage. Everything happened so quickly, less than three seconds. Three seconds out of three trillion seconds that a human can hope for in their lifetime. And those three seconds had changed everything forever. For both people involved.

The young athlete didn't hit the trees as he started rolling down the hill just mere inches away from them. The collision with the man who saved his life was also quite serious, but not as serious as the collision with the trees would be. He broke two ribs, got some bruises all over his body, and twisted an ankle, but he was alive.

After that day, the Person Who Always Carried Guilt with Him had never returned to skiing. He wasn't the Person Who Always Carried Guilt with Him before that heartbreaking day, but by the time that day was over, so much had changed that he, nor any of the closest people around him could remember who he was before that. His family members voiced their opinion that he should not feel guilty, and he also knew he should try to move on from the horrifying memories of that event, but that wasn't easy. Sometimes though he found a way to pretend that everything was good. He also found a new calling, becoming an engineer for a fire alarm manufacturer in the big city, hoping that his products could maybe save a few lives here and there. He got married to a beautiful and kind woman and had two kids, boys, who were three years apart. He did his best to become a good father to them as well.

Most people in his life in the big city didn't know about the accident in the mountains, but the guilt never truly left him. No matter how hard he tried, it shadowed him wherever he went, and appeared most aggressively in the darkness of the night, when he couldn't sleep unless there was enough bourbon in his system to shut down his body for a few hours of rest. He wasn't a drunk, and he tried not to drink at all at social events or anywhere in public. His kids had never seen him loaded; only his wife knew that if he wasn't in bed with her at certain time of the night, then it meant one thing: he was trying to acquire his inner peace through a glass or two of the bitter alcohol.

But for The Person with A Lot Left to Give, that day in the snowy mountains was defining to his ending. He spent a couple of weeks in a hospital fighting for his life through multiple injuries to his back and internal organs until one day his body decided to give him mercy and stopped the fight. The official version was that he died from the internal bleeding, but his soul knew this wasn't a fight he was meant to win.

After hearing the horrible news, the Very Tolerant Person left the university immediately, and spent the whole two weeks by her father's side. She refused to accept his fate and was hoping up till the end that he would come out victorious from this unfair challenge. When it didn't happen, she was mourning for a while and decided to stop her studies. She returned to her parents' house in the village. At that time, she hadn't inherited the inn yet because her stepmother took it over after her husband's death, and the widow tried to continue the successful business that was built by the Person with a Lot Left to Give. But it didn't last. She was an honest woman who lost her husband way too early, and if anything, the inn reminded her of the loss, so she decided to transfer its ownership to the only kid her husband had and then she moved to another state, not any neighboring states, but as far away from this place that was full of the memories that took place and all the memories that she had hoped to create, but didn't get a chance to.

The Very Tolerant Person became the business owner in her home village. As fate would have it, not long after that, something else took place in the village. She met her future husband, the Person with Almost Unlimited Generosity at her father's inn. He was a guest at the hotel, and they started to date shortly after, and got married within fourteen months after that. They both had always accepted it as a sign from heaven, like The Very Tolerant Person's father had sent The Person with

Almost Unlimited Generosity with his blessing to his daughter through the inn he had built. The Very Tolerant Person wasn't as tolerant at that time. She always had a good heart and meant well for people around her, but the level of tolerance was only growing with time because she saw her husband treating people in such a positive and yet humble way that she couldn't possibly not admire it and eventually imitate it.

The main reason she didn't become another Very Generous Person, is because she felt a responsibility to her father to continue building the business he started and to make it the best inn in the state in his honor. So, she couldn't just give away free stays and free food and other perks to every guest, the way her husband seemed to be on a mission to do. But she became a smart business woman who made good decisions while letting her husband do generous things at appropriate times. They had balanced each other well, while also helping each other to grow and be better people.

With time, she became a more understanding person, knowing that every guest may have his or her story, and no matter how happy people seem in vacationing mode while visiting the beautiful places around the village, there could be hidden stories for no outsider to see. It could manifest itself in a drive to be a better person for someone they lost, someone they loved, or someone that they are still hoping to find. Also, she understood with time, that people of all races, nationalities, skin colors and different spoken languages have the same feelings, desires, and dreams. So, she included everyone. There was not a soul who stopped by at her inn who didn't get a chance to open up their true self to the inn owner, and there was no person who wouldn't be worthy of her time that they could spend over a cup of hot tea before bed near the bell desk and talk about their pain that's hidden from the world. She liked to listen and wanted to help as much as she could.

Her and her husband were wonderful together. They made a great team in business and life, but after spending a lovely twenty-nine years together, he passed away over a pile of his fishing rods, and everything had changed for the woman once again. She had to mourn again, maybe even harder this time than the first, but it had to be sustainable to be functionable enough to keep running the inn. So, she continued to listen to stories from her guests.

In doing so, those stories became even more valuable to her. Before the loss of her husband, she listened for the guests' sake, with the drive to be there for them, but after, it seemed it provided a healing power of sorts to her as well. It created a bit of an illusion that nothing had changed, and her husband could walk into the room any moment now and tell her a story that he learned from a guest from room seventeen, and that they should do something to help the poor visitor. Of course, that couldn't happen.

On another side, everything she had learned from her husband through almost three decades about treating others took another level of meaning to her, and the same way that she wanted to continue her father's legacy by building up the business, she felt an unstoppable desire to continue her husband's legacy by spreading the goodness of his heart.

When Granvill reached the inn, it was almost completely dark. He liked this time of the day. It was when the village was taking the role of a quiet paradise. He liked daytime as well, because of all the colors and the greenery that this place had to offer, but the night had always brought extra tranquility to his already comfortable life.

He entered the three-story building and right away was in the middle of a lobby. The lobby reminded him a mix of a professional city hotel with its desk bell, computers, coffee machine and overall cleanliness, and a grandma's house, with flowers and warmth all around. There were a couple of large paintings on the wall, one of mountain tops which were swallowed by the woods around it with lush green forestry and an ocean-blue sky, and another one was of a woman sitting alone on a park bench. She didn't seem to be too sad, as she was submerged in the peace of the place, but she seemed a bit lonely, nevertheless.

Granvill saw only one person behind the desk. It was the owner. She had a couple of helpers to fill in the 24 hours shifts, but for at least a few hours every day, the Very Tolerant Person was at the desk by herself, usually choosing the evening hours so she could catch that famous sharing tea and story time with her guests.

"Mr. Granvill," greeted the woman from behind the reception desk. "How are you today?"

"I am doing great, thank you for asking. I hope the same goes for you." responded Granvill, approaching the desk. "Anything new in your life?"

They had a pretty good friendship before. Granvill had an even closer friendship with her late husband, but after his death, they had spent more time talking about life and important events than before.

"I am doing good, Sir!"

She was smiling and looking straight at Granvill. He wasn't that much older than her, and if she was mentally and emotionally ready to date anyone, he was a candidate for sure. Everyone in the village who didn't think that Granvill was estranged thought he was handsome and appealing. Those two different camps wouldn't agree with each other on Granvill's life, but the mystery he had left as a trail for outsiders guaranteed that everyone just had to assume and create their perception of him on their own.

The Very Tolerant Person was quite a beautiful woman in her younger years, and even now she had two things that every woman probably should have, class and style. She has gained maybe twenty pounds or so throughout the years, but that didn't make her look any less attractive. The only reason she was still single was her memory of a happy, almost thirty-year long, marriage that she didn't allow herself to let go. She would rather spend an evening with a cup of tea and the memory of her husband than in the company of any potential theoretical man. But she did like Granvill. She liked his kindness, courtesy, and charm that were undeniably present in his every motion, even if he wasn't specifically trying to be charming.

"What brought you to this side of town?"

"Actually, if I could just borrow a piece of paper and a pen, that would be great."

"Of course," she was a bit surprised at such a trivial ask but didn't show it in any way.

The Very Tolerant Person provided Granvill everything he asked for without leaving her chair. Granvill accepted it with a smile and thanked her for her kindness.

He proceeded to write the note he felt he should provide to the Person Who Felt Insecure in Relationships as an explanation of his uninvited intrusion to her personal space. After he finished writing it, he gave the pen and the notepad back to the lady behind the desk.

"You look great today!" he smiled.

He wasn't trying to flirt, of course, but he liked to make people feel better about themselves, especially if he noticed in any way that they needed it.

"Oh, thank you, kindly," the Very Tolerant Person accepted the compliment with pleasure. "Would you like to have tea with me? I was just going to make myself a cup."

Granvill thought about it for a minute. He didn't have to go back right away, as the Person Who Felt Insecure in Relationships was probably going to work for a while longer; and even if she showed up at her house now, it was most likely she wouldn't notice anything right away as it was getting dark almost instantaneously. So, he accepted the offer from his friend and took a seat in the chair near the wall just a couple feet away from the bell desk.

They sat together and talked for a while about all sorts of things in life, including the inn, and how the business was going, and eventually the conversation touched on tulips as well. Granvill was eager to share that part of his life: his unconventional vision for the flowers for the village residents. The Very Tolerant Person was intrigued to learn more about it.

"So, you are planting them everywhere? Do you have a specific plan to plant all the tulips you have?"

"No, not a specific plan. You know, I think it would be nice to plant some for you, your guests would appreciate it."

"You are right. It's not a bad idea. We never had flowers here, not naturally grown anyways. We have flowers in pots, usually."

"This could be something different then. Almost fancy."

"True." The Very Tolerant Person was thinking that while it would be nice, she didn't feel like putting any more burden on Granvill. Although, she knew where he was coming from, pure kindness, the kind that she always appreciated in her late husband. "I would think about it, but I can't even call you to tell you about my decision."

She burst into short but sincere laughter. Granvill smiled in response, and then came up with a solution:

"I could stop by any other day and ask you in person."

"No, no, don't be silly. I will gladly accept your offer, but let's do this."

She had an idea, and, in the instant that it came to her, she was committed to it.

"You don't come here tomorrow, not yet. You put all the crates of bulbs you have all around the village, and if you have a couple of them left after that and no good place to put them, *then* you come here and finish it off in my garden outside."

Most of the time she thought about others first, and this idea had satisfied her. This way she got mentally involved in Granvill's project of doing this good deed for other residents of the village. Granvill liked her idea too. He agreed to it, and they proceeded to drink tea.

After talking for a bit about generic things in their everyday lives, they came to another interesting topic, a topic that Granvill would love to avoid if possible, but there was a certain level of respect he had for his friend that he couldn't ignore.

"How come you haven't been more involved?" she asked him.

"What do you mean? More involved in what?"

"More involved…. I don't know… more involved in life, I guess."

Those were the best words she could come up with right now.

"Dating someone, village events, work, community, anything. I know you were quite a businessman before; did you see what the Person Who Wants to be the Center of the Universe is doing? Kind of a competition to me, I think. But you used to do such things. You…. don't work, don't date. You don't get out much, you live on the outskirt of the village, and it seems that you prefer it that way."

She looked at him with curiosity and waited with bated breath. Granvill smiled. It was his usual emotional defense when he wasn't planning to share much of his personal life but was preparing himself to give a polite and courteous answer. He cared about others and didn't want them to feel as though they couldn't talk to him, but he also didn't see any real benefit of sharing private information from his life with people. In about a second and a half of smiling he proceeded with his response, warm in his intonation, but cold in context.

"I like my life. I don't see anything wrong with it. And don't want to change anything in it."

"So, you like being alone? Kind of a peaceful retirement?" She pondered with doubt. He masked it the best way he could.

"So, why tulips then? Isn't it… kind of being involved without really being involved?"

Granvill's smile didn't waver. But the question was spot on, and he realized that he wouldn't be able to brush it off with his regular politeness alone.

"I like the quietness and peace of this village, I enjoy the tranquility I find in my home, my garden, and the nearby woods and lakes."

He started talking seriously now.

"You are right, I lived a different kind of life before, and it has changed a few times since. Sometimes with my consent and other times without it. But I have come to realize one thing about my life. I don't want to be controlled by the *things* around me anymore. I loved working and building a resume of accomplishments, and I felt that I achieved a lot in my life. It was a good period of life for me. But now I don't want an alarm clock to control me and remind me of the time I need to wake up, or a cell phone or some Facebook app to tell me what's happening in my own life, or a bank account and bills to dictate how much I *must* make next month. I earned, through hard work, a certain level of freedom, to do the little things I want every day and any day I choose. And I try to pay little attention to any other noise around me."

He stopped for a minute.

"You enjoy talking to your guests and enjoy running this place, and I enjoy not having a place where I *must be* every day. I like the spontaneity of my life right now. And as for the tulips…. I am not sure how to answer that. I think I have my reasons, but I am not sure I ever went into it thinking about them too deeply."

He smiled again, polite and friendly, as always, but he still wasn't ready to explore the chance of being an open book. She was a friend, and he knew she was coming with questions from a good place in her heart, but he had his own idea about how to express himself, and sharing personal stories wasn't part of it. Despite the fact that he would like to satisfy the good intentions of reaching out to him by his friend, it was more important to Granvill to stick to the little principles he still kept in his life.

The Very Tolerant Person was listening and paying attention to every word of his. She understood what her friend meant in his expression.

"I know where you are coming from. Sometimes I also consider retiring and doing something else, maybe travel. I would love to travel more. See the world. I don't think I had enough chances to do that." She looked at Granvill prudently. "I am glad you have the life you want. That's all that matters in the end. And I hope your idea with tulips will get you the results you are looking for."

Granvill agreed with the woman and thanked her for the kind words. He knew she was a good friend and a great listener. He knew that she would love to hear more from him, but also, she was not going to push for it, and he loved that she could feel his inner mood and respect his wishes. He finished his cup of tea, and decided it was the perfect time to get back to the Person Who Felt Insecure in Relationships' home.

The walk back took the same amount of time as the walk to the inn earlier, less than five minutes, even at his pace. When he reached the house, there was still no lights inside of it, so he assumed that its owner didn't come back yet. He looked around. The street was as quiet as it was most of the day. He thought for a second that it was convenient for him that the road was curvy, and had a curve at the right place too, so even if it was located only five or six houses away from a busy inn, that curve eliminated the chance of seeing The Very Tolerant Person's hotel from this angle, and the trees in between covered the whole three stories of the building. It was also helpful that the main road from the inn was going in the other direction from this street which was directed towards the church he passed on the way and Granvill's house eventually after that.

So, again there was no one around to see Granvill get his body over the fence or witness him push the note through the gem of the door so it hung and would fall when the door opens or take his duffle bag and cross the fence one more time and finally be on his way to his own house. Granvill realized that the note admitted his trespassing endeavor and that fact alone could be enough for him to be in trouble in some legal manner in the case of the worst possible reaction from the property owner, but he believed, in general, the best of people. Even though life has proven him *wrong*. Time after time.

CHAPTER 6

Granvill wanted to step up his tulip planting, because while the tulips could stay fresh in his cooler for a while, the season for planting wasn't too far from ending. When the real cold weather got here, the ground would be frozen, especially at night, and not only would it be almost impossible to sow, but also the bulbs would not have enough time and warmth to break through, so they could come out in the spring. But the old man had a new plan: no more day offs, just pure work until all the crates were gone. He wasn't worried too much though, he figured if some bulbs would be left over, then so be it, it wasn't worth any self-inflicted stress. He ordered twenty-five crates as an approximate without any real calculations, and if he had a chance to empty them all, then it would just give him an extra feeling of satisfaction.

The next day, Granvill decided to go to the local doctor's office. He figured that it was the best place to have flowers next. Patients coming in or going out would appreciate a small field of the vibrant and colorful tulips. The village wasn't too big, so there was only one medical building where the dentist was occupying the east wing, and the doctor had taken the west wing of the building. They didn't have any room for a garden in front of the office, the parking lot was the priority for that, but there was a great space off the west wing of the building.

Granvill also knew that planting the bulbs on the weekend while the offices were closed was a smart idea, and he used this time wisely. He worked both days from morning to sunset and finished just in time. But he was doing it right off the main street, and people were noticing him. Some of them would stop by to ask questions. His response was always simple and direct: "I am planting tulips for the spring". No one asked him, however, if he was doing it with permission. They all assumed that the doctor allowed it, and that he asked Granvill for help. But the next person passing by knew that the doctor didn't allow any of it, and that was the doctor himself. He saw the old man working in the dirt near his office and asked the same question, and hearing the standard response, he *did* follow it up with another question:

"But who asked you to do that?"

It was only then that Granvill realized he was talking to the doctor.

"Oh," he stood up trying to clean up his pants with quick brush strokes of his hands.

"Really no one. But, Sir, I don't think there is any harm in you having a small garden of flowers. They do not need watering, they will make your patients happy, and I don't mind doing it."

The Doctor, who also happened to be the Person Who Needs Affirmation, was deciding what to say next. He was generally a kind person, and he wanted his patients to get the best medical care from him, as well as be happy with his clinic. At the same time, he didn't like that someone was doing something without his permission, but he could take control now. He could either give that permission or shut down the whole project. He was leaning towards the first option but didn't want to give it to the old man too easily.

"This is my property, and it's important to me that I know what's happening on my property. No one just comes in and does whatever they want. Especially in medical practice, there are such things as patients' privacy, laws and regulations. Do you understand?" He said sternly.

Granvill didn't quite understand it exactly, but he realized he didn't need to in this situation. He just nodded and agreed:

"Absolutely, Sir".

"And don't call me Sir! I am at least ten years younger than you!"

"Understood." Granvill was politely curt.

The Person Who Needs Affirmation then thought on what else he could say to the old man. It was too bad that Granvill wasn't arguing with him. It would provide the doctor the needed fuel and momentum to take control of this conversation. But now he really didn't have much left to say.

"If I let you plant those tulips here, it's because I care about my patients. Otherwise, I would stop you from continuing what you are doing. Understand?"

Granvill nodded again.

"Good. Because there are not many things worse than doing things behind someone else's back. So, if anyone asks, I *hired* you to do this from the beginning. Is that OK with you?"

Granvill nodded again. He knew that the villagers would not believe that the doctor hired him anyway. There were at least two reasons they wouldn't. First, Granvill wasn't hired by anyone to do anything, especially garden work, and secondly, there were other people in the village who already received the planted tulips, and they knew they didn't hire Granvill to do anything. But out loud he said totally different words:

"Of course, that makes sense. I wouldn't be here if you didn't hire me."

He looked at the doctor's eyes with kindness, hiding his inside smile. He was getting a bit amused by the doctor's desire to show himself in the best light. Before the Person Who Needs Affirmation could continue and possibly finish this confrontation, they both heard another car screech to a stop next to the sidewalk of the doctor's office. The Person Who is Proud to be Hard-Working had already heard about Granvill's doings from other people in the village. Just by the way he pulled up in his blue Toyota Camry, you could tell that this wasn't going to be a friendly conversation. He rapidly came up to Granvill, not noticing the doctor standing nearby, and started yelling at him right away:

"Do you know what you are doing?!"

Granvill slowly turned to face the angry man.

"Not exactly, no." His response was slow and calm.

The man continued to yell. His face was expressing all his feelings at the same time, and his featured huge forehead was sweating from all the extreme emotions. His forehead was so big that one could be concerned that either his brain was too big, and required all that space, or maybe it was floating freely in there, like a maple leaf in a pool. Either way, there was no way to not notice his big forehead. His eyes, which were accurately placed underneath that big mountain mass of forehead, were usually calm but weren't right now. The eyes and the forehead were playing a game catch me if you can. The eyes were bigger than usual and climbing all the way to the edge of the forehead, while the forehead was protecting its own territory, and trying to climb even further into the haircut of rich dark hair or maybe even completely out of the skull. No one in the village knew exactly that that man's forehead was capable of.

"You are planting free flowers!!!!"

It didn't seem he was ready to throw punches just yet, but Granvill was preparing himself to duck just in case. Meanwhile, the old man connected the dots. The Person Who is Proud to be Hard-Working also happened to be the local flower salesman, and he did well at the farmer's market every day because people of the village really didn't have anyone else to buy the flowers from. The man had a monopoly here, and if people weren't willing to drive to Fish Haven for a bouquet, then he was the go-to man. Granvill realized he was putting that monopoly in jeopardy, even if he wasn't opening a flower business, but planting them for free. *Maybe* that was worse.

"Listen, I am not really following. What's the problem? There are no flowers yet, and there will not be any for months." He tried to be rational, although he knew that would not work. But by starting the rational dialogue, he was hoping to fish out more arguments from the opponent.

The Person Who is Proud to be Hard-Working responded still in a yelling voice:

"Tulips that grow in April will most likely last in May as well, when there is also Mother's Day, on May thirteenth!!! Who will buy flowers from me for Mother's Day if they will have it growing for free on every corner??!!"

Granvill knew that the salesman had a point here, but also knew it was highly exaggerated.

"Let me explain. Please."

He looked at the flower salesman and noticed that he was given at least a second or so to explain himself.

"I have a limited supply of tulips, and some of them will not even grow before they get a chance to bloom. Secondly, not everyone is cheap, and *most* people would still want to buy other flowers than tulips for such a special occasion as Mother's Day. Especially, and think about it, because the whole village will know tulips will be available for free! What kind of mother wants to get a gift from their children that required no effort on their part? And what kind of grown person would want to give flowers to their mother that will make them look like they didn't put any effort into it?"

The Person Who is Proud to be Hard-Working listened to that speech and took a liking to it. He was slowly realizing that Granvill was possibly right. He could see how he could even run a marketing campaign with a couple of posters, in the tone of "Don't Let Your Mother think You Don't Care". It was perfect. He was getting excited again. Then he turned his attention to Granvill again:

"So, why do you do this?"

He finally noticed the doctor standing three feet away, observing the whole interaction.

"Hey, doc. Having a good day?"

The doctor nodded towards Granvill and said:

"I am getting free flowers. I should say that doesn't happen every day."

The flower salesman's forehead began to form wrinkles again between his eyebrows.

"But for Mother's Day I am buying flowers from you!" The doctor rushed to assure the man.

"Good," there was a barely visible smile coming from the salesman's mouth. Then he turned his attention back to Granvill, waiting for a response to his last question directed at the old man.

"I just wanted to do something nice for a few people," replied Granvill with a calming voice. "You should know better than anyone that flowers can make people feel special, they have the power of healing, the power of bringing joy. I just want to be a part of someone's joy."

Granvill's voice was soft and soothing. He was talking about his vision the way people talk about eating their favorite chocolate dessert.

"Yes, flowers do have that kind of power," agreed the salesman. "Are you planning to do it every year?"

"I am not going to promise anything, but no, I have no plans to do it again after this. Just a one-time gesture idea."

The Person Who is Proud to be Hard-Working really did work tenuously to build his business. He also grew some flowers on his own, here in the village. That was one of his hobbies long before it became a business. But mostly, he imported the product from the city, and he was serious about keeping the opportunity to put the food on the table for his family.

"Hmmm. It is a nice thing to do."

The Person Who is Proud to be Hard-Working wasn't sure what else to say.

"Sorry I yelled." He started to throw some strange hand gestures like they could explain the whole thing, the way he angrily parked, ran over, and yelled at the old man.

His eyes returned from his forehead and were feeling a lot more comfortable back in the right place, and even his forehead, while still gigantic, was peacefully hovering over his face like a king on the throne over his kingdom.

Granvill didn't mind it at all. He understood people's emotions better than most, and he also knew that not everyone was good at handling the emotions the way he did.

"It's totally OK," he looked at the salesman attentively and patiently.

"We all have those moments. And I am sorry. I didn't realize right away that I should've talk to you about it before. I didn't think of how it could look from the outside and be perceived in a more negative light than I ever could have thought of."

Now the salesman was getting uncomfortable. Granvill's kindness took away all his emotional weapons. He didn't feel anymore that the old man had anything to apologize for, and hearing the apology was making him feel even more guilty about his own actions.

"No, no, no need." He put his heavy arm on Granvill's shoulder. "We are good."

Granvill was glad they were good, and there was no more tension between them. The doctor also had a good feeling about Granvill right now. He realized that he didn't know the old man very well, despite living at the same village for the past seven years. He also realized that Granvill wasn't even a patient of his. He saw him once in his office, about six years ago, and he still remembered that the old man was extremely healthy with no problems on the horizon of any kind. He hadn't seen him since then, but the old man looked just as healthy today as he did six years ago. But he liked how Granvill handled this confrontation today, and he was curious to learn more about the man. The Person Who Needs Affirmation decided to not pursue it any further. He looked at the old man one more time, then at the half-done soil, and excused himself with a polite "Gentlemen", turned around and started walking to his car parked near the sidewalk.

The Person Who is Proud to be Hard-Working followed the doctor's lead and left Granvill by himself. He got to his car after the doctor reached his but drove away in a quick manner first.

Doc slowly opened the car door, put his body inside, but before he closed the door, he wanted to say one more thing:

"Granvill."

The old man turned around in the direction of the voice.

"Thank you." It wasn't annunciated too loud, but it was confident and firm.

Then he closed the door and drove away.

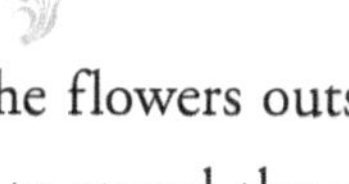

After finishing planting the flowers outside of the doctor's office, Granvill was planning to spend the next couple of days doing the same for the Selfish Person. This task was as difficult as planting tulips for the Person Who Felt Insecure in Relationships. While the latter was a financial advisor and worked the whole day, the Selfish Person was a local Realtor, and while maybe she didn't work as hard, she still put some hours in. In the small town, it was easy to know when she was showing one of the houses.

Most of her business was also in Fish Haven or other surrounding areas, because the village wasn't big enough for a realtor to make money on a consistent basis. She probably should live in one of those places outside of the village too, instead of driving almost every day to remote locations. But her house was passed on to her by her parents, and she valued the history of it.

When she would meet the man of her dreams, who could take her away to a nicer and bigger place, then she would move. Only then she would decide what to do with her parents' house. But for now, there was no such man in her life.

She dated the Person Who Was Obsessed with His Body for a while. He lived in a condo near the largest gym in Fish Haven, the same place he also worked at. He spent most of his free time there too, continuing to sculpt his body in the Greek God mode.

Most girls loved his personality, as he was social and pleasant to be around. The Selfish Person also liked that about him, but the thing she loved the most was the way people would look at them when they were together. She was quite stunning in any outfit and usually wore a tight dress and high heels, and he was taking a lot of females' attention and jealous looks next to her. They were great together, but neither one felt like settling down yet, or starting a family for that matter. Also, she wasn't sure if the Person Who was Obsessed with His Body could afford to give her the lifestyle she wanted for the rest of her life. So, there was a lot to think about there.

But she knew she was happy about at least one thing in her life: her Instagram page. It had a decent following, and most of the pictures were impressive. That was also the way she was beating out her competition. Most of her clients came through the page, and they loved the fact that they were dealing with a beautiful local celebrity of sorts.

Granvill knew the tulips that he would plant for the Selfish Person wouldn't change a thing about her or her life. At least right away. But no one knows what could happen tomorrow, and especially six months from now. They would have to wait until April of the next year before the tulips would even bloom, and by then, the situation in anyone's life could be different. In the off chance that The Selfish Person would have a day where the flowers would make some unexpected impact, that would be worth the effort Granvill was going to put in. In the worst-case scenario, if the tulips will make no impact at all, the flowers would remain flowers. They would grow, bloom and die, no matter how beautiful they would be or no matter of the level of desire to have them from the people around them.

Granvill wasn't going to project or measure the possible impact of his actions, he was just doing this because in his heart, it was important. Something that could end up making some impact on the other person. He knew that The Selfish Person was the kind of person who needed a positive impact to get her life on a better path. That's all Granvill needed to know. The rest wasn't up to him. Not today, not ever.

So, planting for the Selfish Person was done without any adventures or meaningful conversations. One time, the Person with No Imagination, who lived next door, came out of his house to his porch, smoked a cigarette, and saw Granvill working hard on his neighbor's soil, while crawling on his knees in the dirt. The Person with No Imagination looked at the old man suspiciously, but not for long. After his cigarette was finished, his interest evaporated, and he turned away and went back to his house. After all, he couldn't even imagine that Granvill could possibly jump the fence to crawl in someone else's garden, so he let it go. It wasn't his concern after all.

After planting all he could in the free space of the garden of The Selfish Person, Granvill shifted his focus on another house, located just a couple of structures down the street. That house belonged to the Person Without Care for Others. The main difference between the last two people that Granvill picked was quite simple. The Selfish Person did a lot of good things for other people, and quite a few of them didn't even realize that she was doing it for selfish reasons. But the Person Without Care for Others couldn't pretend that other people existed in this world. He was doing his job at the construction site as quietly and as distant from others as humanly possible, and then went back to his cave to simmer until the next day.

The Selfish Person loved her parents, and while they were alive, she was quite helpful around the house. She took care of her sick mother for a few months before she passed away, because having her mother around for a longer time brought her a certain comfort and joy, and she could continue to spread her love towards the people closest to her. The Person Without Care for Others had a mercantile kind of love towards his parents, and after his father's death, he realized he wasn't planning to take care of his mother even for a minute. It wasn't convenient to him anymore, and he found a quick and easy way to put his mother into a retirement home. He wasn't really hiding his one-dimensional feelings from his parent either. He just didn't care enough to think how his mother must have felt at that moment, or any other moment, really.

The Selfish Person didn't do anything that wasn't aligned with her own benefit like promoting her business. But she was aware that to grow her business, she needed many powerful and rich people on her side, and she was friendly to most people around her. One could never know who would end up being powerful or rich down the road. Common folks would buy houses from her too and bring her a nice commission check. If she were to be honest with herself, common folks were comprising the largest portion of her clients.

She also liked to surround herself with people less pretty than her, people who could give her a continuous flow of compliments on how beautiful she was. Less fortunate people would notice her successful career, and people with less followers on Instagram, which was every single person in Fish Haven, her own village or any surrounding area, could comment on her next picture she would share on social media. All of that gave her the attention she wanted to continue to feed her self-centered, although not that unpleasant, persona. People loved her, and they loved her chatty and flirty personality.

The Person Without Care for Others had a completely opposite effect on people. No one really enjoyed having him around, as he was noticeably irritated to listen anyone else's story, and generally was just not a nice person. People knew he was talking far less than pleasant words behind his boss's back, and the Person with Bad Luck seemed to be the only person in the village who wasn't aware it was happening most of the days of every week. People were aware how easy the Person Without Care for Others dumped his mother off his hands into the hands of the professional facility in Fish Haven. Therefore, he had no girlfriend or any real friends. A couple of co-workers of his would get a beer with the guy on a rare occasion, but that was pretty much the extent of any relationship the Person Without Care for Others managed to have in the village.

Granvill knew the nature of both people. He has always been quite detail-oriented, and not much would get past him. He would notice behaviors and words that most people would ignore, and then the puzzle of human personalities would put itself together without his conscious effort. He just knew what certain puzzles would look like and kept that information to himself for the future understanding of what people's' motives were when they did or said specific things. That knowledge has proven to be useful to Granvill many times before. But most of the time, it was information that not really needed as he wasn't interacting with people in the village close enough for this knowledge to pay off in the most effective way. But every conversation was a potential opportunity for him to apply the knowledge so that the conversation would go in the desired direction.

In this case, he was hoping he would not have to interact with the Person Without Care for Others. The simple task of planting the tulip bulbs without the owner noticing would be a perfect result for the old man. However, it wasn't destined to be this way.

On his very first day, a mere hour after hopping over the fence, the Person Without Care for Others came back home in a rush and saw Granvill even from the other side of the fence. He opened the gate in a wild manner, and Granvill quickly realized that the property owner was absolutely and unquestionably aware about his illegal trespassing. Granvill stood up facing the gate, in which seconds earlier, he saw the Person Without Care for Others storming through.

"What are you doing here?!"

The old man could tell that the Person Without Care for Others wasn't happy at all finding him here.

"I am planting some flowers in your yard." Calmly responded the intruder.

"What?!"

"Just planting some flowers for you." Granvill's voice didn't change one bit.

"I don't need your stinking flowers!" screamed the host.

"Maybe not today, but they are free, maybe you could sell them or something." calmly replied Granvill.

The Person Without Care for Others didn't even slow down to think about that opportunity. Not like he could make a lot of money with the flowers, but it still wasn't that bad of an idea. But he had other concerns at the moment, and the main one was this old dude who thought he could just show up on anyone's property and do whatever the hell he wanted to do.

"You don't think I have enough money or what?!" he yelled, almost in Granvill's face now.

"I don't need your stinking flowers! I don't want you in my yard, period!"

Granvill took a breath, then manufactured a smile, not big, but warm and sincere:

"I can leave your property now, and I apologize for crossing the line here, or I could finish planting these flowers in a day and a half, and then you will never see me again."

The Person Without Care for Others was shocked by this man's inability to understand that he didn't want anything from him. And he most definitely wasn't going to wait for a day and a half before he left his property.

"Would you rather I kick your ass?!"

Granvill smiled even bigger now. He wasn't sure if there was no real threat to him in this situation, as he could be here for real trouble. But he said out loud quite a different sentence and in even softer voice than before:

"First of all, I don't think you could, and I don't think you should try."

He continued before the host even realized the audacity of those words.

"Second," still with the same smile on his face. "I really hope you reconsider the offer. I understand you are upset as I tried to pull it off without your permission, but now I am asking *for* your permission. Please, let me work in your garden for free, just for another day and a half, and I will leave nothing behind but some cool flowers for you to do anything you want within a few months of time."

Now, the Person Without Care for Others was really puzzled by all of that.

"You know when my neighbor called me at work, and said someone was in my garden, the last thing I expected was you. I was thinking it was some kids or punks who'd want to steal something. But now I see that I have a bigger problem, some old crazy dude! I've seen you around the village a few times, but what the hell is wrong with you?!"

Granvill stopped smiling and looked directly in the other man's eyes, accepting the serious threat of upcoming confrontation:

"There is probably a lot of things wrong with me."

And continued without losing his temper or hurting his ego:

"But in this situation, the only thing that you should be concerned with is whether you want to let me finish what I started, or would you rather I leave now, and what could have been a nice tulip garden in your yard will never happen?"

The Person Without Care for Others didn't consider the options even for a moment:

"I want you out of here! And I don't need your damn flowers!"

Then he took a breath and felt compelled to continue:

"And make sure you don't ever trespass to my property again! That will not end well for you, old man!"

Granvill understood that there was nothing else left to do here but walk away.

"OK", he said while grabbing his duffle bag and going in the direction of the gate. The unwelcoming host was breathing anger out of his lungs, *a feeling that was so useless in modern society, it was amazing how often people experienced it anyway,* thought Granvill to himself. The trespasser walked out of the gate without turning around and kept walking down the street. He wasn't sure what the Person Without Care for Others was going to do with the tulips that were already planted. Would he take them out of the ground or let them be and tear them off in the spring instead? But that was out of Granvill's control. He knew in advance that not every person would accept the idea of his caring gesture, especially because he picked very specific people in the village. People who, in his opinion, needed to see the beauty of flowers and the humanity behind it, the most. But it didn't mean that they would.

He decided to take the rest of the day off, having enough confrontation for the day, and who knew what the next place he was going to go, would bring. That's how life worked anyways. No matter how much people planned, no one could know what tomorrow would bring. Any direction people take can be redirected or completely turned around in just a few seconds of random chaos. The key was, in Granvill's experience, not letting fears to overcome one's life even before anything could happen.

CHAPTER 7

The next day, Granvill was ready to go at it again. He was back on the same street as he was last week, where the Person Who Felt Insecure in Relationships lived, but this time he stopped one house short and stayed on the other side of the road, where the Person with Bad Luck lived. Granvill didn't know too much about him except that he was a local businessman and an owner of the construction company, which was established by his father. He also knew that the Person with Bad Luck spent a lot of his time in his house. He didn't have as busy of a schedule as other people in the village and didn't have to be anywhere daily, kind of like Granvill himself. So, Granvill decided to approach this situation quite differently than yesterday.

That morning, around 9am, Granvill stood in front of the main entrance to the Person with Bad Luck's house with his duffle bag in hand. He knocked on the door with full confidence, looking forward to the conversation he was about to have. The door opened fifteen seconds later, and he saw the man of the house in front of him. He was about Granvill's age, maybe a bit older, not as tall, and not as handsome, but there was nothing unattractive about him either. He was wearing a dark blue plush thick bathrobe, even though it seemed he woke up a while ago.

"Good morning, Sir," Granvill greeted. "Do you have a minute to discuss something with me?"

The man looked surprised only for a mere second, and then calmly stepped out of the doorway giving a welcoming enter gesture to the guest. Granvill didn't wait too long and walked right in.

"Would you like some coffee? My espresso machine makes a great one, and I was just going to have a cup," asked the host.

"That would be wonderful," replied Granvill as he questioned himself on why he chose the word "wonderful" over any other word in his vocabulary.

"Great!"

Both men walked into the kitchen where, sure enough, a fancy espresso machine that you would find at a coffee shop, was quietly seeping coffee out of itself straight into a white mug.

"So, what can I do for you?" showing his hand gesture for Granvill to take the seat behind the kitchen table.

Granvill looked at the man across the table more closely. He was quite average in everything, but had a kind of artistic face, especially with his rounded forehead and prominent, round cheeks. He usually wore glasses too, which could apply to many different personalities, but fit his generally artistic look. His dark hair was rarely combed, and it sometimes seemed like it grew out from the seventies and never changed since. Granvill was hoping that the artistic side would win out the logical one after their conversation. When the guest started to speak, the Person with Bad Luck stood up to get his cup of coffee out of the espresso machine and placed another cup underneath while loading the fancy coffee maker with another capsule of South American imported coffee.

"Do you like tulips, Sir?" asked Granvill while thinking about why he was compelled to call the Person with Bad Luck "Sir".

"Tulips?" He went into a thinking mode, clearly this wasn't the usual topic of conversation in his house. "I mean, I have some flowers in the backyard, but I don't think any tulips. Not my favorite flower though."

"But you also don't have anything against tulips, right?"

"No, I suppose not." The host sat down back at the table waiting for the cup of coffee to finish brewing.

"I have been planting tulips for a few people in the village, and I would love to plant some for you."

The Person with Bad Luck was expecting rather bad news of some kind rather than what he just heard from Granvill. More often than not, bad news followed the businessman throughout his life. Sometimes, even the good things in his life were perceived by him as eventually unfortunate. He had a different point of view for the most part. He wasn't particularly negative, and it was quite an admiring feat how well the man took the bad news in his lifetime. But he wasn't too positive either, so in his mind, events would never shape up to be great fortunes in his life. Here, he didn't hear anything bad yet, but his life had a way of changing that. He decided to hold on his judgement until he heard more.

"I have tulip bulbs, plenty of them, and would do all the work at no cost to you, all I need is your blessing to do so," explained the old man.

The Person with Bad Luck really put his brain to work now in thought. Interrupting the process, he stood up to get both coffee mugs, now full of delightfully pungent imported coffee, and put one of them in front of his rare guest. He sat back down and tasted the pleasing liquid. He continued his thinking process, and now, with the needed shot of caffeine, he was able to grasp all possible angles of the situation at hand.

"What is in it for you?" He asked Granvill looking at him suspiciously; his logical side was overtaking his artistic side.

"Really, not much. But the pleasure of doing it for nice people like yourself is worth a lot to me." Granvill's' response wasn't completely from the heart. It was more of a nice thing to tell someone, but that's not to say there was no truth in that statement. He didn't know how to explain the motives of his project better for others.

"Hmmm." The Person with Bad Luck wasn't going to give in this easily.

"Listen, it seems like a nice thing for you to do for people, and I do need a bit of upgrade in my backyard. It's been a while since my wife passed for anyone else really cared for it. But let me ask you a couple of questions first, if you don't mind."

Granvill didn't mind at all. He knew that the Person with Bad Luck went through a lot in his life, and Granvill would not want to refuse him the comfort of being okay with the planting. He also knew that one of the things that solidified the host to believe himself being the Person with Bad Luck was his experience with his late wife. They met just a bit too late for them to have an ideal family. She was in her forties, and she couldn't have kids at that point, even though they tried every option available in modern science. They had a great time together, but they both wanted more. And exhausting all options to have a baby in her womb, the couple was considering an adoption, but his wife got sick, and he wanted to wait for her to get better. The time never came. She had complications after a routine surgery, and they had only a few more months of their lives together before she inevitably passed.

That was almost eleven years ago, and in that time the Person with Bad Luck's life only went downhill from there. After a couple of years of trying to bury his grief in his construction business, he realized that he really didn't want to do that anymore and stopped going to work altogether. Money was steadily still coming in to his bank account, and the amount supported his lifestyle, but it bothered him that he didn't even know who would inherit the company after he would be gone. He spent his time mostly at home now, reading and painting, which became the most important passion of his life over the last couple of years. Sometimes he participated in charity and fundraising events and would travel outside of the state two-three times a year, but nothing was fulfilling him, nothing was truly making him happy. He wasn't miserable either; he made his best effort to enjoy his comfortable house, silence filling most of his days, coffee in the morning, a book in the lunch time and painting birds or trees in the evening before bed. He didn't have a bad life, but he had bad luck on the way of building a good one.

"No, I don't mind at all, please go ahead with any questions," Granvill was here for as long as he needed to be to earn the right to extend his help to the man across him. After yesterday's fiasco at the Person Without Care for Other's house, he didn't want to get the same result here, even though it was a different treatment.

"Ok," quite pleased with having a decently interesting person to have a decently meaningful conversation with.

"We haven't talked much before, although we've lived in the same village for many, many years. In your opinion, do you live your perfect ideal life?"

Granvill didn't want to take this conversation lightly and was ready to answer to the best of his abilities.

"I honestly wish I knew what that life was…. Perfect and ideal may not really exist. But… I suppose, there is a certain level of satisfaction from my previous life comparing to some other parts of my current life. But also, this is not the happiest part of my life. But satisfying…. Nevertheless."

The Person with Bad Luck appreciated the effort, and he could tell the guest wasn't going to waste his time with some of the social clichés of inspirational quotes circling around on Facebook.

"You are right about that, there may be no ideal or perfect life. Do you feel the life you have now, you said, quite satisfying, was built by your hands or brought to you by some destiny, or fate?" The second question wasn't easier than the first.

Granvill stopped drinking his coffee and traveled into the deepest parts of his brain. He had asked himself that question so many times before, yet it still needed a deep moment now. Every time, he came up with a different answer to it, depending on the season, maybe; or more likely, depending on the events that shaped his perception.

"Probably both. What's the likeliness of us having this conversation at this specific point in time? And I don't think either one of us had any plans of having one, or even knew about its potential existence just a week ago. So that's something to do with fate."

Granvill's mind was racing through all pieces of knowledge he had acquired in his lifetime as he answered.

"At the same time, if I hadn't made a *conscious* choice to plant tulips, or if you had never decided to open your door and generously offer me a cup of coffee in your house, destiny wouldn't be able to continue this particular path."

Then he thought how likely it was that his thoughts and decisions were controlled by fate as well, but he didn't mention that part out loud.

"My life, I want to believe at least, a lot of it, is my doing," he continued. "And that I made a *conscious* decision to walk away from my old life and choose this one. That's why I enjoy it. The nature, the freedom, the choices I can make every single day, but also there was quite a few events that happened to me that are totally out of my control. Events that if they *didn't happen*, then… I probably would never have been in a position to even want to walk away from my old life. And I probably still would live in the city doing what I did before."

The Person with Bad Luck listened carefully. He was absorbing information like a true artist, with the intention of using it somewhere in some way in his future paintings.

Then he asked the most important question to him:

"Do you think that there could be such a thing like unavoidable fate, despite the wishes and desires that we may have?"

Now it was Granvill's time to absorb the question and try to figure out how to respond to that. He paused.

"I don't know. Maybe all our decisions are not really our decisions, but our *submission* to our fate. Maybe me walking away from my old life was destined to happen one way or another, and me being in this village and my desire to plant tulips. All of that maybe would happen no matter what I did. And maybe the universe knows what your answer to my request is going to be…. But I want to believe, that in the next hour *you* will decide to say yes or no, and *only you*. I want to believe that I decided on my own to choose your house and knock on your door, and I hope we both have real choices on this."

"What about my bad luck?" asked the host. He arrived at another important question, a question that didn't allow him to sleep at night; a question that would make him stop painting and think about all the unfortunate events in his life; a question that would make him feel so helpless that he would want to abandon everything he had and do something drastic.

"I don't want to offend you, but are you sure it was bad luck all along? Didn't your life give something good to you as well?"

Granvill didn't know the answers to the questions he was asking right now. It was a process of thinking out loud together with The Person with Bad Luck.

"And don't you have time now to do what you want to do, paint and create and spend time your way? Honestly, I think we are in pretty similar situations. And I know that we both would rather do our favorite things, like painting for you and cooking or gardening for me, while enjoying the company of our wives and children, but what we have is still not the worst gig on this Earth."

"Hmmm…." the host was really considering all options. It seemed like Granvill did stop by at his house at the right time. Either it was some kind of fate or a mere coincidence, but the timing was curious at the least.

"You may be right. Maybe, we decide only small things, like who to hire on the construction site, how much to pay them, which vendor to use for the materials. But the big things? I don't know. The big things are *bigger* than us. My wife's death, us not having children, my father pushing me into construction… "

"Maybe the big things require more of a resistance from us to withstand the pressure from the universe. It is possible and logical to think that the importance of life events directly correlates to the level of resistance and strength required from us to get it our way, to go against certain luck."

"Are you suggesting that some mysterious strength would've saved my wife from dying? Are you saying that I wasn't strong enough to keep my wife for longer?" The house owner wasn't angry yet, only because he was puzzled by the absurdity of the thoughts.

"No, no, not at all." Granvill realized he didn't express what he had on his mind in the proper words. "Maybe more strength is required to not see your wife's death as horrible luck that follows you wherever you go, but still see the time you had with her, no matter how short it was, as a blessing. And to understand that things do happen, sometimes in a very random order to us, but we have the ability to choose how to react to it and choose what we do after those events. I was trying to say that the bigger the event in our life, the bigger the impact, the bigger the need arises for us to resist the universe. Standing alone with a higher level of resistance to not let that event define who we are for the rest of our lives. I know it may sound like a speech from one of those inspirational videos, but it could be true. And I think you have that kind of strength."

The Person with Bad Luck didn't hear anything completely new to him; he had heard different versions of how he should handle the death of his wife before, and sometimes he wanted so badly to resist to his own belief that all of that was an unfortunate endless flow of terrible luck. But he also heard it this time in a little bit different light. The way Granvill said it resonated with him, just enough to question the way the Person with Bad Luck had lived his life up to this point.

"I am sorry for your loss though, *death* has no logic to it," said Granvill trying to put real meaning in his words. He knew that a typical collection of letters from an alphabet wasn't adequate to express what he wanted to express in this moment, but it never hurt to try.

"Thank you." Calmly responded the Person with Bad Luck.

Both men sat in silence for a bit. The thoughts that were discussed and now floated in air around them weren't born today, they tormented both men for a big chunk of their lives. They handled the perception of answers they had for themselves slightly differently, but they knew too well the price of the burden that those answers came with.

"I don't know how much I have left in this life, but I do know I would really like to find a new way to finish it," declared the host.

"You asked me if I lived my perfect ideal life, what kind of life would that be for you?" Granvill was hoping that the question would propel some positivity. Tulips were still important, but a lot less than this conversation and this moment.

"Definitely more painting. Maybe even do a gallery and get some recognition as an artist. I think that would be nice. Some company in my life would be nice too." asserted the Person with Bad Luck.

"I think you should do that then." Granvill stated. "And if I can help in any way, let me know. I would with pleasure."

The host looked at Granvill. He wasn't going to change his life in this instant or proclaim victorious speech about turning his life around. Deep down he knew it wasn't going to be easy. Not only the part where he wanted to commit to painting, but everything else that would come with it: going against his own nature, against his principles and beliefs, pushing forward and never looking back, and moving on from his late wife and other misfortunes that followed him for decades. But he was seriously considering taking action, possibly even today. He needed time alone to figure out what that would look like.

"Let's start with tulips." announced the Person with Bad Luck extending his right hand for a handshake. "And then we go from there."

Granvill shook his hand with eagerness and respect, also with hope that it was just the beginning of something special.

"Thank you!" said Granvill.

"No, thank *you*. I look forward to seeing the tulips grow. Maybe I can paint them when they come out of the ground."

Granvill looked at the man on the other side of handshake and saw him smiling. Openly and sincerely. That gave the old man a warm feeling. The fact that he could follow up now with planting tulips as well made this even better.

When he started working in the garden, the Person with Bad Luck stayed inside of the house to read a book. A little later, he came outside with the book and watched Granvill plant tulips. After another hour or so, the Person with Bad Luck asked Granvill if it was ok if he helped a little. Granvill agreed, of course, and the host went inside of the house to change into more appropriate clothing for that. When he came back, he looked excited about the new upcoming activity. He felt good to be a part of it now, and together they worked hard for the rest of the day.

They finished with the duffle bag much sooner as expected, mostly because there were two of them now going at it, but they had a couple of more interesting conversations along the way. They had lunch together inside of the house and had a good time. The next day the Person with Bad Luck was in an even better mood, and he looked forward to doing more work with Granvill. They had a morning coffee together and talked about life. They went into deep discussions about expectations, plans, Granvill's experience so far planting the tulips in the village, and many other topics. Then they proceeded to the garden where in the next four to five hours, they accomplished what Granvill had planned. They finished it shortly after a quick break for lunch.

"My friend," the Person with Bad Luck approached his guest. "I want to thank you. First, for the tulips. Second, for the time we spent together digging the dirt."

He was smiling big, like a kid who got his birthday wish granted.

"And lastly, for the conversations. I saw myself as a person in certain circumstances for way too long, and I felt sorry for myself that I didn't get to do what I loved most of my life. And that I lost my wife too soon, and that I never had a chance to have kids, and many other things in between. But the truth is, I am here, and I am free, and I can do something about how I spent today, or the next day, or however many days I have left in this world. I am not sure exactly what I want to do, but I do want to thank you for exploring the options with me."

He looked at Granvill with pure gratitude, and then shook his hand so hard like he had to squeeze the truth about his future out of it.

Granvill was happy about making a real connection with the Person with Bad Luck, and he was glad he made the choice to talk to him instead of surprising him with the tulips in his garden. His approach proved itself to be correct. Granvill left the house trying to carry this feeling in his heart, and the walk home was more pleasant than it had been in a while.

Granvill had one more place in mind before he would be practically done. According to his plan, the last place was going to be the inn for The Very Tolerant Person. But before that, he wanted to plant his tulips at the school. He waited for the weekend to arrive so there were no kids or personnel at the school property and took a Friday off. It was a quiet, peaceful and uneventful Friday, just the kind of day he wished for.

On Saturday morning, he was outside of the school with his duffle bag of tulip bulbs, excited to get something for the kids of the village as well. The local school consisted of two buildings, one for students of elementary school and another for the middle school. There was no high school in the village, and all students had to go to Fish Haven after eight grades.

So, the kids from six years old to about fourteen were in this school, and Granvill was sure this was one of his best ideas yet. Saturday happened to be a sunny cloudless day, and it was one of the warmest days in a while. On one side, Granvill felt marvelous because it seemed like the sun was smiling to his idea of planting flowers for the students, and it could be one of the last warm days this year; but on another side, he was getting hot working in the sun the whole day, and physically, it was quite a demanding day for him.

Granvill was moving at a good pace today. His excitement was driving him forward, and the day was quickly passing by. He took a sandwich from home with him, so the lunch time was easy. He didn't even have to leave the school property, only slightly move under the shadow of one of the trees.

The school was different from the houses he chose before that, because it was government property, and trespassing was probably a bit more adventurous in its right. More punishable, he would assume, in the case of getting caught, but he was hoping that the school being closed for the weekend wouldn't attract anyone's attention. The traffic in front of the building today was quite slow, but tomorrow could present a bit more of a challenge. The local church was located not far down the street, and Sunday morning till early afternoon was the time when the majority of the village would be nearby. Granvill only needed to worry about two timelines: the early morning, around nine o'clock when people were arriving and then later, between twelve thirty and one thirty when people would accordingly be leaving the church. The time in between should be quiet outside.

Long before it got dark today, Granvill was done. There were no more tulips in the duffle bag even though today, he crammed it in as much as he could without damaging the bulbs. It was a good productive day. He spent the rest of the evening on his bench at home with a glass of wine in his hands. He didn't drink a lot, and rarely anything else but wine, but this was a good week and he wanted to relax. Wine did the job.

The next morning, he slept in a bit more because he needed a bit more rest, and because he wasn't planning to get to the school until after the crowd would place itself inside of the church. So, around ten was a perfect time, and he accomplished that easily by timing the walk and jumping over the fence. Most villagers probably would not imagine an old man climbing an almost ten-foot-tall fence that often, but he did it quite athletically and even faster and easier than the day before that.

He worked hard until about twelve fifteen, and then stopped. He moved behind the building without leaving the school prop-erty. Because of the angle of the middle school building, and a few trees in between, he couldn't see people leaving the church from that spot, but he couldn't be seen either. He relied on his hearing instead, listening to voices and discussions, although he noticed that most people usually didn't talk that much after the church.

He ate another homemade sandwich waiting for the time to pass, and then relaxed a bit feeling like he could take a nap, but he couldn't get comfortable enough to do that. Today wasn't as sunny as yesterday, but still quite warm. It was a bit windier, and Granvill enjoyed listening to the wind brushing the tree branches and creating lovely music by swirling through them.

Around two o'clock in the afternoon, it was quiet again for Granvill to get back to planting. Today it was the opposite result than yesterday: the darkness had caught him off guard. He wasn't done yet, and he continued to work in the dark. A couple of street lights not that far from where he was made it easier on him. Another hour and a half later, the duffle bag contents were all in the ground of the school property, and Granvill could take a breath.

Even though he needed still to plant some tulips for the inn and its lovely owner, he felt a certain relief. His project for the village was almost complete. The portion of doing it behind people's back was complete for sure. There seemed to be no more trouble on the horizon, and it made him breath with more ease. He crossed the fence a bit slower than he did in the morning. The walk towards his house was filled with both weariness and satisfaction.

CHAPTER 8

The Very Tolerant Person was ecstatic that her friend hadn't forgotten about her. At the same moment when she said to Granvill that she only wanted the flowers if they were the last ones he had, she was really hoping for Granvill to come back and have some left for her. At the same time, Granvill also knew that he was going to come back here, as the rest of the plans were built around that.

The inn had a beautiful garden already, with some amazing trees and bushes, but no flowers yet, and it had more than enough space to plant them. Granvill came for three straight days to finish his work outside of the inn. In those three days, friends had time to catch up and chat and fool around. The Very Tolerant Person asked Granvill if he had started dating anyone yet and joked about how if he would not find anyone by Christmas, she would snatch him up. She also updated him on what the Person Who Wants to be the Center of the Universe was doing. Apparently, he secured the land for the resort, and they already put up a fence around it, and would be ready to start construction as soon as spring came. The winter was just arriving in the upcoming weeks, and it wasn't a good time to build anything yet.

"I heard he is looking for local managers. I know he offered the Person with Bad Luck and his company to do the development. He is also bringing an architect from the big city, but he needs a local manager on the ground who knows the surrounding area and the people over here."

"I am sure he will find someone," responded Granvill in the way he would talk about the weather.

"That someone could be you, you know," the Very Tolerant Person tried to help Granvill to do more than what he was doing. She always wanted to help people, and she felt while Granvill was enjoying his life, he was still missing something. Maybe he needed just a bit more balance between his old life and his current one. "It could be good for you. It's a one-time project, it's not a job. When you are done with it, you are free again. It could be perfect."

"You are not worried that the new place will damage your business?"

"What does that have to do with anything?" The woman was sincerely surprised.

"I wouldn't want to help a competitor against my friend." Granvill also had other reasons as well, but at this moment, this reason was as true as any other.

"Oh, no," the Very Tolerant Person waived her hand in disregarding manner. "Don't be silly. If it will kill my business, then I wouldn't care at all, if you are helping over there. Business is business, but our friendship goes far beyond that. When I lost my father, and then my husband, I realized I had a couple of things left in my life, and this building is one of those things. But the inn itself… I don't know… it doesn't have to be the inn forever. Maybe I will restructure it and make it something else. A casino with a bordel, maybe?"

She burst into a laugh, and Granvill gladly joined her.

"But really, Granvill, you are my friend, if you need to take on that project, please do. I will be happy for you. And I will do what I can to survive, I may find a niche that the resort can't provide, or I will rebuild it into something else. We always need to grow and adapt. And I think you know that."

Granvill kept the silence, pondering over the new information. The Very Tolerant Person had something else to say:

"Sometimes I think you, maybe, forgot that just a little. You have your life together, you have your past, you have money, freedom, and a kind heart. And the tulips will give this village and their residents something good, but you know what else you could do? You could help this village grow and adapt to the modern world, you could run for a mayor's office, or something else."

She liked her own idea and smiled:

"You would be a great mayor. Did you ever think about that?"

"A long time ago, not in this village, but yes, it crossed my mind." Granvill started to feel that his friend could be right about a thing or two.

Was he going through his days in a sleeping mode and not doing enough in his life? Was he running away from himself? Was he afraid to live life fuller than it was at this moment? He had to ask himself those questions again. Maybe there was something else for him besides living the way he was the last few years. Maybe there was something else he must do before his journey was over. While thinking through the previous words from his companion, his mind had heard the next ones:

"I would definitely vote for you. And with all the changes that people like the Person Who Wants to be the Center of the Universe want to bring to this village, we may need a person on the other side of it to make sure the village is in good hands."

"It's not a bad idea," Granvill admitted. "So, you propose I take on the project to help him build the resort and you propose I go run for office, so I can control how it's done. At the same time?"

"Not at the same time!" she laughed. "I am just throwing options out there in the universe to see what you feel you want to do. I just would like you to use your God given talents for the good of the people. Don't get me wrong, I love the tulips idea, but it will be over now, and you will need a new project soon. You may want to take the time for the holidays and Christmas to relax and think about it, but eventually you will be bored without the next idea or next purpose. I know you."

"You know me too well," he smiled in response.

"If you don't get at least one date with someone by Christmas, I will know you even better," this was the second time she joked about it in one evening.

Granvill burst into laughter. Not because the idea was funny, but because the way his friend was going about it was quite entertaining. He didn't think she was ready to date at all, before Christmas or after, but he did believe that she wanted him to date. And he knew that he didn't have a twenty-nine-year marriage to blame for not dating. Suddenly, he realized that the Very Tolerant Person was pushing him to make real changes to his life, work wise and on a personal level.

"Thank you for trying make my life better." He looked deeply in her eyes. "It means a lot to me. You have always been there for me."

"My friend, you have done for me and my late husband so much more! And when he moved on from this world, you practically saved me and gave me all the support I needed. I will never forget that," her response was as sincere and tender as anyone could be in this world.

In those three days, Granvill felt that planting tulips for the inn owner allowed them to build an even stronger bond between each other. They had a chance to talk here and there a bit more about different topics, and every conversation felt warm and special. He also spent some time thinking deeper about if his life was missing something. He was considering all options now, and he liked all of them to a certain degree. He just needed to figure out if he liked any of them enough to change his lifestyle for. In his mind, the answer was already getting alarmingly close to a resounding yes.

The tulip bulbs found their place in the ground and were already slowly growing, although they wouldn't show until spring. And Granvill was back mostly in his home, cooking, listening to music, reading, sitting on his patio, going for hikes and doing other pleasant daily activities. Christmas wasn't far away, and he was looking to experience new fresh snow that created a sparkling white beautiful winter world all around and related to it pleasantries as well.

He spent the rest of November and the first half of December staying away from people. But this time around, people were never too far from him. He didn't even need to close his eyes to see the beautiful smile of the Person Who Smiled at Everyone, and he didn't need to be in a quiet room to hear the words of encouragement from the Very Tolerant Person. He could also see flashes of the Person Who Wants to be the Center of the Universe, and the tulips he planted in each house, imagining the reactions of the Person Who Felt Insecure in Relationships or the school kids who would no doubt look forward to the end of the school year and into their summer break. Many images followed Granvill no matter if he was busy preparing another meal, sitting on his patio and gazing at the mountain tops, or shoveling snow out of his back driveway. It didn't disturb his peace though. But it changed it. He was no longer alone. For the good and bad of it. In one of the days, about a week before Christmas, he was ready for another casual rendezvous with one of his new friends.

When he came up to the coffee shop counter, the Person Who Smiled at Everyone was there to ask him what kind of drink he wanted today.

"Are you ready for another adventure? Maybe something Christmassy?" She greeted her guest.

"I didn't realize there were Christmassy kinds of coffee out there," responded Granvill with a smile.

"Do I hear sarcasm?" Pretending to be upset for a moment with his sarcastic comment.

"Of course not," playfully serious he responded. "So, what exactly is your Christmassy drink?"

"You will see," she spoke with confidence. "Take a seat, and your treat is coming right up. On the house too."

"That's the real Christmas spirit!" He accepted the gesture with pleasure. "Thank you."

"You are very *very* welcome."

The owner was happy Granvill was back at the coffee shop. She was wondering if their friendship would just die down after he had finished with the tulips at her house. This moment gave her hope that it wouldn't.

Granvill proceeded to take the exact same seat as the last time. The coffee shop was almost full, especially near the fireplace. The winter was in full force for the last few days, and people really enjoyed their time in here. There were not many things better than sitting by the fireplace and sharing a coffee with a friend or a loved one.

"How have you been?" asked the owner while setting down the promised drink.

"I have been really good, busy, with the tulips," responded Granvill while thinking about what kind of drink she mustered for him. "What's in it?"

"Oh, that's a simple drink, Irish coffee with eggnog and some Cameroonian spice. I hope you like it," The Person Who Smiled at Everyone seemed proud of her choice of drink. "I have been good as well. I have thought quite a lot about our conversations, and I think I learned to look at certain things differently. So, thank *you* for that."

When she started this sentence, she was still standing in front of Granvill's table, but by the middle of it, she invited herself to sit across from him. Then leaned in closely and continued with her thoughts out loud:

"I think I found a better balance with my son too, I let it go in some instances a bit and gave him some space for his decisions, but I also got stricter in certain cases, like actually going to school and him being on top of his homework as well as him coming home on time from hanging out with friends."

Granvill was pleased to hear that. Like any good caring mother, it was important to her to have a good relationship with her son, but at the same time it wasn't any less important to know that she was taking the right approach to give him the best understanding of life before he went into the adult world. She wanted to make sure he would grow up to be a decent man. Of course, there was no guarantees that her approach was actually the right one, but she tried different things before, and it was about time for her to try something new. Also, the connection and confidence of her providing a positive and real influence was growing, and unless it was a grand illusion, it was the right direction to move forward. She was definitely hoping that some changes were not going to be wasted, and eventually they would produce the results she was hoping for.

Granvill wasn't sure what to say besides quite generic but nonetheless sincere words:

"I am really glad for your progress, I hope it will turn out very well."

She smiled at him. Not in the usual way she smiled at everyone. This one was warmer and more intimate.

"What are your plans for Christmas?" She asked him, deeply hoping that he hadn't built any plans yet.

He really didn't have any plans yet, but he also didn't want to step in some new plans which were, no doubt, coming his way.

"I am not sure yet if I will be in town. I may visit the city for Christmas."

The Person Who Smiled at Everyone was taken aback a bit by the response. For some reason she was sure he would be available, as if he was supposed to wait for her specific invitation. But she took control of her momentary disappointment and continued with the plan:

"I was hoping we could've spent Christmas together," she said with a little less confidence.

As a matter of fact, as soon as the words left her lips, she felt that those words lost all the meaning that she intended to put in them, and instead they became a loud screaming symbol of her desperation and awkwardness.

"But of course, only if you didn't have any other plans," quickly trying to recover her dignity.

"If you will be out of town, I don't expect… I mean I wouldn't expect you to change your plans. Just thought, it just crossed my mind… that maybe if we are both available, then why not…"

She mumbled through trying to find the right words.

Granvill realized that he created an unnecessary awkward situation, and now he was coming up quickly with a plan in his head how to make this better.

"You know, I would like to change my non-specific, non-existent plans, to spend Christmas with you. What exactly did you have in mind?" he asked in a soft gentle voice.

The Person Who Smiled at Everybody felt hope that this may go the way she wanted after all.

"You would?" She asked trying to not sound insecure, although the question itself made it practically impossible.

"Of course, it would be my pleasure."

"Good," pleasure basking her from hearing the news. "I was going to spend Christmas morning with my son, but then he goes to his father around 3pm, and we can meet up later, maybe at 5pm?"

"Five works for me just fine," smiled Granvill.

"Very good."

She stood up from behind the table and fixed her apron that was covering most of her skirt.

"Enjoy your coffee. I need to get back to work, but I am glad you stopped by today," she said looking at Granvill with blatant adoration.

Granvill was beginning to realize this was more than just a friendly invite, this was a romantic invite. She had an interest in him. Now he needed to figure out if he had an interest in her. He liked helping people, and she was one of his favorite people in the village. She was also beautiful, and interesting, a bit younger, but that was nothing too difficult to overcome. The bigger issue for Granvill was if he was ready for it. With anyone. He lived his life in a certain way in the recent times, and any relationship would probably jeopardize his lifestyle. People tend to have particular expectations. They like other people to act according to those expectations. Granvill felt that this was true in most cases in modern society.

He wasn't sure if even one date was fair to the other person if he had no interest in dating that person. He already accepted the offer for Christmas, but now he was feeling maybe he shouldn't have. Before he went, he needed to figure out where he stood. After he agreed to it, he must go now, it wasn't in his character to go back on his word or make up fake excuses. But he wouldn't want to go if that meant misleading the Person Who Smiled at Everyone. Even though attention from the young and beautiful woman was pleasing to him, he lived long enough to know that honesty in this situation was the best policy. He needed to realize what this honest situation meant to him. He knew that he needed more time to find the answers within.

"Thank you," Granvill smiled, more out of habit than anything else.

The Person Who Smiled at Everyone left him on his own and went back behind the counter to serve other customers. This was the first time after the divorce she would have any kind of resemblance of a date. Because it was a Christmas get-together, it was both less intimate and more intimate at the same time. She didn't feel it would be a rebound of some kind, as she spent a lot of time alone, enough to pass any rebound period, but for the first time she felt some attraction to another man since her ex-husband. She was thrilled and frightened by it all at once.

Granvill was sipping his coffee in deep thought. Recent events had forced him to reconsider certain views. First, The Very Tolerant Person, and then The Person Who Smiled at Everyone reminded him how temporary and fragile his current way of living was. He was on the outside, literally and figuratively, of the village and its residents for a while, and no one was trying to change that, especially him. But his one idea of planting tulips suddenly threatened to change his ways. He wasn't sure he was ready for it.

Doing good for people had certain side effects, and usually one of them was people's desire to do nice things back. Kindness gives birth to the seeds of kindness. Sometimes they grow into tangible actions, other times they get buried in the daily routine of life's mediocrity and self-centered well-being. But Granvill didn't want anything back. One thing that seemed difficult to avoid now was attention to himself. The attention, while well meaning, was kind of unwanted.

Granvill did consider – even before today – the possibility of making new friends or even dating. He loved his wife, and his memories of their life together was enough for him to feel happy. There were days when he was washed over by the overwhelming feeling of sentimental warmth, but generally he looked back at that relationship only with a smile and true contentment inside of his heart. And he didn't feel a need to erase that with new memories of someone else.

One thing was certain, there was enough on his plate to think about. He continued to drink his coffee, while glancing at the Person Who Smiled at Everyone. She was truly a beautiful woman, and it seemed like she had an extra special glow tonight. *Maybe because of him*, Granvill caught himself thinking. Maybe it was that his perception of her was changing, and not her per se. He was lost in his judgement, he was unsure of his feelings, and even less confident in tomorrow's day. While he didn't like the feeling, he wasn't going to let it stress him too much. He had handled all kinds of situations in his lifetime, and this one wasn't harder than the rest of them.

Granvill finished his coffee quicker than usual, thanked the shop owner again, and left. He barely registered his surroundings in his mind on his walk home, as his focus shifted completely to the feeling of unplanned changes coming to his life. Though, there was one thing he didn't like so far. He didn't want any kind of reward from life for planting the tulips. He just wanted to bring something to people of the village, no "thank you" was expected, no gifts or recognition was needed, nothing in return was supposed to come back to him. Him knowing for himself that someone appreciated the flowers would be enough. He didn't feel the need that his life needed to get better, or that his life was asking for improvement; he was happy where he was, he just wanted to do something nice for a few people in the village. That's all. How did it turn into him getting a date for Christmas? Why did the Person Who Wants to be the Center of the Universe have to find him and randomly offer him a job? All of that felt good, Granvill had to be honest with himself, and he was excited to a degree, but he didn't still ask for it. He never wanted any of it. Maybe he was wrong thinking he could easily handle the stress of this. He couldn't even think about anything else.

His current life was kind of perfect. He enjoyed his life. But the question in front of him was if it needed to change to be more perfect? Or an even more important question: what if it stayed the same, would it be still perfect?

CHAPTER 9

The winter this year wasn't too cold, rather mild, but still with some light snow here and there. It was never enough to create road hazards or build snow drifts in people's yards, but enough for kids to throw snowballs and fool around in, making snow angels or building a snowman. Granvill liked all seasons, and for a while, he believed that summer was his favorite one. But he noticed that what he liked the most about the weather was the changes occurring from one kind to another. As much as he liked snow in the middle of winter or the sun during summer, or the rain on a peaceful quiet night, he liked when fall was changing and the snowfall covered grey grounds with a beautiful white blanket even more; or when the trees and plants were growing green at the beginning of the spring; when a really hot summer day suddenly would burst into thunderous rain with lightning; when a five-day rainy stretch would stop and the sunshine and a rainbow would come out and the plants would be crying happy tears of early-dew. All the amazing seasonal changes this world could offer was appealing to Granvill the most.

He used to take life the same way. He knew that without change there is no growth. If he stayed still, but the world moved forward, it meant he moved backwards. But he also knew that he spent a lot of effort to build his current life the way it was now. It didn't happen by accident. Some things were out of his control, but most of the details of his life were planned and achieved by his own conscious decisions and constant efforts.

Today it was a bit chilly and windy. It would be a nice day if the wind didn't present an unpleasant obstacle to deal with. Granvill was sitting on his patio, dressed warmly in a handmade sweater that was good to keep his body in dry comfort. He felt better about the prospect of spending Christmas with a woman, and he started to feel even kind of excited about it. He still wasn't sure if he was up to anything past that evening with the Person Who Smiled at Everyone, but now he knew that one nice date wouldn't be unfair to her and too uncomfortable for him. They should be able to have a good time and see where it went.

But before Christmas, Granvill felt he needed to do one task that was also on his mind for the past few days. He didn't need to leave his house for that though, as he invited a person of interest to come to him instead. So, when he heard the loud knock on his door, he wasn't surprised. He stood up from the chair and walked across the house to open the front door. The Person Who Wants to be the Center of the Universe was, of course, smiling and his whole body shone with enthusiasm.

Those positive qualities were unrivaled to his success, thought Granvill. He invited the guest to come in. They shook hands and after a couple of common greetings, walked back to the patio together. Granvill offered his guest to get comfortable and asked him if he didn't mind being outside in this kind of windy day. To be fair, the wind wasn't strong on this side of the house, as the patio was facing southeast, while the wind was coming from the southwest, and only rare bursts were felt by the people in their chairs. The guest agreed it was a great day to sit outside, still with the same enthusiasm that he was greeting Granvill with two minutes ago.

"So, my friend, how can I help? Or have you decided to help me?" asked the guest without much delay.

Despite his ego, the Person Who Wants to be the Center of the Universe didn't mind sharing credit or asking for help. He knew that alone, he wouldn't have achieved so much in his life and building relationships with other people was his strong side, as well as always finding the best people to complete certain tasks. Granvill never really disliked him, more so, he probably disliked the reminder of his own previous life, the life that he deliberately left behind and walked away from with such pleasure. He didn't want that life back now still, but he was considering if some elements of it could be naturally implemented into his new life.

"I don't have any specific plans yet, but I wanted to discuss with you what exactly your vision was for your project. In about two months, as I understand, you will break the ground on it. How it's going so far?"

"My friend, this is going to be the best project this village has ever seen," responded the entrepreneur. "You have developed land before and built business office buildings, as well as apartment complexes, so you know a thing or two about it. I am not sure if you were a part of resort building before, but it's not much different. There's some licenses, like a liquor license for the restaurants and bars on the territory of the resort, some extra safety measures for pools, there are different standards on rooms quality, buying furniture and designing the place is a bit different, but really, it's all common sense."

"Any obstacles so far?"

"No. Everything is smooth for now, my friend."

The Person Who Wants to be the Center of the Universe felt really close to the host right now and called him "my friend' repeatedly.

"Right now, we're just waiting for the spring to arrive, and then we start laying the foundation, and move forward. All the licenses are ready, and we would need to make sure the work would be done on time. But also, when we invite designers, we need to make sure the cost is reasonable, the style is consistent, and we don't run into any delays. Then we would start working on marketing and promoting it in the city, maybe a commercial on TV, newspapers, and probably organizing the grand opening, inviting local media for that, maybe get a celebrity or two, you know, all the stuff to make the opening successful. I have people working on building the website already, and it should be done before the spring. But I need you, Granvill. I think we worked a long time against each other. This is an opportunity for us to work on the same side for once."

Granvill was listening carefully.

"Have you done any polls in the village to see who supports it and who doesn't? "

"Of course. The great part is, because the tourism business in Fish Haven is growing, and they are doing a pretty good job at promoting themselves, more and more people with each day know about them, and less and less of those know about us. This project will change that, and most people in the village love the idea of changing the status quo to outdo Fish Haven for once. They know I could just as easily build that resort over there, and they appreciate that this choice was made including the village, and not excluding, like everyone else did up to now."

"I am sure you presented it in exactly *this way* to the people before the poll," quietly but confidently pronounced Granvill.

"Of course. Why wouldn't I?" he laughed a bit. "I wouldn't jeopardize the whole project because the residents maybe didn't understand what exactly they were getting. Tourism will be good for this place, the village pride will be good for those people, and the taxes I pay and the jobs I will generate will be good for everybody."

"I guess, everything changes, nothing stands still in this life," the host reluctantly agreed.

"Exactly! But we are the ones who will be driving that change, and people will remember that. Besides, look at the money that can be made," while it seemed almost impossible for guest's enthusiasms grow even higher, right now he was even more excited than his usual self, while talking about his latest adventure.

Granvill shifted his focus to another concern of his.

"I don't want to work full time. If you think I can help doing it part time, in some kind of consulting role, then I will help, only from the moment you finish construction of the building's frame until the grand opening of the place. And I leave the day after the grand opening."

The Person Who Wants to be the Center of the Universe grew serious for a moment to calculate numbers and adjust them in his mind comparing to what he was expecting to offer based on the full-time proposition. His business side took over his identity for a minute, and then – just as serious – he proceeded:

"Agreed. I was going to offer you a lot more, but I can do sixty-five hundred a month to be a consultant. I will hire a full-time project manager and marketing VP, and you can help them both to make sure they avoid any mistakes, and it will all go as smooth as possible."

He looked at Granvill waiting for a response. There were no signs of a smile on the businessman's face.

For Granvill it was never about the money, and that's why he didn't take the full-time position. He wanted to get busy with something, and it was an interesting project after all. He was hoping to keep some of his freedom without the need to be at work every morning at a certain time, and yet be a part of it. His life was already changing, but now he was ready for that.

"A flexible schedule and the ability to take care my errands when I need to," it was his last demand, and he looked at the Person Who Wants to be the Center of the Universe to clarify that they were on the same page. With the clear confirmation of solidarity, the businessman's face changed again with a big smile, and he extended his hand for the agreement and as a symbol of respect between the men.

Granvill shook his hand, and said:

"You know, I was a bit surprised that you wanted me to be a part of the project. At first, I even thought that you just wanted to rub it in."

The Person Who Wants to be the Center of the Universe burst into a sincere laugh.

"I, honestly, never thought you would accept it. But, are you kidding me? You are a legend, Granvill! Before you left the city, there was no one equal to you in the entrepreneurial vision and ability to find the best opportunities. Maybe, besides me," guest was relaxed, and comfortable, like the men were closest friends for a lifetime. "We are not getting any younger, and life will pass us by, like everyone else. No matter how great we are, or were at any point, that doesn't buy us extra time on this earth. I am really excited about the opportunity to work together before it is too late, and we may never get another chance to check off that box."

He looked at Granvill with unmasked respect, probably for the first time since they met over twenty-five years ago. Granvill was a bit dazed by the philosophically deep approach to this situation by his newly acquired partner, and thought, maybe he overestimated his greed and desire to make as much money as possible. Maybe, there was more to him than a desire for a financial gain.

"You really do think this resort will help people in this village, don't you?" Granvill was almost sure of the incoming response.

"I do," said the Person Who Wants to be the Center of the Universe with sheer sincerity. "But don't tell that to anyone. I have a reputation to protect."

And he smiled broadly, hiding his momentary honesty with his own enthused personality. Each side of him was as genuine as the other. One was for a public eye, and the other one was saved for those life glimpses where he felt he could afford to be as honest to the world as he was to himself, before going to bed in the darkness of his bedroom.

Granvill felt even better about the project now, and while there were no guarantees it would go well till the end of it, he confirmed to himself that he was preaching to others so well. Opening himself up to new opportunities and changes could be a positive matter.

"We need to drink to that, my friend," exclaimed the guest.

Granvill agreed and went to the house to grab scotch and he came back with the two glasses already filled with alcohol.

"Scotch?" He asked his guest out of courtesy, but he really didn't have anything else in his bar.

"Absolutely!" Easily agreed his newly established boss.

They clanged glasses and drank for the success of the new adventure. They spent another hour and a half sitting on the patio, savoring their drinks as much as each other's company. Granvill refilled their glasses twice more, before the Person Who Wants to be the Center of the Universe got up to leave. He was truly thrilled about getting Granvill on board, and he felt good about his business acumen and his successful attempt to close the deal with his new consultant. Business was good and promised to be even better next year. Granvill was also looking into the next year with hope and curiosity what all those changes would bring into his life.

There was another day for Granvill in between the meeting with the Person Who Wants to be the Center of the Universe and his date night on Christmas day, and that day was, of course, the Christmas Eve. He noticed after he wanted the date night to be tonight, he was really looking forward to it now. The positivity of the meeting with the Person Who Wants to be the Center of the Universe gave him more excitement and hope that the Christmas day would go well too. But he knew the Person Who Smiled at Everyone was spending today and tomorrow's morning with her son. It was their family time, so there was no way he could be there considering circumstances. He needed another plan.

He wanted to do something different, there was a lingering feeling of change in the air, and it seemed appropriate to do something. If not completely new, then something he hadn't done in a while. He decided to go to the city, mainly for two different purposes. One was to be a part of soup kitchen, the one he used to help a lot during his life at the city, and another reason, if he had time left, he could stop by and see a couple of his old friends who still lived there.

So, that morning, he did get up earlier than usual. He used his alarm clock, which he tried not to use often, and went to a bus station. He could call Uber or Lyft, but he didn't have a cell phone, and he could go by taxi, but in the end Granvill preferred to take the bus. He liked to be a part of people's crowds without drawing attention to himself, and a long-distance bus was exactly that kind of experience for him. He liked trains even more, but there was no train station in the village or even Fish Haven, the closest one you could find was in the big city, but this was exactly where he needed to go, not go somewhere else from there.

The walk to the local bus stop was not long, as it was located not far from the school, and pretty much right behind the church, barely ten minutes from Granvill's house. The wait didn't take too much time either, as the bus arrived right on schedule, and Granvill was just ten minutes early to make sure he didn't come late. The bus was nearly half full, but still with plenty of seats to choose from, and Granvill proceeded to take a seat near the window about four or five rows from the back window. Granvill knew it would take almost three hours to get to the city, and he could use this time to think about all sorts of developments that had happened in his life lately.

He was thinking about all the changes that were coming into his life. He realized by now that he couldn't hold them back. He learned to accept gifts of life, almost as easy as he was accepting life's challenges. But not quite. It was still more comfortable for him to stand up to life's curveballs and unexpected trials than pleasant surprises. While he was a positive person in general, there was a sceptic living inside of him. Did he deserve anything else in this life besides that which he had already experienced? Were the good things at this stage of life even possible? Could those good events last for any significant amount of time?

These thoughts, and many others, had come to his mind while he was on the bus, but eventually he arrived at the city, and there was no more time to think about that. He quickly took a taxi cab from the bus station and asked the driver to take him to Sierra Soup Kitchen. It was almost eight thirty in the morning, and he knew there was breakfast served over there around 9am. He was going to be just on time.

The taxi cab arrival went unnoticed by the people around. Granvill left the cab and walked over to a gray building with old red paint on it where you could recognize the letters of the kitchen's name. The building hadn't been renovated for decades, but it was standing still sturdy and stubbornly, just like most of the homeless men and women who came here to get some warm food in their stomachs. When Granvill came up to the building itself, there were people who looked at him and recognized him right away. A group of six came up to him in a fast-enthused pace, all happy to see the old man who hadn't been here in a while.

Granvill happily greeted every one of them, and they exchanged some common pleasantries, while walking together to the inside of the building. There were tables already set up for the breakfast line, and there were a few homeless people located outside waiting for the food to be served. For most of them, it wasn't an exhausting wait, as they came here most of the days and they weren't as desperate as some, but there were a couple of women who seemed not yet used to the soup kitchens. Maybe they were new to being homeless, or maybe they "lived", or slept somewhere further away from this place and couldn't come here before or didn't even know about the existence of this place.

"What brought you back in our lands? Didn't you move away?" Asked one of the people in a warm greeting to Granvill. His name was Adam, and he was one of the people who was organizing this charity and one of the people who hustled for most of the donations to be able to support the group.

"I came to visit you guys, this is Christmas Eve, and while any day is good to come here, I really wanted to be here today. Unless something has changed, you always need an extra pair of hands."

"We always do need extra hands, and we are always happy to see you!" responded Adam. "But actually, we have been good on volunteers lately, it's becoming a popular trend to be a part of some charity, and between bored higher middle-class housewives and millennials who want to show what they do for the community, we had a pretty good flow of people."

"So, that's good then!" Granvill was happy to hear that.

"Not everything is so perfect, Granvill," another guy standing right besides Adam, who was taller and skinnier than Adam, picked up the conversation. "There are other kinds of problems arising. Mainly, the reasons those people to help us are not great reasons. So, they get involved once or twice, they post on Instagram how cool they are, and then they stop. We have a constant flow, but not many of the new volunteers stick around. Also, even those people who come… they are reluctant to give five dollars or ask their family and friends to donate any money, so financial support is still lacking."

Granvill knew what the guy was talking about well. The guy, or Casey, as his parents had named him, had always been a bit skeptical about people, and it was never easy for anyone to convince him of people's good intentions.

"Understandable. Still, it's a good thing that those people come and help a little bit. Right?" Granvill was more fishing for the response than making a statement.

"It is. To a degree," reluctantly agreed Casey. "It sucks not to have enough hands to give food away, move dishes, and do what's needed. But it also not pleasant to work with people who are not into it, or people who, after an hour and a half, are thinking about when they finally can go home. The people who you have to teach simple things to, just so they can ignore you because they think we should be grateful just because they showed up. There are many things that slow us down, people doing things in the wrong way, and we have to redo something after someone has supposedly already done it in the first place."

"Makes sense," Granvill approved. "Hopefully, while those millennials show up for the wrong reasons, they learn something in the process and possibly arrive to the right reasons."

"Hopefully," settled Casey.

They moved inside now.

"Do you remember where the changing rooms are?" asked Adam, more in laughing manner than serious.

"Of course," Granvill smiled back. "Unless you moved it to another borough."

"Haha" laughed Adam and so did most people in the group. "Not yet."

Granvill left the group and started moving towards the door in the corner. The whole building inside was just one big warehouse, with a couple of offices on the sides and one kitchen, in between offices on the left side, big enough to cook for over two hundred people.

One of those doors was hiding a small changing room with lockers available. No one was getting naked here but changing from a nice dress shirt to an old t-shirt would be ok, which is exactly what Granvill did. He also put on his apron on the top of his jeans and his t-shirt, and he was pretty much ready for the job at hand.

Serving food to people in need was always one of the things Granvill was involved in. No matter how much success he had experienced in his life personally, he always tried to remember where he came from, and what kind of life he had before all the success. He remembered, for a short period of time, he was totally out of money and was not far away from asking for food on the corner. Subconsciously, he was tempted to assume that some of the people didn't make enough effort to get out of their current situation, but he didn't know that for sure. For some of them it was unfortunate and a temporary situation and because they got food, they could have the physical energy to keep believing in themselves, to go out there and get a job, mow a lawn for someone, or do something else to change their life and current situation. It is a tough circle to get out of sometimes, and Granvill believed that at the end of the day, they were still people, and they needed help.

He felt good during the next two hours while serving breakfast. He met a lot of people and started a conversation with some of them. He met Dorothy, who could barely walk because she needed a hip replacement that she couldn't afford. She had been homeless for over a year from the moment her other medical bills put her in big hole and cost her to lose the apartment she had. He met Jim, who fought in Vietnam, then returned home, and though he couldn't find a decent job on a permanent basis, he always found a way with odd jobs here and there to provide for his family until he lost his wife a couple of years back. Now Jim lived on his social security only, losing his house because mortgage was higher than his current income without his wife's supplemented government assistance. He met the Russian immigrant Dima, who came from his country with his parents, as one happy family, but both his mother and his father died in a car accident soon after he turned eighteen, and he couldn't find a job good enough to pay for the place his parents were renting. He dropped out of college soon after he started sleeping on the streets, because he felt embarrassed of his new life. Without being able to go home, he couldn't even take a normal shower or eat something nutritional on daily basis. They all would love to go back to their previous lives, but one way or another that wasn't in the cards just yet.

Most of the people had a story, and Granvill wished he could do more for everyone. Giving them food at this moment was giving them what those people needed right now. In his mind, he was thinking about all the possible scenarios where he could help those people in the future.

By the time eleven o'clock hit, the kitchen was out of food, and all the people were fed. Some people walked off into the light of the day to go do things they did on a daily basis, and some were sticking around because they had nowhere to go anyway, and extra minutes around good people who gave them food gave them hope. It was calming to them knowing that there were people in this universe who were still concerned about them, cared if they are hungry and fed, dead or alive.

Since it was Christmas Eve, there would be a special meal tomorrow morning with some small trinkets for presents prepared by the kitchen, but today, there was a warm greeting and wishing for a Merry Christmas to everyone was as much as the volunteers of this place could afford to do.

Granvill didn't stick around in the kitchen for much longer. He had changed back into his own clothes and said goodbye to the group of people he worked side by side for the last few hours, and then he left the facility. He had something else in mind today. The old man walked towards a bus stop for local transportation and waited for maybe five minutes at the most before the right bus was in front of him. He needed to change neighborhoods to get where he wanted to go, and this bus would help him accomplish that.

Twenty-five minutes later, he was in the richest and cleanest business district of the city. There were three large business districts, but only one had the privilege of hosting the best businesses, and offices of the richest people in the state. This area was located next to the residential rich people housing neighborhood, and combined, it was called Seven Hills. The people who founded it believed there were seven distinctive hills in that area, though in reality, you could count a few more if you decided so. The Seven Hills was a desirable spot for the local entrepreneurs, first to get their office in there and then — as an embodiment of their success — to buy their family home in the same area.

Granvill had spent over two decades in this place, hustling with the best of them, sitting at negotiation tables with every important person in that business circle, making deals and building a name for himself. Lawyers, businessmen, politicians knew who he was, and everyone wanted to make the next project with his involvement. It took a significant amount of time to build that reputation, and Granvill was still proud of his accomplishments. After years of hard work, his name took a prominent place at the top of the ladder inside of Seven Hills. Today, on Christmas Eve, when most offices were closed or closing early, he maybe had an opportunity to catch a few people who didn't leave the city or the country for the Christmas break. It was also possible that every busy person was away with their families or on their annual holiday business trips. Not having a cell phone or social media pages, there was only one way for him to find out.

CHAPTER 10

From the bus stop, he walked a block and a half until he reached one of the local bars. This bar was the hangout of most of the brokers and lawyers, and while one wouldn't see the most influential people of the city here, there were a few distinguished guests, like the city mayor, who loved this spot and came here whenever he got a chance. The bar owner, an Italian whose real name was Riccardo but went by Rikki, was a well-connected man who had a good relationship with everyone.

That was the place to start today, to see who was in town, and who may be able to have time to have a drink or two with Granvill. Interestingly, when Granvill walked into the bar, his walk wasn't the usual slow of himself, but with straight shoulders and a faster pace, without any indication of his actual age. But then, of course, maybe he was just not that old in the first place. Maybe he barely passed "the big fifty" mark and had the full health and strength of the middle-aged man. Whichever was the case, he walked inside of the bar like he owned the place.

The bar wasn't too crowded yet, it was just four minutes past noon, and not many people were done with their obligations before they could submerge themselves into the atmosphere of relaxing, drinking, and company. Granvill wasn't planning to spend the whole day here, but the reminder of the old days was present in the air, and he was hoping that the reminder would be accompanied with some of the people he knew in his previous life as well.

He walked toward the bar counter and took a seat on the bar stool almost in the middle of it. There were only two men sitting on the right of him, three bar stools away, and one lonely guy across on the other side. There were a couple of people sitting at the tables, but no one else at the bar counter. A bartender came up to him right away. He was splendidly clean, and sharply dressed, which was not that unusual for Seven Hills, and of course, highly friendly.

"How are you today? What can I get you? Drinks, menu?" asked the bartender vigorously.

"I will have the Rusty Nail, but old school please, more scotch," specified Granvill ordering his usual drink of choice.

"No problem, coming up," the bartender knew exactly what the old man meant. While not many people still ordered the Rusty Nail here, it was a popular choice between a few older clients.

"Thank you," Granvill thanked the bartender when he came back with the glass half full of the ordered drink.

The bar guest looked around and paid a bit more attention to who was present. He didn't notice anyone who he would know yet. For a second, the thought came to his mind that, maybe, it was a bad idea to come here and try to find anyone. There is a reason why people have cell phones in this day and age, and everyone communicates through them knowing exactly when and where everyone meets. He turned back towards his drink, picked up a glass and took a big sip out of it. The drink was delicious and refreshing. He liked this drier version of it, not like they made it in the modern days with equivalent portions of scotch and Drambuie.

"What's your name?" Granvill asked the bartender. He usually asked people names no matter where he was or who the people were, housekeepers, Starbucks baristas, servers, or hairstylists. Every relationship he ever had, started with a name introduction, and while some of those relationships were over by the time he put the name in his memory slot, others blossomed into productive business partnerships or pleasant formidable friendships.

"Robert," the bartender extended his hand for a handshake.

"It's nice to meet you Robert. Granvill," the old man shook his hand. "Are you expecting a busy day? Being Christmas and all…."

"I think so. He shrugged. "Maybe not as busy as some Friday nights when everyone in the Seven Hills comes to relax after a long week, but I think there will be plenty of people who would rather come here than sit at home. Especially men, whose wives went for a vacation, with children and dogs, haha. Those will be here for sure."

"Makes sense," smiled the old man. "Do you think I am one of those men?"

Robert looked at Granvill carefully.

"No, for some reason I don't. I have not seen you here before, and I think you have better things to do than just being here. But you are probably meeting someone, although I would think you didn't schedule a *business meeting* on Christmas Eve, so my guess is, maybe a personal meeting, an old friend or something like that."

Robert paused:

"Am I close?"

He smiled, just in case, not wanting to offend his customer.

"Oh, you are quite right. Besides one small thing: no meeting set with anyone, but I was hoping to run into some of my old buddies," replied Granvill.

Robert smiled now in a different way, being satisfied to have read the situation almost to perfection.

"Maybe I know them, I will share what I know."

"One of them is Rikki. Do you know if he is going to be in today?" Granvill asked the bartender.

"Rikki, for sure. He was already here in the morning, but he went to run some errands, he will be back probably in a few hours."

Robert was happy he could be helpful. He was one of those people who enjoyed giving a hand or providing useful information, it was possible that's why he chose to be a bartender in the first place.

"Fantastic! I will wait for him then and go from there."

"Sounds good. Let me know if I can help more, or if you need another drink or anything." responded Robert and moved to the other side of the bar to see if the other customers needed something from him as well.

The old man thanked Robert and took another sip of the Rusty Nail. By the time his second drink had only a quarter of it left, Granvill was suddenly approached by a man from behind.

"Granvill?!"

He turned around to see one of the people from his past in front of him. This was Steve Maragos, a half-American, half-Greek local tv station owner, who had always had a warm relationship with Granvill. He was about sixty years old now. He looked healthy and energetic, but his belly grew noticeably bigger in the years since they saw each other last. A few minutes later, Granvill would realize that Steve's wallet and his ego had grew even bigger than his belly.

"Steve!" exclaimed Granvill, stood up from the chair and shook the other man's hand. "Long time!"

"That's an understatement!!"

"How have you been? Sit down, if you have time," offered Granvill.

Steve didn't need a second invite. He took a place on the bar stool next to Granvill and called the bartender right away.

"I will have whatever he is having. What's good for Granvill can't be bad for me!"

Robert disappeared for a minute to get the order and came back just as fast and smooth with the drink in hand.

"So, tell me all about it," Steve started without small chit-chat.

"What exactly?" replied Granvill, not because he wasn't sure what was asked of him, but more because he didn't like sharing, and answering to more direct questions was easier instead of telling his whole life story.

"Everything! What happened to you after you left the city? You had a big position, a lot of people were depending on you, there were rumors you would've run for Congress or at least city mayor, and then you kind of left everything and disappeared. Was it a midlife crisis?" Steve was enthusiastic to see Granvill, but even more so about hearing the story of a legendary disappearance.

"Yes, I had it pretty good," smiled Granvill taking a sip of his drink while recalling the good times in the city. "When I left, it was pretty easy. I traveled first, for almost two years, everywhere. My first place was Bali, then Thailand, Malaysia, Australia, India, China, Japan, I also went to Europe, lived a couple of months in Spain. Then traveled around again, Italy, France, and almost every country in Eastern Europe, dated a girl from Serbia and stayed there for a few months. Then traveled around the U.S. for a bit and made another trip to the south of the U.S, Mexico, Costa Rica, Cuba, Colombia, Venezuela and Brazil. Didn't make it to Peru or Argentina though. I returned, found a small town where no one knew who I was, bought a house, and settled down."

Granvill decided to skip mentioning his trip to Venezuela, in the time between Colombia and Brazil, as to avoid any political questions that could arise.

"So, what do you do over there?" The big tv station owner was hoping to hear something ambitious and fascinating. Nothing but disappointment was coming his way instead.

"Honestly, not much. That's the point though. I spend time in the mountains, or at the lake, or I walk. I cook, I read books, have read many, many books that I didn't have time for till now. I go to a coffee shop and have a coffee at my pace."

A month ago, this response would come out of Granvill with a lot more confidence and tranquility. But now he was hearing himself from the outside of his body and felt that he was missing out on something else. Maybe he needed a balance. It seemed like he jumped from one extreme of chasing a career and money to another extreme, of doing nothing at all. He felt truly at peace and happy for all that time though. Was it a mirage of some kind? A lie to himself about his newly found purpose?

"I heard about your wife, sorry about it," said Steve.

Why did he feel a need to bring it up right now? Was he starting to feel bad for Granvill?

"It's totally ok, it's a part of life," responded Granvill. When he saw his counterparts face, he realized that there was a little belief, if any, from the other side, in his last words, so he decided to expand an explanation. "Listen, I changed my life not because of what happened to Paige. I changed my life because I *needed* a change. While all the success looked great from the outside, it started to burn me from the inside. Let me ask you something."

Granvill turned his body more towards Steve, so his eyes could be looking directly at him.

"You have by now probably even more success, more attention from others, and more money than ten years ago. Do you really feel happier than ten years ago? Don't you have moments when you think you could throw all this away and do something else with your life? "

Steve got quiet for a moment, taking a big sip from his glass:

"That's what women are for, to make your life interesting. My last one, Amber, is super-hot, and she has so much energy, she always wants to do something. It's amazing. But when I am by myself," his smile turning serious. "Yes, there are moments when I think what the hell I am doing with my life…. You know, you think children will be there for you, to make your life fun and worthwhile, I have four of them, and none of them spend with me more than one day a month! And usually it's only when everyone gets together for a birthday party or a holiday, so I have twenty-nine days when I barely see a text from them. Four kids!"

"Why can't they spend more time with you?"

"The same thing. On one side, we want to be proud of them and see their success, on the other, it's exactly why they don't have time for you. Only one is still single, and she is in all kind of charities, sits on four board of directors, besides running her own interior designer company. The other three have families and children on the top of their careers! They are all busy… I am proud of them, don't get me wrong. Engineer, lawyer, and a TV producer, great careers! But that's not what I expected it would be like."

"How old are you now?" asked Granvill.

"Sixty-two. And believe me, not getting any younger. I am very happy with what I have built in my career, but not too happy about…pretty much, everything else."

He took a mouthful of his drink and finished the glass. Right away, he made a sign for a refill.

"So, that's why *you* left?" he asked Granvill.

"I think so. It's not like I have everything figured out, and I don't have a wife or four children to spend the time with." Answered Granvill. "But at least I wake up in the morning, and my schedule is not dictated by my success. I remember waking up, knowing I have six meetings and seventeen calls on my calendar… and I asked myself, if I go by my feeling only, and don't follow what's the best to advance my career, how many of those meetings and calls I would choose to do? I said to myself, I would be happy to see two of those people and make another four calls. The rest was needed because of where I put myself in life, and because I wanted to get somewhere even higher than that. I don't have that anymore. I needed that feeling of certain freedom in my life. At least, at that time."

"I still think it's, at least partially, because Paige has left you," the half-Greek made the statement stubbornly. "Women make our life more bearable. And alcohol."

And he took another mouthful of his second drink, as to prove his point.

Granvill thought to himself that it could be true.

"Do you think there is anyone in this world who is at sixty-two years old who thinks their life is exactly what it should be?" asked Granvill.

Steve looked at him, first, surprised by the question, then his face changed to something like a "who cares" attitude.

"I honestly don't know. But this drinking is becoming depressing," he burst into laughter, which was quite sincere and not as awkward as people would expect it to be in this situation. Maragos was a master of diplomacy and an expert of putting a good face on. He also gave thousands of TV interviews in his lifetime and learned to look ready for the camera at all times.

Besides his large belly, he was quite an attractive man, maybe not Apollo attractive, but not ugly by any means so a girl like Amber and many others before her, could spend a few months swimming in luxury and a lavish lifestyle with him.

"I am glad you are getting what you want in life though," continued Steve. "I wouldn't want to live without all the little perks I got accustomed to in the last twenty-five years. I like to be in the middle of things that are happening here. I like the attention of beautiful women, I like the extravagant parties and my toys."

By "toys" he meant all the material objects he owned; expensive cars, watches, suits, his yacht, and other items on which his money could be spent for.

"Thank you. Everyone has their own path," concluded Granvill. "But more so, that path tends to change. Just when you think you figure your life out, the time of tranquility just ends on you, and you are forced into the rat race all over again."

Granvill thought about possible upcoming changes in his life. He already took a position with the Person Who Wants to be the Center of the Universe, and who knows what tomorrow will bring when he got to spend Christmas with a beautiful woman who had enough courage to invite him to a private date.

"Honestly, just a few months ago, I thought that this is it, this is my life now. But I think it may change again at least one more time," Granvill was speaking to himself as much as to his counterpart, and the words seemed to carry extra power within them.

"If you ever want your old life back, let me know. You still have some powerful friends in this city," announced Maragos. "I am one of them."

The station owner burst into laughter again. In his mind, he was the most powerful friend anyone could have in the city, and he was shamelessly proud of it. He wouldn't say that out loud, but more than his lifestyle and his toys, he wouldn't ever want to give up his level of influence. He worked way too long and way too hard to get here, and only the grave would be able to take it away from him.

Granvill did have some powerful friends, and if he wanted to come back to the city, he could easily slip back into his old life without a hitch. But he knew he wasn't ready for that kind of backward change. He was wondering how people really knew what they wanted. Or what they didn't want, for that matter. Was there some kind of feeling deep in their gut that would tell its owner which direction to go? Could it be that that feeling was really directed by fate? And was that how people ended up in places of this universe where fate wanted them all along? His gut feeling was barely comfortable with the idea of the changes that were coming to him.

The upcoming events still gave him shivers, once again taking him out of his comfort zone. The strange part was that he was the king of living out of a comfort zone when he lived his city life. He made a name for himself for that alone, always challenging the status quo, always creating ambitious new projects that made waves in the whole state. Yet now, after the last few years of living in the village, he got used to a different kind of life. His comfort zone kind of settled on its own. Was it real freedom if he was trapped in this new warped comfort zone? Was he fooling himself of who he truly was?

Granvill didn't understand what was happening to him. Why, instead of enjoying this trip to his past, was he questioning his choices; why, after all those years, was he not sure that he was living his life the best way possible; why, suddenly, was the comparison between his old life and his new one so clear and staring right into his soul? He was too mature to not know what his life purpose was, yet he felt more lost today than seven years ago when he left this city behind him.

He and his old buddy Steve had a couple more drinks together. Granvill sipped it slowly and stopped after three glasses, and his powerful friend was only getting into the groove after three drinks. He ordered at least as many more before he felt it was time to slow down. He held his liquor well though, Granvill noticed, while trying to remember if he was the same back in the day, or if that part had also changed. Probably a mix of both.

By the time it was ten minutes to three, Steve was still on his fifth glass, and the slowing down hadn't occurred yet, but one thing interrupted the two men. Rikki, the owner, came back, and he quickly recognized Granvill sitting at his bar.

"I can't believe it! That's you!" His loud voice boisterous, and most people in the bar looked in his direction to see what he was screaming about.

Granvill stood up from his bar stool, and made a few steps toward the owner, before their bodies met and quickly clinched in a big bear hug. Rikki was smaller in stature than Granvill, but he spent a lot more time in the gym, and his arms seemed like they could hug even a large Sequoia tree. Granvill's lean body wasn't even a challenge. Rikki had one stand out feature on his face, his huge smile, from ear to ear, with sparkly white teeth blinding anyone in vicinity of the Italian hospitality.

"Happy to see you!" exclaimed Granvill. He suddenly felt a relief to see the old Italian friend, as if his worries and doubts about his future just evaporated.

"No, no, no, I *am* happy to see *you*, my friend!" proclaimed Rikki, finally letting his bear arms let go of Granvill. "I didn't expect to see you today, but I knew I would see you someday! You disappeared from planet Earth!"

Rikki told Granvill to walk with him, and he was directing the direction with his arms. An extremely articulate person already, Riccardo was already feeling extra excited, as he took control of the situation. Granvill wasn't sure where they were going, but his trust in Rikki was unwavering. They walked behind the bar, and into the small, not very organized, office. Riccardo came up to the only desk and reached out to the bottom drawer. He moved a few papers from the top of it, reaching for the object he was searching for. He took out a white envelope and showed it to Granvill.

"I hope you don't think I forgot!" He was smiling even bigger than before, if that was possible at all.

"Forgot what?" Granvill wasn't sure what he was talking about.

"The money." Rikki didn't even blink to his guest's reaction. "My friend, I remember the time I had a tough stretch, with recession and my ex taking me to court for child support, and me not being able to see my boys… I almost lost everything! Then you came in and saved my ass. Don't you think I would ever forget that! Fourteen thousand five hundred dollars, not too much today, but oh boy, I felt it was like millions on that day! You saved me, my friend! I see the boys now, they are seventeen and fifteen now, great boys! So proud of them! I have my bar now, and it is prospering!"

Rikki spread his arms showing the invisible riches that were attached to this physical place. Granvill now remembered the event that took place more than eight years ago, and he was happy that it turned out so well for this hard-working Italian immigrant who always was there for his family, and his children, even after the ugly divorce with their mother.

"So, here is a check I wrote probably like five years ago! Left the date blank, but I knew I would see you again. It's for double the amount, twenty-nine thousand, hope you don't mind. I owe you a lot more than that, but I didn't want to measure all of it in material things."

Granvill was touched, by everything that was happening here. Rikki's great enthusiasm, him writing the check for Granvill years ago, him keeping it in the drawer ready to go, him doubling the amount, the old man wasn't sure which part was more thrilling! It wasn't about the money at all though. Understanding that almost no one would have done it *this way*, because there was no any interest whatsoever attached to the loan Granvill made to his friend in need.

"Thank you, Rikki," Granvill was grateful. "It means a lot to me. You are truly a great person, and you have only confirmed that you deserved someone to help you when you needed it, and I am happy that your business and your kids are in great shape."

They hugged again, and this time, Rikki held his friend in his bear arms for a second longer. He really couldn't find a way to really express his gratitude. It was so much bigger than this moment or any other moment they potentially could have for the rest of their lifetime.

Rikki took out a pen out of pen cup holder sitting on the desk and wrote down today's date on the check. It was a minute of triumph for him, to thank the one man who he waited to thank for over thousand days prior to today. Rikki gave his guest the envelope with the check and hugged him again.

"Ok, let's go celebrate with a drink. You know, it's on the house, right?" Rikki was not asking but ensuring that Granvill understood that the bar owner's gratefulness didn't perish into the past with writing the check.

"Thank you, Rikki," acknowledged Granvill while walking out of the office. "Truly."

They came back into the bar and rejoined Steve Maragos, who was getting buzzed but was ordering his sixth drink anyway.

"I am sure you have a lot of questions. I will answer yours first, and then you tell me your story," Rikki was not going to get distracted by the bar business while Granvill was his guest. Who knew when the next time he would see that man would be, and he was eager to spend time with him and catch up on old times.

"Yes, I do," smiled widely Granvill.

That was exactly what he came to the city today for, to learn about his old friends and colleagues, to touch the past that was so good, yet so tempting to escape from. He spent a big part of life side by side with these people, and losing connection with them was his choice, not theirs. And his choice on purpose, more as a direct consequence of him not having a cell phone and wanting to disconnect from the world to live in the present.

"Go ahead," encouraged Rikki.

"Ok, where do I start? First, anyone from my company, the owner, other partners, do you know anything about them?" asked Granvill.

"Yes. Ok, your owner, William Bradford, is still the owner, but not as active in the business itself. He got sick about two or three years ago now. I think more like three years, had some heart problems. He had to have surgery, spent some time in the hospital, recovered completely, more or less. But doctors told him not to work so hard, and he practically retired. Junior took over."

"Billy Jr.?"

He remembered the owner, who never wanted to retire. He loved to develop new buildings, buy land, and be involved in all processes, from permits to construction to the sales of the built units. He bragged about how he would be ninety-five years old cutting ribbon on his next project in downtown. Today, he wasn't even seventy-five yet. His son, William Junior, was quite the opposite kind. He grew up with money, and probably didn't spend a day of his life thinking about how that money was made. He may have passed many office buildings in the city that he never even knew were built by his father's company. How he took over the company, Granvill wasn't sure. Unless the old man just decided that risk of crashing the business in his son's hands was better than the risk of not getting his family involved and not passing on his direct legacy.

"Yep," Rikki's response was short and telling. He also knew what kind of person Billy Jr. was.

"Did he change at all? How is the company now?" Granvill was almost afraid of the answer to that question.

"Company is struggling. He has changed a bit, accepted the responsibility of being a boss, but the lack of ideas and leadership are still there. The company is not doing nearly as good as at your times."

"What about the partners, don't they help?"

"As much as they can, sure," Rikki shrugged his shoulders. "But don't forget how stubborn that guy can be. When it comes to big polarizing decisions, he manages to make the wrong one three quarters of the time. I don't know all the details, but last year, he decided to buy land across the state history museum, planning to build a new office building. He planned to make it like fifteen floors high. Then the city only permitted to build no more than eight, and after he couldn't expand the parking lot space for it, because of the territory of the museum, he stuck with a tiny parking lot. So, at the end they built a three-story office space to match the parking and lost a bunch of money. When he bought the land, he paid top dollar, being sure of fifteen floors of renters. Later, everyone found out that all the partners were against the idea, but he went on his own to prove to everyone that he was right and made the deal anyway. Joseph, – remember Joseph? – almost quit the company after that. At the end he didn't, but I think that's what made him start to look for other options. And maybe six, seven, maybe nine, not sure, months later, he accepted the director position at Suropak."

"Wow, he couldn't stand them back in the day!" exclaimed Granvill.

"That's right, things change, and he figured it was better than working for Junior. Anyway, so the other two are still there, Mark and Chase. But Mark is working kind of part time, and he drinks a lot now. He comes here all the time. He may be here today too. His wife left him, his teenage son, unfortunately, overdosed on drugs and passed away, and he became a shadow of himself.

I think he goes to work so he knows his routine, otherwise he would be lost. Sometimes I try to stop him from drinking the whole night, but other times, I feel bad. He has nowhere to go. All he has is that crappy office and this bar."

Granvill remembered Mark quite well. He was eight years older than Granvill and started at that company a few years earlier than him. He was the guy who took Granvill under his wing at the beginning, and mentored him on the land development and construction, taught him a few tricks of the trade, especially how to recognize good deals from average ones.

"That's sad." Granvill was hoping to hear better news about his old friends.

Rikki agreed. He poured two glasses of expensive scotch and offered one to his dear guest.

"But Chase is doing really well!" He wanted to talk about something positive. "He is finding deals, making money, doing charity as well, there are rumors of him running for office someday. He is happy. Married, two children. Rarely comes here. Usually when he closes another big deal, he will stop by with some employees, and have a drink or two, at the most, and rushes home to his family. Every time."

Granvill thought about how Chase' life right now sounded a lot like his own life eight years ago. Does that mean that Chase' life was not necessarily perfect, but he caught a glimpse of it at the right time and then it all went downhill from here? No, he couldn't think like that. *I am a positive person*, Granvill told himself, forcing a smile out of himself.

He remembered when Chase just met his future wife, and everything seemed to be going in his favor at work as well. They were a good couple, she was ambitious yet warm, and complimented him perfectly, although he complimented her wit and charm just as well.

Granvill was happy for Chase. He was a good honorable guy, and maybe he could keep this life he had for a long time, maybe forever, if such a concept existed in our modern world. In the past, things worked in a different way. Slavery could be forever, for a lifetime of a person; kings were born into their royalty forever, there were many things that used to take place in human history that were forever, but not today.

In today's world, a person could be rich one day and beg for a dollar on the corner the next, a person could be free and, in a blink of an eye, earn time in prison, married or divorced, alive or dead. Every day could look exactly like all the previous ones, and any day or time, it could all change with no return.

"I am happy for Chase, he always wanted to be a big shot and make a lot of money. But he also did it the right way and always had a good heart," admitted Granvill.

"Absolutely! One of my favorite boys after you skipped the city," agreed the bar owner.

"No new partners, huh?" asked Granvill.

"No. Junior has everything in his hands, he would gladly take the power away from Mark and Chase, but they were promoted before his time. And he needs Chase to keep whatever good deals and positive production happens in the company. If he leaves, the company will truly be in shambles. I think the father also told Junior to not mess with Chase, especially after Joseph left. It hit him hard, but he knows it was because of his son."

There was so much talk about his old company and his old job, that the air started feel like the air inside of the office of Bradford Development. Granvill had good memories of those times, but today's conversation was hardly positive. The luck had changed, and life at the company had as well.

"Tell me, what about Kristine? She was an up-and-coming dealmaker. Did she get anywhere?"

"Oh, Kristine is doing ok I think."

Rikki paused here for a moment preparing himself to say out loud what was coming next.

"But life hit her hard. She got married, after dating a guy for almost five years. It seemed like she knew who she was marrying. But the bastard cheated on her with her own cousin, and then took most of the money from both of them and left the country."

"Wow!" Granvill couldn't find any other words. "*Men* do that?"

"Apparently. That's not it, I am afraid. She buried herself in work and kept doing well. But after that, her mother died, and that kind of threw her in a tailspin. She battled a painkiller addiction for a bit, went to rehab, she took all of that pretty hard. She had to leave Bradford because of that too, I hear she is ok now, but she moved somewhere across the country or something."

"That's crazy. Bad things happen to good people just as much as to bad people. It all seems so random," Granvill went into a philosophical mode. "I really hope she is ok."

Granvill liked Kristine. He was married to Paige at the time, so no extra activity was ever possible, but Kristine was always nice, easy going, and delightful. She looked astonishing too! She was a few years younger than Paige, and single at the time. Granvill always kept a distance, but they were working together quite a bit, and formed a good kind of selfless friendship.

Kristine was kind woman, who everyone thought would advance well in her career, then get married to a successful ambitious man and have a great power-couple happy life. But she never got married at the time when Granvill was around, she lost a relationship or two, because she worked too hard, and had no time for personal commitments, and in the end, she ended up picking the wrong guy.

And it's not like a woman needed to get married to be happy. And the same applied to men. *Successful people want to have families to share their success with someone, just like miserable people want to get married to share their misery and bitterness at life. Only people in the middle stay single*, thought Rikki while he was telling this story. Like him.

When he got married the first time around, he was extremely broke and not that happy. But he was bubbly in his nature, as he had the best moments of his life when he worked as a bartender. Then he opened his own bar and got divorced a few years later. Since then, he survived the tough times, and now he is in the middle. Not miserable enough to find a gloomy at life girl, and not successful and rich enough yet to marry some local model type or a gold digger, which was almost the same thing. And he undoubtedly wasn't attractive enough – from the point of view of social status – to create a power couple with anyone. He was still a bartender after all, just now he didn't have to share his tips with anyone.

"I hope she is ok too," replied Rikki.

For a minute he started to wonder if Kristine dropped from the top echelon to the middle where he was, or all the way to the bottom, where life really seemed to be an unpleasant struggle with yourself and your doubts. He heard she was still quite positive, and since she got her life together again, she was probably right in the middle with him. Too bad she wasn't around and decided to move away from here.

They talked a bit more about all the people Granvill used to know well and spend a lot of time with through work, friendships, charitable causes or big parties. It was interesting to get a glimpse of their lives many years later, but it also was interesting to think about what his life would look like today if he had stayed on his path of socially acceptable success.

He had spent a couple more hours with Rikki, Robert, and Steve Maragos. He stopped drinking roughly an hour before he decided to leave the bar. Everyone wished him well and asked him to stop by more often than once every seven years, and maybe even get a cell phone, which Granvill replied that he would think about it. Riccardo hugged him one more time and reminded him that his debt was not paid off. The next time the old man was around, he should take advantage of drinks on the house again. Granvill was touched once again.

The old man took the bus back to the village, the last bus
for the night; he walked still straight and at a faster, more confident pace, without really noticing the change in himself. His
confidence wasn't higher than usual, his awareness of what kind
of image perception he projects to the world, however, was at
a different level. This life in the big city was a totally different
kind from the life in the village, and they both had advantages
and disadvantages, like anything else. Granvill needed to figure
out if it was possible to balance the two acts at the same time.

CHAPTER 11

Christmas. A fun holiday for the children of the world, a meaningful one for the parents and the religious kind, and a tremendously chaotic one for everyone else. This was the kind of holiday that when one didn't have a family to celebrate it with, it wasn't a happy celebration, but a brutal reminder of one's lonely place in the world. People spent a lot of effort and money to escape from that kind of reminder. They would go shopping, spend their time at big parties, embark on cruises around the world, or otherwise try to change the dynamics of that day; dynamics that otherwise overbear them by creeping deep into their hearts.

Granvill had spent the last few Christmases mostly alone, but not miserable.

He was at peace with himself back then, and he wasn't looking for anything else from the world besides his freedom and tranquility. The more peace and tranquility he had, the more of the goodness he could spread from his heart to the people around him. That was the way he envisioned his life. And that was an almost perfect plan.

But life tends to change on you every time you think you've settled in. It's like if he was sitting in his lazy chair of existence, protected by the walls of his serenity, and after a while, the universe decided to rock the chair a bit to wake him up to new challenges. And when he didn't listen to it, it started to pull the blanket off him and made him feel less comfortable. Then it turned off his fireplace, and finally finished it off with tearing the walls around him down. Now, Granvill was still sitting in his favorite chair, but with no comfort around it anymore. No blankets, no fireplace, and no walls. He wasn't alone in his comfortable place anymore. He was in the open for anyone who could possibly pass his house to see. And he was feeling exposed to the brutality of the weather with all the rain and snow storms that it could muster.

This Christmas, he wasn't comfortable anymore. But he was also not alone. On his walk to the Person Who Smiled at Everyone's house, Granvill didn't bother to think about any of that. He was focused on nothing more than on the evening ahead and going over in his mind all the positive scenarios that could take place tonight.

Granvill was back at the white house, arriving just in time for the Christmas encounter with the beautiful woman who resided there. When she opened the door in response to him ringing the doorbell, he was pleasantly taken aback by her physical appearance. He was quite aware of the beauty that the Person Who Smiled at Everyone brought with her into this world, even if some of her beauty started to fade, just a tad, but he also had never seen her like *this*: extravagantly fabulous. Her makeup was done to perfection, specifically to highlight her already perfect cheeks and the smooth silky skin of her face. She was wearing a gorgeous blue dress: simple, but elegant, with a low décolletage that was adding to the effect. It was quite long, reaching her knees, tight enough to show off her form, yet loose enough to be comfortable.

She was smiling, not in a shy way, but in a happy to finally-get-together way. Granvill smiled back and complimented her on her look tonight. They moved inside, and she was excited to tell him how Christmas Day was going for her so far. She invited him to sit on a couch in the living room. Although the dinner was ready, she didn't feel like eating at the dinner table, she had an idea in her head that they would be more comfortable in a less formal setting.

Granvill got comfortable within the cushions of the grey-greenish couch of the living room. He felt a bit out of place dressed in dark grey dress pants and a light green dress shirt, but his appearance matched the look of his date, and that made him more certain. She asked him if he wanted some wine, and while he rarely drank wine, he gladly accepted the invitation. After less than a minute, the Person Who Smiled at Everyone came back with two glasses, each half-full, and provided one to her guest.

She placed herself cautiously on the same couch merely ten inches away from Granvill. It seemed like a safe distance for the first minutes of the evening, yet close enough to connect with the man. They clanged glasses and tasted the wine. It was Beringer Luminus Chardonnay from Napa Valley, one of her favorites. It wasn't the most expensive one, but she really hoped he would enjoy it. He did, considering he wasn't a big wine drinker. Although, he enjoyed tasting wines from all over the world in his travelling days, and he was still open to experiences that were pleasant for other people. Also, he wasn't picky about getting exactly what he wanted. At least, out of the material things.

"I will bring dinner. I hope you are hungry," mentioned the Person Who Smiled at Everyone, while standing up to move to the kitchen for the plates.

"Thank you," Granvill smiled at her, enjoying the host's kindness.

They continued to chat about Christmas while she was getting dinner on their plates. Granvill asked her if she needed help, but she politely refused, and they continued with the conversation. She really wanted to make sure this evening went well. She spent a delightful morning with her son, and they had such a good time without managing to offend each other. Because of that, she was in extra good mood, and she had full expectations that the evening would go just as well.

When she came back to the living room, she was carrying one plate which was for Granvill, and she had to make another trip back to the kitchen to get her own plate. When she returned, she sat at the same exact distance from the man. During the meal, they chatted more about Christmas, children, the new generation, the old generation, good old times, their favorite music from the good old times, their favorite movies when they were growing up, and many other topics. Granvill realized that the age difference between them wasn't big at all, and their interest differences were even less noticeable. They did have a lot in common and talking about everything was easy and extremely comfortable. They were like good old friends or high school sweethearts who happened to get together again trying to rekindle their flame.

The dinner was delicious too, the Person Who Smiled at Everyone prepared chicken marsala and Granvill could easily call it the best chicken marsala he ate in at least ten years. It also went well with the chardonnay, and the conversation kept flowing smoothly over food and wine. After taking the empty plates to the kitchen and pouring more wine in their glasses, the Person Who Smiled at Everyone sat down on the couch and cut the ten-inch improvisational distance between them in half. Granvill felt comfortable with it.

By now, he was going with the flow and not thinking about the changes that were coming rapidly into his life. He felt close to his date tonight, and spending time with a beautiful and kind woman who made dinner for him reminded him of a feeling that was well forgotten, but dearly missed. Although, he never even realized it was missing. By the time another glass of wine was gone, he took her hand in his, and held it warmly and gently.

"You are really an amazing woman!" he said. "And this is a great evening!"

"Same here." She practically whispered the response.

Her lips were getting a feeling of dryness, the kind of feeling that only Granvill's lips could help to bring back to their normal existence. Granvill noticed that, but he decided that this was a perfect moment for something else first.

"I do have a present for you."

"Really? I got something for you too," she smiled, talking still three quarters down of her normal talking tone.

Granvill took a box out of his pants pocket. It was a tiny and quite generic box, the kind that usually contained jewelry, like a necklace or a bracelet, wrapped in bright Christmas paper, not too precisely, but with care. She unwrapped the box carefully with her beautiful fingers and opened it with excitement. There was a set of beautiful blue crystal and silver-toned earrings, in the shape of a raindrop, and they created the desired effect on the Person Who Smiled at Everyone. She was excited and gave a quick emotional hug to her friend. Just for an extra second, she kept her arms around Granvill's neck, and he had a chance to take a breath of the smell coming from her, a mix of her perfume and her natural body aroma. He knew that her sexiness was now overtaking everything inside of him, and the urges were getting too strong to resist, although he had no plans to object them anyways.

"Thank you! They are so beautiful!" exclaimed the woman. "Let me get yours."

She stood up quickly and left the room. Granvill had a few seconds to collect his thoughts and ask himself if the evening was going the way he liked. *The evening was magical so far, in the real*

Christmas spirit. When she came back, she had a large box in her hands, and she was thrilled to give it to Granvill. She sat down on the couch next to him, in such a way that the side of her thigh was practically touching his. Granvill started to unwrap the box and teared off some of the red and green wrapping paper. The box itself didn't present itself as anything recognizable. It was a plain beige box that could hold absolutely anything. His curiosity with that kind of thing normally wouldn't be triggered, but right now he was sincerely interested in what the present could be.

He opened the box and finally revealed the present. It was a tan leather color weekender duffle bag that looked really fancy and the timing of this gift couldn't have been any better. Did she know about Granvill's changes? She couldn't know more than some random details, but a travel bag was kind of a symbol of him accepting a new work position. He really liked all the pockets, and the size was perfect. It seemed big enough to fit everything he usually needed as he traveled light, yet not too big to take as carry-on inside of the plane, which was always an extra benefit to not have to deal with cargo luggage.

"Thank you," Granvill said to the woman. "It's a generous and thoughtful present. I love it. Perfect color too."

He put his left arm around her back, clenching her body in a half hug. She leaned into it a little, and her face, with soft dry lips in close distance, were already in his space. He had nothing left to do but the most natural thing in the moment. His lips went after hers and they met and collapsed into one hot kiss. There was enough passion left in them to feel like people in their twenties, and the kissing quickly escalated with his right hand under her dress.

They woke up quite early, not even 6am. She was in his arms, her naked body was only half covered by a comforter, and her hair sprung from the sheets to his shoulder and his left arm, that was holding her tight. She opened her eyes just minutes before he opened his. She asked him if he wanted to get up or sleep a bit longer. He felt like both options were good, but sleeping was better. She was happy with the answer. She turned around and got into a comfortable snuggling position with his arms around her from the back. She closed her eyes and, with a smile on her face, she dozed off again into morning sleep.

The next time they woke up, almost two hours later, they both decided it was time to get up and start their day. He kissed her passionately, moving from her lips to her neck, her breasts and her stomach. She moaned a bit, and just when he was ready to leave the bed, she pulled him back closer to her, and they quickly engaged in sensual morning sex.

That was a great Christmas, thought Granvill.

That was an unbelievable and unforgettable night, thought the Person Who Smiled at Everyone.

They had a morning coffee together with croissants, and eventually, around eleven o'clock, he had to leave her. She closed the door behind him, bit her lip in the memory of the night, smiled to the Universe and went on to take a shower.

They didn't see each other again for two days, and Granvill had time to think about what exactly took place. There was unquestionably a connection, but was it a one-night wonder multiplied in effect by the holiday? Was it an intimate chemistry of two souls? Was the Person Who Smiled at Everyone expecting him to stop by and ask her out again? And what did he want for himself in this situation?

Granvill went to the coffee shop in the hope that he would catch his Christmas date there. He didn't have a plan, but he knew that he wanted to see her again. Of course, he happened to choose the coldest day this winter season yet. Not like it bothered him personally; he was used to any kind of weather, as he took most of the surrounding circumstances out of his control lightly. He knew that there was nothing he could do about it, so it wasn't even worth his attention. It was the same mentality he applied to many other things in life: if a store was out of his favorite scotch, or the animals ate some vegetables in his garden, or there was traffic in the city, if the post office was losing his mail, an airline company delayed the flight because they had no available pilot, or his sports team lost a big game. All of that and much more was out of his control. And all of that and much more wasn't going to ruin Granvill's days.

However, today, it seemed that the fact of the coffee shop being crowded as most people were either sitting in their homes or coming over here for a cup of hot chocolate or cappuccino, was creating an extra inconvenient atmosphere for him to get a minute with the shop owner. It bothered him more than it usually would. However, when she saw him in line, everyone else disappeared from her vision. She could only see Granvill. He was more handsome than she realized before, although all women in the village would agree that he was generally quite a handsome man. But right now, in this line of this coffee shop, there was no one else but this man, who suddenly introduced her to the magic of a great date again. She was married for seventeen years, so her last date was more than eighteen years ago. The first five or six years of her marriage were also great, but since then, she forgot what it felt like to have a man who could make your day, to have a man nearby who could make you feel like you were the most amazing person in the world.

She gave her last coffee order to a customer on complete auto-pilot, and then she asked the Girl Who Knew Everything to take over the line. She stepped away slowly, barely breaking eye contact with Granvill. Of course, she was smiling. But her smile wasn't of the confident kind. What if he didn't come here for her? Since he didn't have a phone, they didn't talk for two days, who knew if he wanted to see her at all?

Granvill was smiling too. He was happy to see the Person Who Smiled at Everybody, but also, he was happy with her reaction: she was truly excited to see him. Granvill had the same doubts, although maybe a little bit less of it. He was as confident as he was on day one, knowing they had a great time. He was still confident the second day thinking that this was a normal period to not see each other after a first date, but today in the morning he started to feel some doubts like if he waited too long to connect again, or if she was interested in connecting at all. Her reaction right now gave him a boost. He smiled at her and left the line towards the woman.

They both weren't sure how to greet each other properly, but they embraced in a hug, which seemed appropriate.

"How are you?" asked the Person Who Smiled at Everyone.

"I am good. You?"

"I am good as well. Very busy. Christmas season is a good time for coffee and such, but also a very busy time. I am glad you stopped by though. I waited."

"I wanted to see you. What time will you be done?" asked Granvill.

"I close the shop at 9pm, but I can leave around eight, I think, and leave the guys to finish it up."

She wished it would be possible to close the store right now, right at this moment, and go embrace Granvill somewhere else. But she knew she needed to be here. It would be a busy day, and the shop wouldn't be ok without her being here.

"Would you like to go to my place after that? I have a nice patio with tulips as well, and a great view of the mountains."

She nodded yes. She embraced him with a hug again, and said she needed to get back to work, but that she would see him after eight. Granvill turned around without getting coffee. It didn't even cross his mind again to get a cup of a hot drink. After seeing the Person Who Smiled at Everyone, he was happy.

Granvill decided to cook tonight. What he didn't already have at his house, like candles and flowers, he picked up at a local store, and then cooked his version of a romantic dinner. Sea Trout was nicely and evenly baked in a lemon butter sauce and crab cakes were added as the alternative, also baked in lemon sauce, so he didn't have to make sauce twice. He only needed to separate the basis to add butter in one of them.

The Person Who Smiled at Everyone arrived just before eight thirty. She left her shop just a bit later than planned, and then stopped by at her house to put a different dress on. Now she was wearing a shorter black outfit, that was simple yet not as casual. She had never been in Granvill's house before today, and she felt a bit nervous. More nervous than the Christmas evening, for some reason. Maybe it was the fact that now they both knew where it was leading to. The first time around it was not a certainty, but rather a possibility.

They had another amazing evening though. Dinner and wine under a candlelight, great conversation, more wine and talk at the patio with the view of the mountains, and hot explosive sex on the same patio under the moonlight. The house was in such a remote destination that there was no one who could see them here. Being outside really made the Person Who Smiled at Everyone feel free. She had never done anything similar with her ex-husband, and in her mind, something like that could never take place. But here it was, happening today and now. The moment was spectacular. *Each and every moment.* Him taking her dress off. Him grabbing her body. Him executing his form. Her having an orgasm, one after another, each time howling at the moon. She had never felt that free before today!

All her doubts were erased on this patio. She liked Granvill, not only for his passion, but for the kind of man he was, considerate, calm, pleasant, and intelligent. Everything she always respected, and everything she had never received. She couldn't believe her luck that that man was interested in her.

She couldn't believe that after a seventeen-year marriage with a disastrous ending, there was still enough time in her life to find that kind of relationship.

Granvill and the Person Who Smiled at Everyone kept seeing each other for the rest of the winter. They never spent time with her son though, and never talked about taking it to the next level. Sometimes he stayed in her house, and other times she stayed at his. Granvill felt young again, and he was enjoying that adventure. He also really liked the woman, but he didn't know where the future would take them. One thing he was certain about was that he didn't mind that kind of change in his life anymore. Everything that he was so sure he didn't need in his life, he was happy to have now.

Valentine's day they spent like most other nights. He cooked a romantic dinner, and they had time to take a bubble bath together and exchange massages for each other. It was a quiet, intimate night which they both enjoyed, but not anything more than that.

Granvill started to think about the spring, and the resort project with the Person Who Wants to be the Center of the Universe. Granvill was getting excited about it, almost anxious. It was amazing to him how easily his peace was replaced by a hunger to accomplish something worthwhile and work. It meant to be a productive member of society, and he always appreciated that part of existence. But it also took his harmony and perfect sleep away from him long before the work even got started. Granvill had no idea what exactly he wanted out of his life anymore.

Most of the village residents were ready for the spring to come. While the winter was mild and not that long, there were not many people who really loved it. Mostly kids. Adults, however, were living in the near future and were hoping by April it would be warm and sunny.

The Person Who Wants to be the Center of the Universe started laying foundation a week after the snow had melted, and he was focused on work and the impact he would make on this province. After he finished this project, he would be the largest land developer in the whole region, and while his presence in the big city was also significant, he would be the guy to go to when big people out of the state wanted to build anything substantial in this area.

Meanwhile, he started dating a new girl from the city, the Person Who Preferred the Status over Anything, and while he knew it probably wasn't going to be a long-term commitment, he enjoyed her personality. Her way of approaching life with joy and pleasure appealed to him, as much as her body and energy in bed. She was almost a full ten years younger than him, but he gave her the thing she wanted the most: status in society, especially within the city.

She was also excited about the resort because more exposure meant more status for her. A girl like that was born to be the First Lady of the country, which meant she still had class and some brains, but she just didn't want to work for anything in her life. She realized quite early in her life that her beauty would get her further with less effort than anything else she could offer to the world. That was as much on the society she lived in as her own doing, at least that's what she was telling herself. She was just playing the game with the hand that was given to her.

Besides business and his new girlfriend, the Person Who Wants to be the Center of the Universe used this winter time to travel a bit and made two big trips. The first one was to South America, to the extremely popular tourist destination of Machu Picchu in the Peruvian mountains, which he wanted to do for the longest time, and he enjoyed that trip without his girlfriend; and the second one was at the beginning of February to the beaches of Bahamas, the destination his girlfriend picked for them. This was the location where she loved to take selfies and pictures together as a couple to show off to all her followers how perfect her life now was.

Not everyone's life was even "fake perfect", and not everyone in the village could take a vacation to Bahamas. The Person Who Felt Insecure in Relationships took a short five-day staycation at Christmas time, and then went back to work. She tried to set up a meeting with the Person Who Wants to be the Center of the Universe, but to no avail. The man was busy, especially for any kind of salesman, or saleswoman.

She continued to work hard through the winter, prospecting, servicing her current clients, and trying to grow her business. She didn't like to be stagnant, and since she practically had no personal life to attend to, her work was defining her life. By the spring, she was behind on her goals, both personal and set by her financial firm, though it wasn't like her job was in jeopardy.

She had proven herself over and over again in the years prior. But she didn't like the feeling of not doing the best she could, and since her life wasn't filled with something else relevant, the work put quite a bit of pressure on her. She reset her goals for the second quarter of the year and was hoping to catch up to the point where she should be.

Her neighbor, the Person with Bad Luck, had a completely opposite kind of winter. Very little work, although he wasn't doing nothing. He painted more canvases in the last three months than in the seven previous years combined. He painted almost every day, and he finished over sixty paintings. Beautiful landscapes of the village with trees, animals, gardens, and woods were mixed in with some portraits and even abstract attempts. His portraits also included his late wife, and that wasn't as painful as it used to be and was even kind of therapeutic. He woke up most days with the excitement to face daylight and looked forward to what he could do next. He found a couple of new hobbies as well.

One of those new hobbies was golf. He always wanted to play more golf, but when he started to spend more time with his wife at the time, golf took a backseat. He played some in his twenties and early thirties, and he was quite good at it, shooting ninety to ninety-four in average, but he never took the next step. The Person with Bad Luck decided that this was the time. Of course, in the winter time, there was little, if any, golf he could do, but there was a practice facility in the city, and he went twice a week over there, so he could prepare his game for the summer.

The other hobby was a totally new thing to him. He joined a local chess club, and started learning all the openings, gambits and other strategy tactics of the game. He never realized how fascinating and complex this game really was. What grabbed his attention the most was the infinite possible moves that could be made by both sides and how people plan five moves ahead yet are forced to adjust their strategy every time when the opponent makes an unexpected move. He was truly amazed how at the beginning, a player had only twenty options to start the game but had four hundred available moves after two ply moves, and that number grew to a remarkable seventy-two thousand eighty-four positions after only two moves apiece. He learned that there were over nine million positions after three moves apiece, and over two hundred eighty-eight billion possible positions after just four moves apiece.

That infinite amount of choices was mesmerizing to him and moved his train of thought in the other direction of fate. The control of the situation that one player could have on the board over the other player despite such unpredictability really inspired him to believe that life – maybe, just maybe – is a bit like chess, and he had something to say on what his next move in his existence on this Earth would be. Chess came to his life at the right time, and it gave him more than a hobby. It gave him hope.

Between those two hobbies, his painting and some local volunteering that he started doing together with his late wife and continued even after her passing, he was suddenly a busy and quite content man.

The Very Tolerant Person was less content with her recent life developments. While she took many events that were happening to her in quite a philosophical way, she sometimes felt that there were just too many things that were out of her control, and it started to create a feeling in her that there was nothing she could do about it. She had seen reduction in the occupancy of her inn in the winter time, which was normal for her business in this village. This place was great in the summer, but not really built to have fun in the snow. But the difference this time around was that normally, after a slow season a booming season would come. Spring would move into the summer, and it was always busy enough with nature lovers, families who want to get out of the city, fishermen, jet ski hobbyists and honeymooners who couldn't afford to go to Mexico or Hawaii, so they would go somewhere closer and more cost friendly.

This year though, she was worried that the new resort would eat a big portion of that business. She had heard that they would try to open in the middle of the summer, around Independence Day. While she had some time before that, there was no guarantees of long-term survival. Fishermen may still prefer her place, for two reasons, prices and loyalty. But the rest of the people, especially families and people celebrating their love, would surely prefer a fancy resort with more options and better rooms than her small inn.

The business was much better for two other people: The Person Who Needs Affirmation and his doctor practice and The Person Who is Proud to be Hard-Working and his flower business. The local doctor did well this winter season, because not only it was a flu season, and people regularly came to him for a quick fix of stronger medicine than over the counter, but also because he happened to have a couple of patients who were at the late stages of their respective diseases. It meant they were pretty much dying, and while it was awful for his patients and their families, and he felt bad for them personally, it gave his clinic an extra boost of continuous checkups, prescriptions, and tests which he could sent to the big city for analysis. He was also hoping to be recognized for the Person of the Year in their county, and while the competition was quite stiff, especially candidates that were coming from Fish Haven, he was expecting to be nominated at the least.

On the other hand, the business for The Person Who is Proud to be Hard-Working was good for more positive reasons. Most people would buy presents without flowers accompanying them, but the Christmas season was ok for him because many were filling their cold houses with artificial warmth through flowers of all different colors. Fresh lilies, tulips, roses, and orchids that were delivered from greenhouses all around the country were a good option for that.

Then the Valentine's Day came, the best time of the year for his business. He knew that lust was stronger than love of parents and mothers specifically, at least based on the flowers sales of each holiday season. Valentine's Day usually made his whole first quarter, and this year it was slightly better than usual. He was extremely satisfied. He did work hard to provide for his wife and three children, and he made sure all his customers were happy with the service he provided. Timely deliveries, even if he had to drive his family minivan himself in addition to the two regular vans he employed, and fresh flowers were trademarks on which he built his company. Valentine's day rewarded him financially and was positive in acknowledging his quality work.

The Valentine's day, unfortunately, wasn't great for everyone. The Selfish Person decided two days before the holiday that the Person Who Was Obsessed with His Body wasn't as good for her image as she thought and decided to break things off between them. At the end of the day, the downside of being with him outweighed the upside. While it was great to take pictures together, which she wasn't sure if it gave her more Instagram followers or not, but if did, not necessarily of the right kind. Him trying to overshadow her and show himself off was too much for her and her supporters. Plus, she couldn't flirt with single rich men, or go with them to a dinner to close a deal on a house, which worked so well for her in the past.

She was sad a bit to let him go, especially before the Valentine's day. She was even considering doing it right after the holiday instead, but she decided it wouldn't be right and too cruel, even for her. One thing she would miss though was the jealous looks of the women who wanted to be with her man. They already were envious of her personally, her beauty, her lavish lifestyle, her Instagram page, and her business career but the extra attention that she got a perfect man by her side as well was giving her extra pleasure. That was gone for now though. Until she found her next target.

Her career was moving up though. She managed to sell a few big and expensive houses in the area. Only one of them was in the village, but she did more in Fish Haven and the surrounding territory. Her Instagram grew quite a bit, which made her happy. The more followers she had, the more important she felt, and the more she worried about the quality of her content. She had to continue to create interesting and fabulous posts, and she made sure her real life was up to the standard of her photo desires. If she had a choice if she should eat at a local sandwich shop, or Fish Haven country club, she would drive an extra forty-five minutes to take a picture of herself eating lunch next to the beautifully green golf course. Even in the winter time, there were spots in the village that offered better views, or a more original menu, and that's where she would go.

That desire worked tremendously well for her career. Her houses website presentations were flawless, not only because she knew how to decorate houses, but because she also knew the most expressive photography angles and what worked and didn't work on social media. She made average houses look good, nice houses look amazing, and mansions looked, in her skillful hands, like king's castles. During live demos, she used her sexy dresses, white teeth smile, and adorable laughter in timely moments to connect with each buyer, and that made her the best realtor in the county. Her Instagram page was three-fold: a vast source of her real estate business, the confirmation of her success in her industry, as well as her affirmation of being popular and relevant in this universe.

One of her devoted followers was the Person Without Care for Others. Not much had changed in his life though. He still had no girlfriend or any real friends. A couple of co-workers of his would get a beer with the guy on a rare occasion, but that was pretty much the extent of any relationship the Person Without Care for Others managed to have in the village. His mother was still hanging on for her life, trying to enjoy her new home at a retirement home in Fish Haven, and her son would still visit her once a month or so. He still worked for a paycheck at the construction company, dreaming about owning one someday in the future. While Granvill's life was all about changes this winter, the Person Without Care for Others didn't want to change many things in his life, and the one thing he wanted to change, his job, he didn't really know how to go about changing.

CHAPTER 12

The Very Tolerant Person woke up as usual at exactly six o'clock in the morning. Her alarm made sure she did. Days when she woke up by the alarm meant it was a good night of sleep for her. Some nights she would be up at five forty-five or even worse, she would lose sleep in the middle of the night, something like three thirty in the morning and wouldn't be able to go back to bed again. Those are the things that people from the outside could never see. They saw a woman with an optimistic outlook on life and a smile on her face. Her having a good relationship with everyone around her also was noticeable to people in the village. What they didn't see was how much effort was sometimes needed for her to get up in the morning and be that person that everyone loved. Being nice and tolerant was in her nature but being always positive about her day wasn't necessarily the same thing.

After taking a shower and getting dressed, she made her morning coffee, with one sugar and one hazelnut creamer, as usual, and proceeded out of her room to the lobby of her inn.

Her room was on the first floor of the inn, around the corner, with a private entrance to the garden. She loved that garden and spent a lot of time there. She was excited about Granvill's tulips as well, as they would add a nice extra dimension to the place. Another advantage of her place from the rest of the rooms in the inn was the fact it had two extra quarters, though not large, but not too small to put their functionality in jeopardy. One room was a kitchenette, where she had a fridge, a stove with an oven and a counter big enough to prepare her meals.

The other room with time became a mix of a dining room and game room. It had a proper dining table, a square one, able to fit four people, with an ability to recline to fit in eight, though there was no space in the room to ever use it for that purpose; and a smaller coffee table in the other corner with a chess set standing on the top of it, covering more than three fourths of the table top. This chess set was used often by the Person with Almost Unlimited Generosity and was never used again after his passing. Besides chess, there was a dartboard on the wall and a deck of cards on a shelf of a small cabinet underneath it. The room didn't have many more games other than that. The woman and her late husband used to invite friends here, and spend lovely Friday nights over dinner and chess, or a rare poker game.

In the last five years, the Very Tolerant Person had not eaten in here once. It was never a conscious decision though. At first, she just didn't feel like eating in there alone, after twenty-nine years of eating in there with her dear husband. She has been eating in her bedroom suite since then, on the sofa in front of a tv. Sometimes, if it was late dinner, even in her bed. She was sure in her mind that with time, she would start eating in the dining room again, but week after week, then month after month flew by, and eventually it was a whole five years and counting that had passed. If anyone would ask her now, she may even say that sometime soon, she would go back to the dining table, but the reality was that, though she didn't want to admit it to herself, there was no place in her life for that extra room and all the memories that came with it.

The only time she would come here was to pick up the next book to read. She would walk in, look around, always glance with a deep level of sentimentality at the chess set, then find the book she wanted on the shelves of the larger cabinet on the same side of the wall as the door to the room, and walked out. The next time she would come back to the room again was to exchange the book she had finished for a new one. Her library wasn't big, but then again, she wasn't an avid reader. Although she enjoyed the process, she would read maybe a book a month at the best. If it was a thicker manuscript, then the actual reading process could stretch to five, six, or even seven weeks.

When she walked into the lobby, she greeted the person at the desk, who happened to be the Person Idolizing Celebrities, and asked if everything was in order. After receiving a positive confirmation, she walked passed the desk into the coffee area, and took two croissants from the inn's continental breakfast offer. The owner did that almost ritually every single morning, and there was no reason for an exception today. She looked around the area. There were no guests in the breakfast area yet. It was Friday morning, and most guests would typically get up after seven. The breakfast at the inn was served until 9am, so there was enough time for everyone to get some carb energy before they would start their day adventuring into the local nature, which is where visitors would usually spend their time in the village.

The Very Tolerant Person also looked at both paintings on the wall, the one with mountain tops first, and she admired the natural beauty of this world, and then she glanced at the painting with the woman sitting on a park bench. That woman had reminded the owner of the inn of herself so often in the last few years; the woman in the painting wasn't too sad, yet like the owner without a companion, completely on her own.

The Very Tolerant Person took her croissants and walked back to her suite. After she had her breakfast and finished her coffee, she put her shoes on and walked out of the inn. Today, she wanted to get some grocery shopping done. The fridge was almost empty, and she didn't like having no food at her home. Food was usually a comfort thing for her, and she needed comfort at the beginning and at the end of most days of her existence. She knew that the need of that comfort had a lot to do with her gaining twenty pounds or so. But her weight didn't bother her. Comparing to the torturous feeling of missing her husband and her father, a few extra pounds was the last thing on her mind. Even when she looked in the mirror, she didn't notice her body, she didn't see physical traits that she possessed. Instead, she saw a glorified image of herself and the Person with Almost Unlimited

Generosity standing next to her, hugging her. Sometimes the image of her husband would glance at the mirror with her and smile to their reflections. He was always there. Every single time. And that was the only thing that she could see in the mirror.

Walking to the local store was usually a pleasant routine for the Very Tolerant Person. She never bought too much at once, so she would have to walk to the store four or five times a week. During that walk, she transformed herself into the person who everyone loved in the village; enthusiastic, optimistic, and approachable. Before her morning coffee and mental preparation, she wasn't ready to be who she always was. The death of her husband had changed her. Her routine didn't. She felt her hotel guests and local village residents deserved to see her best, so she continued to be that person *for them*. Maybe it would be better for her to acknowledge the transformational change in herself. On the other side, without continuing to be a pleasant person for the outsiders, that new version of her could very well get depressed or could feel not needed, without a concrete place in this universe. Her connection to other people who cared about her kindness and tolerance was one of the matters saving her from herself.

The walk would normally take about twelve minutes in one direction, and with each passing minute, the Very Tolerant Person was becoming more and more of a happy person. It was a sort of a self-therapy. By the time she would reach the store, she was all smiles, and she would greet every person she met like a dear friend of hers. She did care for all people in a sincere manner, and if anyone would ever need her help, she would step up to the occasion and do as much as she could. She also felt stronger to take on her own challenges when she was active and helpful.

She bought a few things and walked back to the inn. Her walk back didn't mean she was transforming herself back. *No, Sir!* She wasn't going to let herself be weak. She was ready for the day now and was thinking in her head about all the things she needed to get done. She was starting her shift at the desk at 5pm today, which was her regular time to start. She worked mornings as needed, but she really preferred evening shifts as it allowed her to interact with her guests more.

Until then, she had the whole day in her disposal to do something else productive.

She could do invoices today or could also place orders for any small objects from the vendors which usually needed to be refilled like coffee filters, packets of sugar, creamers, bath towels, cleaning supplies for their housekeepers, and other items needed for their business. And then she could start preparing for the Spring party. Twice a year, she would throw a party for her guests and the whole village, one in the spring, hence the name, and one in the fall. The party always took place in the inn's garden, and usually consisted of good food, some raffle fun with prizes, and live music. She would find a performer who was talented enough to make the party fun, yet not snobby enough to donate their time as one-time appearance. Some of the performers liked coming here so much, they would keep volunteering their time and keep coming back to the village. She could decide today whom she wanted to invite this year. The Very Tolerant Person was getting excited about the thought.

By the time she had reached the inn, she was even more enthusiastic than she was twelve minutes ago. She walked into the lobby and smiled to the Person Idolizing Celebrities. After receiving a smile back from her, she was planning to walk past the desk into her home arrangement, but the Person Idolizing Celebrities stopped her with a body gesture of needing the owner's help.

"Yes? What do you need?" She smiled at the desk worker.

"Actually, someone is looking *for you*."

The reply had puzzled the Very Tolerant Person just a bit. But the employee continued:

"There is a gentleman who checked in just five minutes ago into room nine, and he specifically asked for you. He said he hopes to get to talk to you whenever you have time."

"That's odd. What's his name?" The owner was quite intrigued now. Could it be one of her old friends?

"His name is George Bronson."

That name didn't say anything to the Very Tolerant Person. It wasn't one of her old friends. She asked if the Person Idolizing Celebrities could call the room and ask the guest if he wanted to see the owner now. The employee followed the instructions and easily reached the guest. After exchanging a couple of phrases back and forth, she hung up the phone and confirmed that the guest was eager to talk to her and would come down right away.

Even more so, the Very Tolerant Person was anxious to meet that guest. Sales people and vendors did not check into the rooms, and returning guests, while excited to see her, rarely specifically asked for her in that particular manner.

Not even two minutes later, the guest did come downstairs and right away approached the owner. He looked completely unfamiliar to her. He was tall, some people would find him handsome, with black short hair, honest eyes, and a softly featured jawbone, with an almost round shaped chin. He eagerly and passionately shook her hand and started to speak:

"I realize you don't know me, and we have never met before, so there is no reason you should."

His voice was even softer than his chin. He sounded almost too fearful to speak.

"I mean, you shouldn't know who I am. But I have something important to talk to you about."

The man with the soft chin looked at her with confidence, yet also with a bit of distress that she may reject him. Maybe that fear was driven by something else entirely though.

"Sure," she said, still sounding uncertain about the new stranger.

"Is there some place private we can talk?" asked George Bronson.

"Definitely! In the garden would be a wonderful place to chat," she smiled at the stranger. "Would you like some coffee?"

"No, no, thank you so much," his mind was clearly focused on one thing right now.

They proceeded out of the lobby and walked through part of the garden until they reached a nice-looking bench underneath a gigantic old oak. This oak was one of the few trees that was here even before the owner's dad built the inn here. He chose this place specifically because of this oak. When he bought the land, he built it around those trees and saved them all. The Very Tolerant Person used to love listening to her dad tell her that reminiscence, as well as many other memories dad used to share.

They sat on the bench and he continued with the conversation.

"I really hope that you will let me tell you the whole story," he began with little confidence.

The Very Tolerant Person thought, that if he knew her at all, he would know that she would always let him tell her his story. She nodded in affirmative agreement.

"I will start right away with the main point, I was thinking how it would be better, and what is better, and I think there is nothing better. I mean, there is no perfect way how to tell you. But I...."

He stopped talking, and the woman noticed that whatever was on the guest's mind made him feel quite emotional.

"It's alright, I am here, I am listening," she gently touched his forearm with her hand.

The words that George had practiced thousands of times prior to today were not coming out, and when they finally did, they came out in a totally different way and much harsher than he ever planned to say it out loud:

"Ms. The Very Tolerant Person, I am the man, who…. who killed your father."

He looked at her with as much mental strength as he could muster, but there was no holding it back now. Two tiny precious salty tears started to go down his cheeks. His eyes were piercing the woman with all the hope and honesty he had in him, yet disgust toward himself at the same time.

She gasped at the news she just heard. She stopped breathing for the next few seconds and then reached out for the air with the full power of her lungs. A weird exhale sound left her soul, and then she froze in space and looked at the stranger. Was this really happening right now? This person just showed up here like a ghost from the other dimension and told her that he was at fault for her dad's death.

"You were….?" She tried to put a sentence together, but then the griping sound came out of her body again.

"I am the person who was skiing that day, and I am the one who your father had saved…. He saved my life…… "

By now, the Person Who Always Carried Guilt was in full tears. He was trying not to sob, to let the Very Tolerant Person process the news. This wasn't about him right now, but about the person sitting across of him. A person who lost her father a long time ago due to the unfair life situation, and who was now forced to face one human being who was guilty of the whole situation to begin with.

The Very Tolerant Person recalled her sweet father's face. She could clearly envision how happy he was, how much he loved his only princess, and she burst into tears, then put her face in her hands and exploded into crying. The guest had no idea what to do in this situation, would she get angry at him after the initial reaction, would she hate him? *Of course she would*, he thought. She hated him for the last thirty plus years! She just didn't know who exactly *he was*. And now she did.

Despite those thoughts, he slowly and carefully put his arm on the woman's shoulder. He felt her sobbing through the convulsing movements of her back. He kept his hand there. His tears were continuing to stream, without a sound, letting deafening silence express his agony. He didn't feel his own heart, but he could only think about the heart that he just broke again, the heart of this – probably amazing – person. The heart of a person who he happened to just meet minutes ago. Yet, the lack of knowing the woman for any significant amount of time didn't stop him from inflicting on her a world of pain.

She cried for a very long minute, and then she lifted her face and looked at the Person Who Always Carried Guilt. He took his hand away from her body and froze in space.

"Tell me how it happened. Tell me why you are here." she demanded in a loud, but struggling to materialize into eloquent sounds, voice. "You asked me to let you tell the whole story. Then tell me."

He looked at her with the full intensity of his feelings, then took a deep breath, wiped the tears on the left side of his face off, and continued:

"I am here because I wanted you to know that his life…." He subconsciously decided to change the words again. All his mental preparation was out the window now. "That there was not one day in my life since that day that I don't remember the sacrifice your father made for me. And now, as I am a father myself, I understand how brave a person needs to be to disregard himself to save the life of a complete stranger. Your father is a hero, and.... I never, *never* felt that I deserved the exchange of my life for...... his."

His tears intensified, and made it difficult, almost impossible to see anything through them.

"I spent my existence trying to justify what happened, trying to live up to... I don't know what.... The second chance I have received for some crazy unexplainable reason, and I guess I am here to tell you that I will never be! I will *never be* enough to balance the scale of your loss. And I am so, so sorry."

He continued to cry, now uncontrollably. He tried to inhale the air, but instead his crying went into a human emotional collapse when the words were getting swallowed up in the magnitude of the moment. It was the woman's turn to put her hand on his back. She was in shock hearing all of that, but she also had a good heart that wasn't prepared to give up its life principles in the most important minute of her life.

"I will go get coffee for us now. Stay here," she commanded.

Still in tears, but with a bit better realization what was taking place, she was coming out of the tremor state, and was slowly recovering her senses.

She stood up and started walking towards the hotel. Before she got to the front door and walked away too far to lose sight of the bench, she stopped for a second, and looked back at the man who showed up, so unexpectedly, at her inn today. She saw him trying to take control of his emotions, but totally failing. She knew that the man – maybe, just maybe – did deserve the second chance that the universe had given him for that horrifying day, but she still wanted to hear more from him. She needed to hear more.

CHAPTER 13

'I became an engineer, I work for a fire alarm manufacturer. We are working on a few things right now, like a software that is making use of video cameras for smoke detection by analyzing digital images. We also work on mass notification, where even neighbor buildings can be notified of large fires. And we monitor live situations from the fire stations and notify them on the exact conditions inside burning buildings, and many other things that can protect people. I really like my job. I don't know if I would be doing that though if not for your father."

Those words didn't come out as easily. It took a while. After they had some coffee and sat in silence for a few minutes, The Very Tolerant Person asked her guest to continue. And he did. First, still trembling about how sorry he was about what had happened thirty plus years ago, then she directed him to more of the current moment. And he shared his story.

"I got married, I have two kids, all of them are here with me. The boys think it's a vacation, but my wife knows the main reason why we are here. I try to be a good father, and I don't take a moment with them for granted. Every minute I have with them is for one reason only, *your father*."

His tears started coming up again. He held them inside for three decades, being strong for himself at first, and then for his family. But now he had no more control over them. His heart was getting the release it needed. The Very Tolerant Person wasn't sure if she supposed to be angry and hateful, or if she should try to understand the man. But she did like to hear that this stranger didn't plan to waste his life. That would be a shame.

"I would never have asked your father to sacrifice his life for me," his tears intensified. "I would give my life back for his at any moment if I could."

The last word was swallowed up in his emotion and disappeared deep into his lungs.

The hero's daughter started to feel for him. She could tell that this stranger carried this emotional weight for way too long.

"It wasn't...."

She couldn't say the words that came to her mind. Of course, it was *his* fault! If not his, then *who is* to blame?

She didn't want to accept the randomness of the incident. It was *someone's* fault, and that person was in front of her right now, crying about his pain and drinking her coffee!

She felt anger rising in her chest and getting ready to spill over. Shu turned her face away from the man, trying to collect herself. Maybe, to buy a little time, so her mind could recoup its sanity. She looked at the magnificent gigantic oak that reminded her again, as it was accustomed to, of her father. Then, she moved her eyes to the sky. She took a breath, and turned back to the guest:

"Things do happen. Out of our control," she mused out loud.

He tried to control his sentiments. He made a stout effort to pull himself together.

"I wish it was in my control. I wanted to tell you that I spent thirty years trying to be a better man, for your father more than anyone, but I failed. I can never be enough to replace the good that he could do if he stayed alive. If he didn't try to save me."

"That was my dad," she recalled what kind of man he always was. Before he became the Person with a Lot Left to Give he was the Person with Honorable Principles.

Her dad was too young to be in World War Two, but he volunteered for the Korean War and spent the whole time in the Marine Corps. He retired soon after the war was finished, with a couple of medals. He volunteered again for the Vietnam war, although this time, he got a bullet in his lower back early on in 1965 and had to return home early. After two surgeries, he recovered fully, received the Purple Heart among other military awards, and retired again. He went on to flight school, and eventually became an American Airlines commercial pilot. He was flying for them for almost a full ten years till the day he was at the mountain enjoying a gorgeous sunny winter day of skiing.

She remembered that he was always ready to help anyone, and that he went the extra mile for so many people. He had military friends who were grateful to him for his approach, his comrades at the Military Order of the Purple Heart, and his colleagues at

American Airlines. During his pilot days, he was loved by everyone for his honesty, treatment of others, and willingness to give a hand.

The best story she could recall from those days happened about a year and a half before the tragic event in the mountains. One of his coworkers at the airline, a flight attendant, was diagnosed with cancer. That flight attendant had a wife and a two-year old son, and while the health insurance provided by the airline was good, and it covered almost all medical expenses, there was a big question on how he would be able to support the family. The Very Tolerant Person's father first started a fundraising campaign that went beyond his coworkers. It spread through every club, group or friend circle he belonged to or associated with, and the effort ended up collecting over twenty thousand dollars for the family. Then, on top of that, he made a few calls and helped the wife find a better job that paid decent wages and was flexible in hours, so she could continue to be at the hospital for her husband's treatments.

He didn't stop there. Then, he hired a babysitter for their son and told her to send the bill directly to him for as long as needed for the flight attendant to recover. He paid that bill for eight months without ever asking anything in return, till the flight attendant had beaten the disease and could get back to work. The family ended up financially in an even better position than before the illness came to their life. The wife had a better job and better income, and the husband received a raise from American Airlines. Since then, they put the official recovery date on the calendar to celebrate, and they invited the Person with

Honorable Principles and his family for the one-year anniversary of that remarkable day for their family. The Very Tolerant person was present at that party as well, and she could recall, even today, how proud she was of her father. That day was the first time she had even heard the story. Her father never brought it up at home, beyond health updates of the cancer survivor. All other details of his involvement she learned that day only.

The Person with Honorable Principles didn't make it to the second anniversary. He was stopped by another remarkable event, the day when he saved the life of another human being, this time, a stranger.

"That's who he was," she repeated with firmer voice. "Always."

She practically was in control of her state of mind right now.

"I wish I knew him," the response of the Person who Always Carried Guilt was genuine and touching. "I wish I could tell him in person what kind of man he was, and what kind of example he is *to me* in life."

The woman nodded. She wished she could say that and so much more to her dad as well. She realized as she left for college, while she always loved her father, she didn't tell him often enough how proud she was of him.

"Did you know that he spent two weeks at the hospital fighting for his life?" a pride of his constant battles sounded in her voice.

"I do. I was *there*."

Those words sent another vivacious shock through her body. She never expected to hear *that*. She never even considered the possibility of the stranger who killed her father to be at the hospital at the last moments of her dad's life. She looked at the Person Who Always Carried Guilt with wide open eyes, silently demanding, with the strength of the look, an explanation.

"I was there. They brought us to the same hospital. I had some injuries, minor…. I spent three days in bed, and then the doctors released me… I asked them to see the person who saved my life. They agreed to it, but only on one condition: that I wouldn't talk to his family members, and *especially you*. They weren't sure how you would take it, and they wanted to avoid the drama.

The hero's daughter was still in shock, listening to this. "So, they would tell me when you would go to grab something to eat or something, and then I would come to the room and spend ten or fifteen minutes there. I wasn't there every day though. I came maybe four or five times, including his last day, and would sit in the hall for three, four hours sometimes to wait for the word from a nurse that I could go see him."

"But…"

"I wish I could've told you back then. But also, it was probably for the best. I hated myself, I hated that I survived! I hated that I could stand while seeing him lay in that bed."

"Oh my god," the Very Tolerant Person was trying to comprehend this new information. Her mind was getting overwhelmed with what she had learned today.

"I am sorry,"

He shut his mouth after that apology. He was running out of things to say. Now the Person Who Always Carried Guilt was feeling like his muscles relaxed for the first time in three decades. He still felt guilty, but there was a glimpse of self-forgiveness at the horizon of his existence.

"Did he ever wake up? Did he say anything?" She asked him in the hope of hearing something.

The Person with Honorable Principles woke up twice with *her* being around. One time he moaned something before moving his eyes in her direction, while wincing from pain. He then made a grimace that looked a bit like a smile to her and lost consciousness again. The other time, he was awake for a couple of minutes, and clearly recognized his daughter. He told her he loved her, and life was good, and he had no regrets.

"Don't be sad, life is good," exactly what he had said to her. "No regrets. No regrets...."

She remembered every word of it. For the last thirty years. Like it was yesterday.

"He woke up once but didn't say anything. I thought...." The Person Who Always Carried Guilt stopped talking. "No, it's silly...."

"Please, tell me!" She begged the stranger.

He looked at her and saw through the expressions on her face that she *had to* know. There was nothing silly about any of it, and he had no right to make that call.

"I thought... he smiled at me," he responded, unsure of himself.

She exhaled the air with so much uncontainable power that the whole garden could hear it. The Very Tolerant Person burst into tears. She covered her face with both of her hands and spent the next fifteen seconds reliving the moment of pain, pride and memories. All at the same time.

"That was my dad."

She repeated those words full of magic and power that meant so much more than the stranger could imagine and smiled through her tears. Then she cried again, but seconds later she started to wipe the tears off her cheeks relentlessly and made another subconscious effort to smile through the pain of her loss. Then she looked at the Person who Always Carried Guilt, paused for a moment, and gave him a warm smile, full of humanity.

He looked at her in astonishment.

"Thank you," she expressed her current state of mind to the man.

"For *what*?"

"For coming here today. For... "trying to find words that would be right to this situation. Her hands started to dance in the air attempting to replace the speech with some expressive circles drawn in space. "For becoming an engineer, for caring about my father for as long as I have and not forgetting about him. For *visiting* him at the hospital."

She continued to fight off her tears and tried her best to be faster wiping them off with the new streams that were surely coming.

His tears were a bit slower than hers, but his heart was always ready to burst. He knew that the daughter of a great man was demonstrating to him *her own greatness* at this moment, and he was grateful to be in the presence of that greatness.

"I don't know if that's too much to ask, because God knows, I don't deserve anything, and I have no right to ask anything."

"Go ahead, please ask," she insisted.

"Would you want… would you mind meeting my family? My wife and my boys…"

She smiled at him still fighting her watershed.

"You know what? I would *love* to meet your family!"

They gave themselves a few more minutes to finish their coffee and sit still on the bench under the magnificent oak, mostly to get their emotions in order. It seemed that together with the oak, there was the Person with A Lot to Give there too, feeling the moment between them, sharing their emotions, telling them that it was ok.

They agreed to meet for lunch at the cafeteria of the inn. The Very Tolerant Person wanted to clean up, fix her makeup, and the Person Who Always Carried Guilt needed a moment or two as well to consciously realize what took place on the garden bench this morning. Both adults just grew their souls quite a bit, and while for different reasons, they were now united by the open and tearful conversation they had shared.

The Very Tolerant Person had a chance to change her clothes to a bit of a fancier look. For some reason, it now became quite important to her that the kids would meet her at her best. There was some connection between her father, lost too early, and those kids. They represented everything that survived in this universe after the moment when he didn't.

The guests came down to the cafeteria all at once. The Person Who Always Carried Guilt was walking carefully, almost afraid to continue down this vulnerable path. It still wasn't easy for him, but on the other hand, he did carry those feelings under his heart for way too long.

When they came up to the table that the Very Tolerant Person was sitting at, he introduced his family to the inn owner. He introduced his wife first, who was maybe not as beautiful as some models on Instagram, but her face was shining with warmth, and her blue eyes were as welcoming as the warm Caribbean Sea in Cancun in the middle of a hot day. When she got introduced, she smiled openly and affectionately, and shook the Very Tolerant Person's hand. Then the man introduced his boys, Arthur, who was eleven years old now, and Thomas, who was eight and a half. Both boys were curious about who they were meeting and why they were doing this right now instead of exploring the countryside they came to see. They wanted to go to the lake, but they were a little hungry, so they would get some food before their adventure started. The boys were energetic, but polite and pleasant.

They sat down and ordered some food while chatting about the many simple things in life, the children's school and their summer break, their plans for this visit, and many other topics. Arthur was excited about fishing and camping and anything else they could do outdoors on this trip. He was dressed accordingly: camouflage pants, a tight t-shirt, and a baseball cap. His younger brother seemed to be less interested in fishing, but he wanted to run around anywhere he got a chance this summer. He wanted to climb trees, maybe find some rare rocks – that would be the best! – or footprints of some cool animals, like a wolf or a fox. He was wearing jeans and sneakers, and a light hoodie on the top of his loose t-shirt. He wanted to be outdoors, but he didn't care if it was at the lake or right outside of this cafeteria window. He had the energy to spare.

The Very Tolerant Person quickly fell in love with both boys and their attending mother. She was getting an understanding of what kind of man their father was too. It took guts to bring his family to meet the woman who he probably was expecting to hate him. He was ready to take any fire she could unleash on him, and he was ready to do it in front of his family. That man cared about principles, and he seemed to care about the second chance life gave him. Not that life gave to him, to be correct, but her own father, with the most selfless act of kindness anyone could demonstrate.

The Very Tolerant Person was watching the kids eat. She could feel her father's energy present. That made her feel happy. For the first time, she wasn't focused on the random cruelness of the passing of her father, but rather, his heroic nature, the day when he was faced with that dramatic decision, and this family, right in front of her now, who benefited from her father's action. Who knows how many people this family impacted in their lifetime? Their parents, their friends, their coworkers, their children's friends, and those two precious boys who would continue to spread the goodness – hopefully – as they grew into mature kind adults. She could only see the positive at this moment, and there was a certain kind of peace that awashed her body.

"Granvill!" she exclaimed, in an even happier voice, when she suddenly saw the old man approaching their table.

She stood up from her chair and made a few steps toward the man to greet him. Granvill was looking for her, and already was moving his body towards the table. When he was close enough, the Very Tolerant Person had a chance to introduce him to the family of not so strangers.

They invited Granvill to join them at the table. He had no idea who those people were, but knowing the Very Tolerant Person, and before that, her spouse, The Person with Unlimited Generosity, he was never surprised to see other people around those two.

He sat down at the table and asked the waiter to bring him some coffee.

"What brought you here? You don't stop by that often," asked the Very Tolerant Person.

"I was looking for you, actually. We are finishing the foundation of the resort in a couple of days, and probably by Monday or Tuesday the latest, I will start working for the Person Who Wants to be the Center of the Universe. I wanted to make sure you knew that."

"Oh yeah, we knew that moment was coming for a while now," she smiled at him.

She really wasn't concerned with the business right now, but Granvill couldn't possibly know that.

"Good. Is anything I can do for you before that?"

She thought for just for a short moment, and replied happily:

"No. We are good. I am still waiting for the tulips to bloom. They already looked nice when they came out of the ground, but I want to see them pretty and full of life."

She smiled again.

Granvill found her state of mind just a bit curious. She was always an optimistic woman, but she had a different aura about her today. He liked what he saw, but he couldn't pinpoint his mind on the reasons for that change. Then he looked at the guests. They seemed normal, there was nothing special about them; the adults were listening to the conversation just in case they needed to pitch in an opinion, and the kids were fascinated with the food which they both were devouring in a rapid pace.

"You have a good inn here," the old man started the sentence while moving towards the inn owner, then he shifted his focus and turned his face towards the guests. "Right, guys?"

They all agreed right away.

"I want it to be ok. For a long time," Granvill continued, turning back to the Very Tolerant Person.

"Thank you, Granvill, you are too kind. But as we talked before about it, everything will be just fine. Everything will work itself out," assured the inn owner to her dear friend.

And she believed in those words even more so now. The Very Tolerant Person even started to think that maybe the way that the Person Who Always Carried Guilt showed up here today was another sign for her. A sign for a change. She wasn't sure what kind of change yet, but the air was aromatized by changes for a while. First, with Granvill and his tulips, and then him working for the resort, and then the resort itself, and the complications it was surely going to create for her business. Changes swirled around, and she could feel them. There was only one thing left to do: interpret them in the right way and decide a course of future action.

The kids were done eating, long after the adults were finished, and the waiter took the dirty plates away. They ordered some ice cream for dessert, and while they had a moment of time waiting for it to arrive, the Person Who Always Carried Guilt decided to do something that he had planned in his head to do.

"Boys, do you know who this person is, besides being the owner of this wonderful hotel where we are staying? "

The children looked at their dad with their full attention. Granvill was also curious. The Very Tolerant Person had no idea what exactly the guest would tell his children, but butterflies rose up somewhere deep in her stomach.

"Boys, when I was fifteen years old, not much older than you, I was skiing in the mountains with my friends and my father, your grandfather Paul."

The kids recalled their grandpa and continued to listen. They were not aware yet that there was a connection here.

"And that day, something bad had happened. I lost control, at full speed, of my ski, then the second one kind of followed. I tried to change direction, but I couldn't. I would have crashed into the trees if one brave man wouldn't have seen me and, in the last second, stepped in front of me, extended his arms and pushed me away into the safe area."

The kids were feeling like it was a thriller story, but the intonation of their dad made them feel that instead, it was a very serious revelation, maybe even quite a scary one.

"That man crashed into the trees after saving me, and he paid for it with his own life."

He looked at the Very Tolerant Person. Her tears were already collecting at the bottom of her eyes, like soldiers in trenches, waiting for the order to go to the attack.

"That brave man saved your dad's life."

The kids were in a wow moment but were not sure how the inn owner was involved.

"And that brave man was the Person Who Had A Lot Left to Give, and he was the Very Tolerant Person's father. So, we came here to show how forever grateful I am to her father, and to her."

The Very Tolerant Person was crying now, but with more happy tears than the previous times of this full of emotions day.

Arthur, maybe understanding the magnitude of the moment, maybe not completely, looked at the Very Tolerant Person and said:

"We wouldn't have our dad if your dad was less brave."

The Very Tolerant Person burst into tears. The parents of the kids gave their children a hand gesture to go give the woman a hug, and they gladly followed the encouragement of the action. The inn owner hugged them with her whole heart melted.

Granvill was touched as well. He was happy to see his friend getting so much needed closure, and he was hoping it would help her move on from that terrible experience and take life's randomness with more acceptance.

He also thought about how many things had changed in the recent months. Not only his personal life, which he lived a certain way for the last seven years, but also the tragedy of the Person Who Had A Lot Left to Give, and its effect on his daughter which had happened four times as long ago.

While still embraced by the Very Tolerant Person, Thomas then whispered just loud enough for people at the table to hear:

"Thank you!"

CHAPTER 14

Granvill left the inn after the lunch with the Very Tolerant Person, the Person Who Always Carried Guilt and his lovely family, in a positive mood. While he already knew that his friend would not be upset about the resort progressing to the next stage, and him being involved in the project – hey, she did encourage him to get involved! – but it was also good to see that she had something else to concentrate on instead of thinking over and over about the same problem in front of her. He knew that she was a bit fearful to face the changes and that she loved the inn business too much to walk away from it, but maybe there was some solution in the long term. Meanwhile, it was good for her to be focused on something more positive. Besides, the shift in mentality that maybe her father's death was something more than a random showing of life's unfair foundation, something more than a pure tragedy. It was, after all, his own choice, no matter how spontaneous, to be the man who he always was, which resulted – by life's' destiny – in giving a chance to this wonderful family who she got a chance to meet today, to build their life together.

Granvill was happy for the Very Tolerant Person. Another person who he was thinking of in this moment was the Person with Bad Luck. He heard that the man continued to paint and really enjoyed it as well as his new hobbies, golf and chess. Granvill decided that this was a perfect day to go and play a game of chess with the man. This idea was planting in his head for a few days, but he didn't have a specific time in his mind to go see the Person with Bad Luck. Today felt like a perfect day for that.

He walked from the inn to the Person with Bad Luck's house. They were located on the same road and were not far from each other at all, so three minutes later, he was at the door of the house he needed. He wasn't sure if the resident was home, but he was hoping for the stars to be aligned. Some days, things just fell in the right places, and he felt that energy right now.

The Person with Bad Luck opened the door, and as soon as he saw Granvill, he got a big grin on his face.

"Granvill!" he exclaimed. "I am so happy to see you!"

"I heard you play chess now, and I wanted to see if you needed a partner for that today."

Granvill was happy that the Person with Bad Luck was home and seemed available.

"Of course!"

The two men walked inside the house and proceeded into the depths of the home, coming to an end at the living room.

The room was located in the next turn after the kitchen, where they had their last conversation. Granvill was wondering if the fact they were meeting in the living room now was a compliment to him personally and a symbol of a closer connection, or the sign of the transformation that the house owner went through in the last weeks, being more open to having guests in his house. Either way, it was a pleasant change, and Granvill accepted it with a certain level of excitement.

"I will bring the chess set," the Person with Bad Luck made the comment and disappeared back into the depths of the house.

Granvill thought for a moment that maybe he got excited about being invited to the living room a bit too soon. It was possible the real reason of the invitation was the fact it was a more convenient place to play chess. But nevertheless, there was something different about the Person with Bad Luck today.

The house owner came back with the chess set, and he carefully put it on the coffee table in front of his guest. Granvill was sitting on the sofa, so the Person with Bad Luck moved an armchair closer to the coffee table, in comfortable reach for him to sit on and still be able to move his pieces on the chess board.

"What's new?" asked the host.

"Quite a bit of news, actually," replied Granvill while moving his white pawn two squares forward to start the game.

He then proceeded to tell him about his new involvement with the resort, as well as his personal connection with the Person Who Smiled at Everybody. The Person with Bad Luck listened it with a friendly courtesy.

"I am glad you are making changes. I think that was the one thing that was holding me back. I spent too long thinking about how unlucky I was to lose my wife, and the fact that I never had a chance to have kids and thinking that the business I had I never truly wanted."

Granvill nodded in understanding.

"In reality, I was blessed to never be in need of money because of my company," continued the host. "I was blessed to spend great years with my wife and get a glimpse of understanding of what true happiness was. And her death forced me to make changes again, which I resisted. I lived in denial and got stuck in the past, but I realized that to keep living was in no way disrespectful to our memory and life together, it's just what it is. Moving on and living in the present the best way I know how. But I needed to make changes for that. And the main thing for me was to be able to begin to enjoy the things I like to do, paint, play golf and chess, and among a few other things, like having guests in my house."

He moved his hand towards Granvill with the last remark to show that he was one of those welcomed guests.

"I was so sure I liked my lifestyle, and I didn't feel like I needed any changes," Granvill tried to explore his personal situation through the prism of what he just heard from his chess partner.

"Then changes found you at the right time of your life. But at least you paid attention to the sound of them, you heard them, you didn't try to deny and reject them. I think that's important."

Granvill nodded in agreement.

"By the way, talking about changes. Did you hear the news about the Person Without Care for Others?"

Granvill wasn't sure what kind of changes his friend was talking about, as he didn't seem to hear anything new about the Person Without Care for Others, so he responded that he wasn't aware of any news.

"His mother died in the Fish Haven retirement facility, poor woman."

"That's sad."

"Not so much for him. Funeral is tomorrow. And I heard he didn't spend a dollar on arranging it. He left it to the city to take care of everything."

"That's even more sad," observed Granvill.

"Apparently, she left him quite a bit of money, but it will take a bit of time for him to get his hands on it. And he didn't have or didn't want to spend money out of his own pocket. She had a will and certain things in it that he wasn't aware of. She had old stock certificates and some bonds she held for thirty years or more."

"That's interesting," all Granvill could really say hearing that kind of news.

"They are worth over two hundred thousand now, and that bastard for a son got all of that!"

"She left everything to him?" Granvill was a bit surprised, considering the kind of treatment she received from her own son and yet she still decided to leave him everything she had built up in her life, instead of giving it to some charity or something of that sort.

"Yeah. He already quit his job in my company, and apparently wants to start his own," replied the Person with Bad Luck.

Granvill was again a bit surprised by his friend's mentality. The old version of the Person with Bad Luck would surely mention how it was his misfortune that his employee was now preparing to start a company that's going to compete with his business, but nothing of that kind left the mouth of the house owner.

"You are not concerned?" Granvill wanted to make sure this change he was seeing was real.

"No. Not at all. Let me show you something."

With those words, he stood up and beckoned to his guest to follow him. They walked out of the living room, then out of the house to the patio located right in front of the house garden. There, spread over the dirt in the garden, were hundreds of tulips with long green stems, trying to reach the sky.

"You started this process," said the Person with Bad Luck. "Remember we talked about fate back then?"

Granvill nodded again.

"The way I see it now is that you had a plan to plant the bulbs for those tulips, and we did the work. And there are certain consequences to our actions, which is *this*."

He spread his arms showing off his new addition to his garden, ready to bloom soon.

"If fate would have it, then those tulips wouldn't break the ground and would die long before we could enjoy the results. But after that it is our choice to give in to that fact and never plant tulips here again, or try again, with no guarantees of a positive result."

He had a certain confidence about him.

"I don't know what fate holds for us, I don't know what's kind of destiny is written for the rest of my life personally, let's say, but I do know that I want to try to make it the best ending I can possibly write."

Granvill was proud to see this man change after all that time. And he finally realized what he had seen in him as soon as he saw him opening the front door. That man wasn't the Person with Bad Luck anymore. That was a *new kind of man*. That was The Person Who Painted while Moving Forward in Life.

"I still believe in fate, and a certain degree of preprogrammed factor to our lives, but I also believe in *the Unknown*, the things that we can't know about our future. And the fact that we don't know how our lives will turn out to be if we make one decision or another, *is* the best thing in life. Not knowing what our fate is somehow became the beauty of this world for me. There are many wonderful things in this universe, and I try to capture some of that now through my paintings. And I am ok not knowing where it leads me."

He looked at Granvill with a certain clarity that only The Person Who Painted while Moving Forward in Life could have, and it was not *ever* given or revealed to the Person with Bad Luck.

"I am very happy for you!" said Granvill with a sincere heart. "And it reminds me to ask you something."

"Shoot," responded the host.

"As I mentioned, I am now running certain aspects of the new resort we are building. And I would be honored if we could put some of your paintings on the walls of the resort, the lobby especially, and some public places for everyone to see."

The Person Who Painted while Moving Forward in Life looked at Granvill with childlike excitement.

"We can't pay too much, pretty much at slightly above the rate of reproductions rather than original art, but we would get like ten paintings or so…"

The Person Who Painted while Moving Forward in Life didn't even let him finish the sentence and quickly hugged the news bearer.

"That's just fantastic!! I would be so happy to sell you my paintings for any price you offer me!"

He let him go, looked happily in his eyes and then extended his hand for a handshake. Receiving the hand extension back, the host shook it with all the gratitude he could possibly collect in his body in one blink of a moment.

"Thank you for everything, Granvill! If you ever need anything, anything at all. Please, contact me. Don't hesitate."

Granvill was happy with the way the whole conversation went.

"But, we have unfinished business. Let's go finish our game, I must know if there is a chance I can turn my bad luck around in chess as well," smiled The Person Who Painted While Moving Forward in Life.

Granvill ended up winning the game, but not with a big advantage. It was a close match till the end, but Granvill's experience of playing the game made the difference. After the game, he and the Person Who Painted While Moving Forward in Life agreed on how they were planning to deliver the paintings to the resort, and Granvill wished him all the best.

"I also have some unfinished business to take care of," said the guest and shook the host's hand. "I am going to take care of it first thing tomorrow morning."

"Whatever it is, good luck to you as well," the host didn't believe in the bad luck as his life compass anymore, but he knew it still existed in this world and it tried to sneak up on the people not caring for it or suspecting anything. He only wished good luck to be brought to those people.

Granvill woke up the next morning by his alarm clock. He had a quick breakfast of two boiled eggs and a cup of coffee, and he quickly left the house. He walked to the bus stop behind the church and waited for a bus to arrive. Not even ten minutes later, he was on the bus to the city. Less than three hours later, the old man was in the city and he took one of the many taxi cabs waiting outside of the bus stop. Like the last time he was here, he arrived at the Sierra soup kitchen just in time for the 9am breakfast serving.

Adam and Casey were both there too, as were about ten to twelve volunteers, most younger people, really young people. A couple of girls who seemed to be in their late teenage years were arguing with each other about if using plastic gloves was necessary. One of them was worried about blisters or getting something unwanted on her hands, while another one said the pictures on Instagram wouldn't come out the right way if they were to wear those blue ugly gloves, and that was more important than a possibility of a blister. *At least they were here*, thought Adam.

Why are they here then, thought Casey? Granvill greeted everyone and moved his body across the warehouse to the changing room at the end corner of it. He changed into one of the old t-shirts he brought with him and put on an apron that the soup kitchen provided for volunteers.

Serving breakfast to people in need had always humbled Granvill. He had never thought he was better than the people who he was serving food to, although sometimes those thoughts crawled into his mind. But every time it would happen, he made a conscious effort to disregard them as soon as possible, because at the end of the day, he knew that each person had their own story. And yes, different people showed a different level of resistance to life obstacles. Different people demonstrated different levels of hard work to overcome those obstacles, and showed off different levels of positivity, ability to fight off depression, as well as adapting skills. But each human soul did what they could in their power. They weren't hurting others, they didn't decide to become criminals, and steal or assault citizens, and some of them needed extra help to get their life back on track. And giving them a meal in the morning gave them more than a combination of protein and carbs, it gave them hope in humanity, it gave them a belief that they could survive another day, it gave them an assurance that they were not alone in this world.

Some of the people who came to the breakfast today were the same people who Granvill saw on Christmas Eve, but most of them were new. Two of them were totally new to the streets. Granvill could recognize them from the rest by both fresher clothes, and more panicky, fidgety and unsure behavior. When an opportunity presented to him to give them their plates with eggs, sausage and hash browns, Granvill told them both that everything would be alright.

When the breakfast was over, Granvill stayed to help to clean the space up. At the same time, he also had started a conversation with Adam.

"I didn't see the Russian guy today," said Granvill.

"Dima? The boy who lost both of his parents in the car accident?" clarified the soup kitchen organizer.

Granvill nodded.

"I haven't seen him in three or four days. I hope he is ok," continued Adam. "Those kids sometimes get in trouble, by trying to steal food or a blanket, or they get accused of it even if they didn't do it."

"Was he around before that? Any progress in his situation?" asked Granvill.

"He was around. He would come here a couple of times a week. He still didn't go back to college though, which he should've done. But it's not easy. I think sometimes he would mow lawns for people in the neighborhood and get paid a little bit. He would buy food on that money and we wouldn't see him for a couple of days. So, nothing to worry about yet, but I do hope he is ok. We should see him tomorrow maybe. Or even later today, dinner time."

Granvill was thinking about Dima for a while. His story stuck with him since Christmas Eve. The kid's life had turned upside down in literally seconds of time. He was an eighteen-year old young man full of promise, a college education, a family, and a good stable life on the horizon, and the next minute he loses his parents. Everything else that followed later was written in the stars at that tragic moment: the loss of his home, dropping out of college, and being forced to figure out how to get food for his own survival while mourning his family. No future, no plans, no dreams to come true for him anymore.

"I can tell you a good story if you wish," continued Adam. "I think you could use one."

"Definitely! It's always nice to hear a good story," easily agreed Granvill.

"We had another boy here, Caesar. We called him many different names, all with love. The Little Caesar, Pizza, Pepperoni, and any other name that we could connect to the franchise of the pizza maker," he smiled. "He started to help us out with that! When he had good, and not ordinary days, he would say that he was not a plain pepperoni today, but a pizza with mushrooms, olives, green peppers and extra cheese. That guy was funny."

Adam's wide smile was reflecting his love and care for the boy.

"People at the local Little Caesar's actually would feed him, would give him a whole pizza when they could. He loved sitting in front of the store too and offered to wash people's cars. He would always carry a couple of rags and wash spray, so he could make a few extra bucks. So, one time, he was sitting there, and he approached one of the Caesar's customers to wash his car, and he said "Yes, sure". Then that guy gave him a twenty-dollar tip.

So, naturally, our Caesar wanted to be there even more often, in case that man would come back."

Granvill nodded, agreeing with the natural desire to make more money washing someone's car for twenty bucks.

"So, a week later, that man comes back, but this time he says "No, I don't need my car washed", but gives Caesar a five-dollar bill anyway. So, Caesar is happy. He even bought a pizza and brought it here to share with a few of his friends. And then naturally he goes back there. But for two weeks the man did not come back. Caesar started to think, maybe the man wasn't even local, or maybe he moved away. Or maybe he wasn't that big a fan of pizza. But in the third week, the man shows up again. And this time he gives nothing to Caesar, but he sits down with him on the ground and starts asking him questions. About Caesar' life. And then at the end of that conversation, he offers him a job!"

Granvill was delighted to hear where this story was heading so far.

"What happened then?"

"This man was apparently a rich successful guy, who had built a pretty good business with real estate development, investments and so on. So, Caesar first started as his chauffeur, then his protégé, and now he is taking a real estate exam to sell real estate to get experience and knowledge to help his boss in his business."

"That's amazing!" Granvill was happy to hear the story especially considering what he was planning to do.

"Truly is," agreed Adam.

"That's one of the reasons you do what you do, isn't?" Granvill asked the man beside him.

"Definitely! We just buy time for people who need it and encourage them to change their life when they do get that chance. But mostly, we buy them time. Any day can be their last, and we try to make sure *it's not*. Because any day their life can change for the better as well."

Granvill thought it was well said. At the end of the day, all we have is today's day, and tomorrow is not guaranteed to anyone. While less fortunate people can see the dangers clearly in front of them, the well-off people conceal their lives behind their job security, money, status and power. Those mundane things decrease the risks of something bad happening to them, no doubt, but they do not promise tomorrow to be here for them, and they do not protect them from the possibility of something bad happening in their lives.

"Those stories are few and far between though," said Adam. "What happened to Caesar doesn't happen to anyone. *Ever*. He got very lucky."

Granvill agreed out loud that those stories should happen more often. They finished the conversation and separated for a bit to their own activities. Adam needed to make a few calls to donors, which he was doing almost every day between breakfast and dinner at the kitchen, and Granvill wanted to help start preparing for dinner. The dinner time came upon both men quicker than they thought. Adam made a few dozen calls, talked to one donor for a good twenty minutes only to get a promise that he would receive a donation sometime in the future, and only one person donated something. It was fifteen dollars more than they had in the morning. There were some donations that were coming online nowadays, and a couple of people who would give money on the monthly basis. So, it was always *almost enough*, because in the other sense, it was *never enough*, but between a few volunteers buying some portions of food on their own credit cards, and their fundraised budget, they were ok. But those fifteen dollars a day was the reason why they were. Adam knew all too well how each dollar had counted, and that one donation maybe made the difference between them having enough food one of those mornings, or cutting down the nutrition, or reaching in his own pocket.

Granvill was busy helping to do any physical job that could be done in the warehouse of the kitchen. He fixed the door to the locker room which creaked every time it was being opened. He painted the locker rooms in a bright red color; he found old unused paint sitting in the warehouse, which one of the employees brought a few weeks back as a leftover from painting the shed in their apartment building. No one got to it till Granvill did. And he had time to hang a wooden suggestion box on the wall near the tables where they served food. This was Adam's idea, and the old man decided to execute it while he was here. This way people who would come here had a chance to ask for certain type of food or suggest something else they felt needed to be improved at the kitchen, without asking for the impossible, shrimp with lobster for example, which there was no practical chance for the kitchen to serve.

When Granvill was finishing hammering in the last nail to permanently incorporate the box into the wall, he was approached by a boy with an accent.

"I heard you asked about me."

When Granvill turned around, he saw Dima standing right in front of him. He was dressed in wrinkled but not too dirty clothes, a dress shirt that used to be a light blue color, which was now faded and looked even more light than any kind of blue, and brown khaki jeans, which were ripped on one side near the pocket, but otherwise still looked good. His sneakers were in the worst shape out of his outfit. They used to be white, but now they resembled mudslide boots. Dima cleaned them up once every couple of days, but some shades of grey and black were not possible to remove in the street conditions. Dima had no real expression on his face, not even slight curiosity on why Granvill was asking for him. But Dima felt he needed to come up and politely ask how he could help.

Granvill offered the boy to take a seat somewhere. It was about twenty minutes until the dinner, and they had time to leave the premises for a bit. They walked out of the grey building and found a spot on the top of a pile of forgotten construction bricks lying about fifty yards from the soup kitchen.

"I don't want to assume anything. Maybe that's not what you want or need. But I heard what had happened to you. My condolences," started the old man.

Dima quietly thanked the man for expressing his sympathies and then continued listening, unsure of where the conversation was going.

"I know many people have a tough time here. And I also know that sometimes they need just one chance to turn their fortunes around. I would like to extend you an offer for that chance. I *hope* you take it."

Dima was still listening, but now with a real sense of curiosity.

"I have a house in the village two and a half hours from here. The house is not huge, but it has three bedrooms, a kitchen, and a dining room. There is a patio with a view to the mountains. It's in a very nice safe area. You can stay there for as long as you need with only one condition."

"What is it?" Dima started to feel dizzy anticipating big changes in his life.

"You would enroll into an online college program right away and be on track of graduating. Later we will figure out how to get you either to the dorms or maybe live somewhere near the school. But you can start online. I will get you a computer, internet and will pay for the college if you will not get sufficient government aid."

Dima couldn't believe what he was hearing.

"Seriously?" his accent was not too strong, but still noticeable for sure.

"Absolutely. I hope you will accept it. I really want to help."

"Wow!"

Dima went into a silent mode trying to comprehend what was happening. Granvill waited for the moment of shock inside of the young man to pass and then continued his thought:

"If you need to see the house first, before you make your decision, we can make a trip any day, maybe tomorrow."

Dima got his thoughts together. It really struck him on the emotional side. He suddenly understood that he may have a real home again. He could have a place to put his things down. He could go to bed in the same spot. He could have a place to go to where he belonged. He thought about how he could still go to college and have a normal future. He had so many worries about his future lately, and now this was a load off his shoulders.

"I accept," he responded emotionally, barely holding his tears back. "I don't need to see the house."

Granvill was happy to hear that. Since Christmas Eve, there were some thoughts brewing in his head, and somehow it evolved into this idea. He had no real conscious control over the idea, he was merely being the man he was, and his mind made the rest happen. A couple of days ago, while eating breakfast in his house, he suddenly knew that he could share more than his tulips with people, he could also share his house. And Dima was the best logical choice, considering how much impact the story of the eighteen-year-old Russian kid and his poor parents made on Granvill the last time he had visited the city.

"Let's go get some food," said Granvill while standing up from the pile of bricks. "And then we go home."

Dima followed his example, and they both started moving back towards the Sierra soup kitchen. Dima stopped for a moment, then Granvill did the same seeing young man's confusion, till a moment later the boy launched himself on the old man and embraced him with a hug of a lifetime.

CHAPTER 15

Granvill woke up on this beautiful April morning, and went to the kitchen to make himself a morning coffee. He already learned two things about Dima. One, the boy didn't like coffee, and preferred tea. And the second, the boy could sleep! So far in the few days that he had been in the house, he never got up before ten thirty in the morning. Granvill wasn't sure if that was normal for Dima, or he was recovering from the countless sleepless nights that he had spent on the streets. Either way, Granvill wasn't going to interrupt that.

So, Dima was still sleeping, and Granvill was left to himself. He never minded being alone. There were worse things than that in life. It was a lot worse when people you loved and cared for made you *feel like you were alone*. Maybe that was one of the reasons why he never felt comfortable letting anyone get close after Paige had left him. He saw being alone as the control he needed over his own happiness. He was happier when he was married, but it wasn't meant to last. Both he and his ex-wife made enough mistakes to not make it work.

Granvill stepped on the patio and inhaled the fresh mountain air of the village. This air and coffee were all he needed right now. Helping Dima was also a good step. He was hoping for a positive result of this action. He was hoping it would change the boy's life. Dima already registered for the online university and was thankful to Granvill for giving him a roof over his head. *That was a good start*, thought Granvill.

The old man looked over the field beyond his patio, and a smile took over his emotions. A beautiful multi-colored sixty-yard-deep and thirty-yard-wide field of tulips was looking right at him. They all were at the early stages of blooming, and they already made the old man's day. He thought about the moment where it all started. He then remembered every place he planted them. He was hoping the kids and the teachers at the school were enjoying those same tulips right now. And the other residents of the village.

He smiled again and sipped his coffee. This was a beautiful mix of the sun and clouds kind of day. Not too hot, but warm enough, with a light breeze traveling through the trees of the valley. He had a plan for today; it was going to be a busy day. First, he wanted to visit the Person Who Smiled at Everybody. It had been over a week since he'd last seen her, and this seemed like a good day to go.

It took him just over thirty minutes to get ready. Taking a shower and getting dressed were two simple and quick activities for men, and Granvill was a classic example of it. Then he wrote a note for Dima and left it on the kitchen table, the one place he knew the boy would easily find it. Granvill got a cell phone a couple days ago, and people could reach him now, including his new co-occupant, but he still felt more comfortable leaving a note containing information on when he was planning to come back home.

Granvill still didn't like cell phones but working for the Person Who Wants to be the Center of the Universe required him to have one. He wasn't going to give the number to anyone outside of work-related contacts and a couple of people in his personal life. He was also hoping to not destroy the balance in his life by using it too much. He could remember how much attention a cell phone required from him in his previous city life. Looking back, not much of that attention was worth it.

Reaching the white house, like any other place in the village, didn't take Granvill too long. Since it was Sunday morning, he was hoping that the Person Who Smiled at Everybody was at home. She usually would sleep in on Sundays, and later decide if she should go to the coffee shop to help or take a day off. Right now, at nine fifteen in the morning, she should be awake, but not ready to go to work just yet. If she was sticking to her Sundays routine that is.

Granvill ended up being right about everything, almost to the minute. The Person Who Smiled at Everybody woke up at eight forty-two today and had enough time to make her coffee but didn't change out of her pajamas yet. She also hadn't pushed through her Sunday relaxed state of idleness to take a shower and was watching tv in her living room. Her son was away with his dad, and she missed him, especially on days like this, when she had a bit more free time, but she couldn't do anything about that. On the other hand, she was taking advantage of the peace and quiet in the house. It was when such simple things in life, like walking in her sleeping clothing for an hour or two after getting up, seemed like some sort of simplified, yet not less satisfying, heaven.

Seeing Granvill in the morning was another feeling she had missed a lot. Granvill had mentioned to her that he would be busy for a few days. He had some things to take care of with his new position at the resort, and he also shared with her his plan to bring Dima to the old man's house. But outside of that, Granvill still seemed a bit distant, and the worst scenario sometimes would overtake her thinking process, or, at the least, distract her from the everyday joys of life.

So, she was happy that he came to see her today. He knew that Sundays were good days for her, and maybe they would get a chance to spend it together. She didn't think about taking their relationship to the next level yet. Of course, it has crossed her mind. She liked him a lot, and who he was as a man, and she liked how she felt around him, free, without judgment, and she loved the way he treated her, with gentle care. He always seemed to put her interests in mind first, and he always had adapted to her situation, either her work, or her son, or her slow ability to let go of her past and be able to be in the moment with Granvill.

But there were also signs of warning for her, signs that held her back from wanting this man around her for a long time. For one, he didn't have a cell phone, and while he was supposed to get one through his work, it would be probably a temporary solution only, considering Granvill's attitude towards them. In this day and age, without a cell phone, it was tough to build a closer relationship. It hasn't been easy so far to update the man when her plans were changing. And her plans changed often. Plans when her ex was going to pick their son up, or when they planned a trip and she was going to be at home for a few nights by herself. Because of that simple reason alone, she felt that he wasn't always there for her, that despite his adjustments to her, it was a bit of a one-sided relationship, and she wanted more. She also felt that Granvill's need for freedom would be tough to change.

The Person Who Smiles at Everybody invited Granvill in, poured him a cup of coffee out of the still hot pot of the coffee-maker, and apologized for being in pajamas instead of something more presentable. He didn't mind that fact at all though. They decided that a good place to enjoy their coffee this morning was on her patio, with the view of the gorgeous pink tulips that she was anxious to show him. And the tulips were definitely and undeniably gorgeous!

They were not as big as Granvill's own sea of flowers, but the all pink garden, the house owner's favorite color, was blooming with hope for the future. It reminded the Person Who Smiled at Everybody that everything in this life would come together somehow, and the steps she was making now would give her the life she wanted. It gushed with the excitement of today and gave her a reeling feeling of encouragement for tomorrow. Granvill smiled again, the second time in the last couple of hours that he couldn't resist the power of those flower fields. He was also happy that those tulips didn't die and made it through to expose their beauty to the world of the village.

They got comfortable on the patio and started talking about the events of the last few days. Granvill shared a few things and especially the Russian boy's story. He told her how Dima ended up being homeless, and how he had been becoming acclimated to living in the village. The Person Who Smiled at Everybody thought for a moment *what a great man Granvill was after all, and he was the kind of man that she was always looking for.*

"I wanted to share something else," said Granvill after finishing his story about Dima.

"What is it?"

"It's not as pleasant as the boy's story though. And I wish I had better timing with this. But there is probably no good timing for it."

Maybe he is breaking up with me, thought the Person Who Smiled at Everyone. Her insecurities spoke louder than anything else in her right now.

"It's ok. You can tell me."

"I feel that we need to stop our relationship. You are a great woman, but I am not the right man for you."

The spoken words reached into the woman's rib cage and squeezed her heart with a tight grip. She winced from the physical pain of her blood pumping organ but continued to look at Granvill straight into his eyes.

"I am sorry if I misled you at any point," apologized the man.

Her brain raced through time, collecting all information through the last four months. He really didn't, although she still felt like he kind of did.

"If I can still be your friend, and do anything for you, I would be happy." finished the old man.

She was realizing consciously what was happening to her at this moment. This is not the Sunday she was hoping for. Was she falling in love with him? Or was this just her ego getting bruised a little bit?

"You chose the "it's not you, it's me" routine..."

She smiled. That's why she was The Person Who Smiled at Everybody after all.

"I don't want to do *any* routine. But it's also not honest for me to continue this relationship romantically. And not because I don't like you. But I don't know how to change my life enough to make it work into a real and lasting relationship. And I don't feel that a casual dating situation is a good thing for either one of us."

"I understand," she replied in a quieter voice than usual.

She looked at the tulips. Their strong power was now sending healing qualities to her heart, and she was glad they were there. *They will not be there forever though, as her relationship with Granvill,* it crossed her mind at the same instant. The flowers were going to die. But not today. She took a deep breath and looked back at Granvill.

"What are you going to do now? If I can ask."

"Of course, you can ask," responded calmly the old man. "I have a trip coming up. I am going to the city again in the next a couple of days, and then I will come back, and I think a few more things will change again. The next few months, I hope we will finish working on the resort. And then I will decide what to do professionally after that, if anything."

He continued to speak about his plans, and while it was hurting the woman to hear all the things that she *would not* be a part of, she continued to listen with politeness and courtesy.

"I want to put Dima through college, and I want him to go to real school where he can interact with other students, so he can make new friends, maybe even meet a girl. So, I need to make some moves to make that happen, get him to one of the schools, hopefully by August, so he can start the next school year on campus. And then.... We will see. Life has surprised me many times before. Every time I think I am in control and I know what I want, life has thrown something else in my direction. I am sure I am not alone in that. That's how it probably works for all of us."

"You are probably right," she responded with more calm in her voice.

Although deep down she suddenly felt that maybe she was *falling in love* with that man. *What unfortunate timing for that,* she caught herself thinking. There were so many things she loved about him, and so many things that she would miss. But she needed more time to figure out if that was the true state of her heart.

"You are a good man," she said out loud. "And it's a nice thing you are doing for that boy."

"Thank you."

"I hope you find what you are looking for. And if you decide to change your mind, you *may* ask me out again."

She looked into his eyes, maybe for the last time in the role of more than a friend.

"I may or may not say yes to that though," she smiled, and Granvill followed giving a smile back.

"You are a good woman too. There will be a lucky man somewhere to be a part of your life. I hope you will be happy. I hope you will continue to take chances, open new doors and explore your life," said the man, sincerely wishing all of that to the only woman in the village he cared for in a romantic way.

"Thank you."

She leaned in with her body towards him, and kissed him on the lips, for the last time. For now. *Till life possibly throws more surprises their way.*

Walking out of the door, Granvill still didn't feel good about what just took place. He felt he let down certain expectations. He realized it bothered his core. He wanted to be perfect for the a few people in his life who he truly cared for. Living in the village in such a way that he could keep the distance from everyone meant two things after all: his freedom to do what he wanted and no failed expectations of his own self-perceived perfection. Since he decided to plant tulips for people, he let that distance be narrowed, and the Person Who Smiled at Everybody was one person who closed the gap. The developments after that quickly reminded him that *he wasn't perfect after all.*

But there was another direction in life to explore for him. He took a chance on the eighteen-year old young man, and now he hoped to be perfect for him. Deep down, Granvill realized that the relationship with the boy would bring him even more sadness of failed expectations on himself, for one reason or another, but he was ready to do that. He was ready to be the disappointment in Dima's eyes, which eventually things could come down to, in exchange of the boy's safety and *his* chance for a new life.

From the white house of the Person Who Smiled at Everybody, Granvill walked towards the local inn where he hoped to catch up with the Very Tolerant Person. He felt it might be a good thing for him to be around a friend right now, and he also wanted to give her his cell phone number, which she may use anytime in the future if she needed Granvill's help. The Very Tolerant Person greeted him from behind the front desk with a smile.

"How are you, Mister Granvill?"

"I am doing great. I hope the same for you," responded the old man.

"I am doing fantastic, and I have news for you."

"Really? What kind of news?"

The Very Tolerant Person seemed eager to tell.

"You know, meeting the Person Who Always Carried Guilt and his family opened my eyes on many things. I loved my father, he was everything to me, yet after high school I wanted to run away from this inn, his creation…. I wanted to go to college and live in the big city. But then his death gave life to a stranger and let him be happy with his family and raise his kids, and it also returned me here and let *me* be happy with my husband. I spent a great twenty-seven years of my life in this inn with the love of my life. And now that chapter is over too. It's been over for a while…. I have grown as a person and became who I am today in those years."

She interrupted her own thoughts for a second.

"Would you like some tea? I think we need some tea."

Granvill smiled warmly and nodded his head. The inn owner hurried to make two cups of tea for them. When she came back, she gave one cup to her friend.

"We have talked about changes before, and I am so happy that you are changing your life," she continued to share. "And it is time for changes in my life too. The Person Who Always Carried Guilt gave me a certain closure, which I needed more than I could have imagined. And now I am ready to do the two things I have always wanted: to do something for myself and travel a bit around the world. I know you have done that for a couple of years before you came to the village. And I also want to continue bringing people joy, but I can do it in better ways now than through this hotel."

Granvill was very curious about what the news was, he knew the big boom was still coming.

"So, I have decided to close the inn on the last day of June, and then travel."

Granvill raised his eyebrows in a surprise.

"I didn't see that coming. Are you sure?"

The Very Tolerant Person was looking happy and confident.

"I am very sure," her tone confirmed her inner confidence.

"Good then. I am happy for you. I know how much you always wanted to travel, and I think the world is ready for you to be out there. You will love it!"

"Thank you, Granvill."

"Is there anything I can do?" asked the man.

"I hope you will be around in the summertime. If you could help me close the business, maybe sell some furniture, maybe come up with an idea on how I can use the building after I leave. I don't want to sell the building."

"You could do an Airbnb with it or something," proposed Granvill. "You would need to upgrade the lock system, and put separate electronic locks on rooms, but it could work very well without the stuff or you even being here. All you would need to do is to find someone to watch over it and clean the room after guests leave, you could pay part-time to a couple of people and still be profitable.

"That's a great idea, Granvill!" the Very Tolerant Person elevated her level of excitement even more.

"We can still think about details till July, I am sure we will come up with everything we need. I would be happy to help," smiled Granvill. "I am really pleased that you found a way to continue your life in a direction that you can be happy about."

"Me too. Believe me," assured the inn owner. There was another chapter coming to her life, and it could be just as good as some of the previous ones.

The Person Who Always Carried Guilt was spending his last day in the village before heading back home. His boys were thrilled to spend that day in the woods after going to the lake of Fish Haven for the last three consecutive days. They did everything they wanted in this countryside and everything they never had a chance to do in their hometown. They went on a boat around the lake, they rented out a small two-person floating unit with pedals, which they didn't even know the name of, they tried zip lining across the lake, and of course a lot of swimming and beach soccer. They also did a bit of fishing from the offshore on the east side of the lake, which made Arthur, the oldest boy extremely happy. The boys didn't miss out on the chance to beg their parents for a consistent flow of ice cream, fruit popsicles, fruits and any other kind of snack they could find at the nearby kiosks.

Going to the woods today was their father's idea. He wanted a bit more of a peaceful goodbye to the village, and it was the easiest sell to the kids. Arthur, besides fishing, also liked camping, and even before his dad could finish the invitation sentence about the woods, he was already asking if they would stay overnight. The Person Who Always Carried Guilt wasn't prepared to camp, as they didn't have tents or any camping equipment with them, but he agreed to stay up as late into the night as they could by the campfire site that they would be able to start on their own. Thomas easily accepted the idea too. He was looking forward to climbing some trees and maybe seeing some wild animals. Staying up past his usual bedtime also sounded like a great idea to the eight-year old boy. Their mother was happy to join the kids and her husband anywhere, and while the forest wasn't, at least in her mind, as comfortable as getting a tan by the lake, she was content with the idea of sitting by the fire and sharing some stories with the people she loved. The family bought some marshmallows in the village before they left and were ready to go.

They went on a hike into the western part of the woods, going unknowingly towards and eventually past Granvill's house on the outskirts of the village. They only took two backpacks with only necessary stuff: water, some food, a couple of blankets, two light summer raincoats, a flashlight, matches, paper to help start the fire, and a first aid kit, just in case. The kids had nothing to carry, so they were free to have fun on the way. They chased after each other, told each other jokes and did other brotherly things that were quite normal to any parent of two boys.

The day in the woods did have a calming effect on the Person Who Always Carried Guilt. It wasn't an easy week for him. While the Very Tolerant Person accepted his story, and wished him well, he still felt ashamed to be happy. He did his best for the last three days to put on a happy face for his children and his spouse, but deep down, the heavy weight on his heart, that was sitting on him for the last thirty plus years, wasn't completely off. He was glad he came to the village and had an opportunity to be honest with the one person he wanted to tell the truth to, but he needed a reset button to help him start his life with a clean emotional slate. That day in the woods, he was hoping, would serve the role of that button.

They spent most of the afternoon hiking and getting deeper into the woods. The forest in this area of the world was not a tourist spot like the lakes in the area, and there were only a few signs that showed the visitors the right paths to walk. People in the village told the father of the family where to find the campfire spots, and he was moving towards one of them, not far from the small fresh water stream moving down from the top of the mountain.

By the early evening, they were at the right place. The campfire site was big enough to fit in five to six families, but there was no one here. It seemed there would be just four of them here, which fit perfectly with the Person Who Always Carried Guilts' motivation for tonight.

Thomas right away went exploring the ground around the campfire to see if he could find anything unusual, either animal footprints or rare rocks or a human civilization object left behind by the previous campers. Arthur got quickly focused on the task of building a fire. He assessed the situation at the firepit inside of the large white stones creating a shape of a circle and asked his dad if they should bring more firewood. The Person Who Always Carried Guilt agreed with his son that they should. They left the boys' mom to watch over the younger one, and the two went into woods to bring more timber.

There were no bears in this area, or other animals dangerous to humans. The biggest threat to the family would probably be coming from a couple of different kinds of wild cats and coyotes, although none of them were supposed to attack the human kind. The man of the family felt comfortable enough to leave his wife and his youngest son by themselves for twenty minutes. When they came back with full arms of the firewood, they saw only a slightly different picture than the one they left behind less than a half hour ago. The boy was examining some rock the size of his palm that he found near the firepit, and his mother was putting sandwiches together for the family before they could get to the kids' fun foods like cookies and marshmallows.

After successfully building a fire and eating their simple but delicious dinner, the darkness has arrived, and it covered the camp site. The fire was the only source of light now, and the kids loved it.

"Daddy, can you tell us a story?" asked Thomas.

"Of course, Tommy. Do you want a cute one or a scary one?"

Here the boys disagreed on which story should be told. They ended up, as it often happened within family units, on a compromise. First the father would tell a "cute" one, and then proceed to the "scary" one. That seemed to make everyone equally satisfied. The "cute" story was one of the stories that the Person Who Always Carried Guilt had invented through his improvisation skills. Sometimes he would change certain events and characters in the same story and other times, he would invent a totally new story altogether.

Tonight, he took one of Tommy's favorite characters, an elephant, and put him together in a castle with a prince and told the kids how, throughout the years, they had built a close friendship. The prince was smart, funny, and was loved by most around him. The elephant was quite simple, he wasn't as smart as humans, and he didn't have many friends. The prince really liked the elephant, and they stayed loyal to each other throughout their lifetimes.

Until one day the prince got sick, and no one knew what was wrong with him. The elephant volunteered to leave the castle in search of a medicine for his friend, and he traveled many miles, through the woods and deserts, mountains and seas, to find a famous healer, who no one seemed to know in person, but the legends were traveling about his level of skill and his ability to treat anyone with any disease.

While the elephant was looking for a healer, he went through many obstacles, being cold and hungry, being chased by bad people, falling into a ditch and struggling to get out of it, but he persisted on his journey, finding a way within himself to stay strong. Till a day when he got sick as well. Moving forward was becoming almost impossible for the poor elephant who didn't care at all about being sick, he was just worried about not being able to help the young prince. When the elephant couldn't walk anymore, he laid down and eventually lost his consciousness on one of the hills of a green countryside with no one around him. But he was awakened by an old man who happened to find the elephant and who had been treating the mammal for the last twenty-four hours while he was passed out.

Very soon the elephant got better, and in a few more days, he completely recovered. He learned that the man who had found him on the hill was that same healer who he was looking for his whole journey, and he started to beg him to share the medicine for the prince. But to his complete shock, the healer refused to help.

"But why?" asked the elephant.

"I helped you because you were right in front of me. Also, because I know you are a good elephant who put himself through a lot of struggle to help his friend. Your prince is far, far away, and there are many people and animals I can help between here and there. Instead of helping him only, I can focus on others. And I also don't know if the prince is a good person or not."

The elephant wasn't sure how to argue with the healer. He felt that he was just an animal, and how could he possibly teach wisdom to the wise healer of the land? So, he didn't try. He hid in one of the tents of the small village and started to cry. He cried for a day and a half, practically non-stop. He didn't eat, he didn't sleep, and he didn't come out to see people in the village. But a day and a half later, he suddenly knew what was on his mind. He went back to the healer and told him:

"I know you are the wise and skillful healer, but who are you to judge others? You don't know who my friend is, but he has many good qualities. He didn't have to be friends with an elephant as he could pick anyone in his kingdom to be his friend, but he is a good friend to me, at all times, and he has been since the day we met."

He took a deep breath and continued:

"I also know that he is sometimes a bit spoiled and he doesn't treat everyone in his kingdom as well as he treats me, but everyone is capable in changing, growing, and improving. Everyone can learn not only a skill like riding a horse, and shooting a gun, but also life skill, like how to be a better friend, how to treat a stranger, how to offer a hand of help to someone, how to forgive and understand someone who made a mistake, how to love and how to make the most out of a second chance."

The Person Who Always Carried Guilt teared up while saying those last words of the elephant's speech. His own memory started to recall many moments that took place from the moment of tragedy in the snow mountains to the moment of the conversation with the daughter of the man who saved his life. He knew now that he did everything he could to make the most of the second chance given to him by a stranger.

"So, if you have the power to make a difference, you should not shy away from the responsibility to bring that difference to the world," continued his speech of the elephant. "If that feels right in your heart, then you should let me take the medicine to my friend, so I can save him like you have saved me!"

His words had touched the healer. He listened to it carefully and after the elephant was done speaking, the healer took his time to think it through what he just heard.

"You are right," his response was full of respect for the animal who taught him a new truth in his life. "Everyone is capable of changing. However, most are afraid to do so. Most see the changes only in a negative light, forgetting that without changes, they would die being the same person they were as a teenager. Reacting to negative events in life is easy, because they leave you no choice to do so. *Changing because one strives to be better is a gift that's given to everyone but wasted by most.*

He stopped talking for a moment and thought through his next decision.

"But I will give you the medicine. Because I am not in a place to judge anyone's life. And because you are an example of someone who can do better, and I hope the prince will learn that from you too. Please, don't be afraid to share with people what's on your mind. You are not just an elephant, and you are smarter than you think."

And the healer gave the medicine to the elephant. The animal left the village and walked many miles back to his castle, where his friend was getting worse and worse with each passing day. But the elephant made it back just in time to save his friend. The medicine did the miracle they hoped for, and the prince was fully healthy in just a few days. He was eternally grateful to the elephant for saving him. They became even better friends and they continued to teach each other how to be a better friend to the rest of the world too.

"The end," finished his story the Person Who Always Carried Guilt.

The kids loved the story, especially little Tommy. But also, his wife was deeply touched with the new twists of the old story. Her husband happened to tell that story before, but never with the exact plot as tonight. She understood, of course, some parallels with their own life, and her husband's journey, and she was grateful to the Very Tolerant Person for the understanding she showed to her husband and to the universe for giving the love of her life another chance for irrefutable peace in his heart.

They shared a few more stories over the campfire, and the kids told their own improvisations, which were both funny and adorable. They burned some delightful marshmallows and had a great time. At some point in that evening, while listening to Arthur trying to scare everyone with his coyote who happened to be a ghost as well, the Person Who Always Carried Guilt suddenly realized that this beautiful evening had given him exactly what he wanted and maybe even more. A lot more. As of this moment, he wasn't the Person Who Always Carried Guilt anymore. He just became the Forever Grateful Person. With that self-realization, he smiled at his kids, then turned his head to his gorgeous wife, and reached out to her face to give her, a warm and thankful for everything she ever brought to his life, kiss.

Adam was a man in his mid-forties. He was the kind of man who wouldn't impress you with his life accomplishments, or his extremely high level of intelligence, or great looks which could create havoc across the whole county, or anything else that common people usually bragged about. Deep down he knew all of that. He perceived himself accordingly to that description. No matter where he would go, he would be no more than one in a crowd, like the person next to him, or in front of him. The one place where he always felt different from the others was his second home, which is what the Sierra soup kitchen became for him.

He worked in different capacities for that kitchen for over seventeen years. First, he joined like most volunteers would, asking how he could contribute, and of course, ended up serving breakfast and dinner to the needy. What was distinctive about Adam comparing to the ninety-nine percent of the volunteers who would come through the doors of this gray building was his consistency. By the end of the second month, he saw about one fourth of the volunteers stayed the same, and all others have come and gone. By the end of month six, there was only three people who volunteered at the same time that he came in that were still there. By the time of his one-year anniversary of volunteering, he was the last man standing. New volunteers would show up and then disappear without a notice, wave after wave. He started to take on a bigger role and manage those volunteers. By year three, Adam was running all operations. The project almost died at some point from lack of funds, and Adam had brought in new donors and saved the place from going under. Since then, he felt like he belonged here and nowhere else.

Adam came in today to work at about his usual time, seven twenty in the morning. Breakfast was served at nine o'clock, and a cook would come at eight twenty. Adam liked to come one hour early to give himself time to check yesterday's mail, plan for both meals of the today, and think through any issues that may be going on in the kitchen. That was his hour of control when he felt the place needed him as much as he needed that place.

He took the mail from his desk in one of the corner offices across the locker rooms. He made this office his; he wanted to have a small corner which he could call his own. It was a bit of his ego dictating the order in this case, but it seemed fair to him since he did put seventeen years of his life into this project. He sincerely cared for the kitchen itself, its role in the community and every single homeless person who ever came here for food. He could name the majority of them by name, and sometimes even could name what month and year he saw them first, and how many times they have disappeared for a better, although temporary, life just to come back a few weeks later. He knew if anyone had allergies, although they rarely served anything that people usually had allergies to. He knew their life stories, and who those people thought about, who they missed and who they prayed for.

He also knew all the previous donors, and all the future ones he hoped to encourage, and he reached in his personal pocket not once, or twice, to save the day and ensure the kitchen was doing what it was meant to do. He paid himself a modest salary, but not big enough to move apartments. He lived in the same one-bedroom condo now as he did seventeen years ago. There was not much else he could do for the organization and for the community. He was just hoping that somehow this place would never die and continue to serve people in need. The better solution would be to not have any homeless left on the streets, but with the way capitalism worked so far, there was little hope for that. As long as there was a demand, he wanted to provide the supply.

He sat in the chair and started to shift from one piece of mail to another. One letter grabbed his attention. Most envelopes with the handwritten address of the kitchen and the addressee were from donors, which was a lot more pleasurable or him to open than any kind of bill or letter from the IRS.

On this letter, there was no return address at all. Adam opened the envelope and reached into it with his hand. He pulled out a check, – of course, as predicted. But the sum written on the check stunned him. He straightened his back in the chair and looked at the payee. The name was unfamiliar: Riccardo Ventura. But then he looked at the "written to" line, and the check made more sense now. The check was originally written to Granvill. He turned it around and saw Granvill's signature allowing a third party to deposit the check as well. Underneath of the signature was written, in small but clear letters, "Thank you, keep doing what you are doing". Adam choked up a little and turned the check around again. This was a significant amount of money that would provide him and the place some breathing space for a long time. The check was for exactly twenty-nine thousand dollars.

Granvill was at the airport of the big city, the place where he spent the most years of his life. He built his career here, he met his wife here, he made enough money in this city, and at some point, he was happy here. All the way until it was the time to change things around in his journey. And this kind of time had come again. He left Dima enough food, house supplies and money to ensure the boy would enjoy his alone time at the house till Granvill would come back. For Granvill, there was one more trip to make.

From the moment he left this city and traveled, and then settled in the village, he had one regret. And fate seemed to have something to say about it. Till now. Now, fate was on his side. At least, he had that kind of feeling. His regret was the fact that he wasn't a part of one person's life, the life of the human being who was carrying his gene, who was brought into this life by Paige, his wife at the time, twenty-six years ago. Just about eight years ago, his own daughter, Victoria, told Granvill she didn't want to see him again. Back then they lived in this city and had a – what most people call – successful life. He was a decent father when Victoria was a child, but a fallout started to happen when she was a teenager, and then an unrepairable disruption took place when she was a freshman in college.

Since then, he tried to reach her many times, he sent her birthday presents, Christmas cards, random letters but to no avail. Until now, Granvill thought that Victoria was just as stubborn as her mother, and there was nothing he could do to repair the relationship with either one of the women. In truth, she may have been even more stubborn than her mother. And that part probably hadn't changed. But now Granvill was different. Granvill was focused on something else instead of his daughter's flaw. She was *his daughter*, period. Even if she felt she didn't need him in her life, he was going to be close by, just in case she ever did. He figured if the tulips approach made such a big difference in his own life, and in the lives of many people in the village, there was no way it wouldn't work on his own flesh and blood.

Then he thought about his journey in the last few years. How much of it was his own doing, and what was the likeness of his actions leading him to this airport today? Could he not be here now if he had made some different decisions, or was he going to end up here no matter what he decided in the past eight years?

It seemed for a minute that no matter what he would have done, he would be *here*. It made Granvill feel smaller than a grain of sand in the universe, yet important enough for fate to care about the outcome of his life at the same time. He wasn't sure if any choices he had made lately were of his own creation, or was he fulfilling some kind of predetermined prophecy. It also could be a combination of both, maybe, choices he made on a smaller scale, but fate interfered when it came down to the important things, and it ensured he made the turn when it was needed. To be there when he needed it to be. *And he needed to be here*. Right now. He knew that much.

Granvill thought about how the universe could be so simple, yet impossible to understand. He wanted to choose his life and the way he was living, he left the city for that, he changed after the divorce and the fallout with his daughter. But maybe, the only thing he could really control was what kind of person to be in this world. The only thing that was up to him was how to react to all the turns on the way, both unpredictable and the ones he could see from a mile away. *And maybe, all he could do was wake up in the morning and do the best he could, one day at a time*, thought the old man.

There were many things in his head right now, not in a chaotic way, but a quite peaceful and tranquil mode where many thoughts were clear to him. Not because he had all the answers, quite the opposite. But because he was ok with not knowing them. He was ok with taking the next step while looking forward with a certain level of excitement. He was ok with his life changing again; he felt at peace with his place in this universe. He remembered the words spoken by the Person Who Painted While Moving Forward in Life. *Not knowing what our fate is somehow became the beauty of this world for me.*

Going through the airport security he was confident and optimistic. Before approaching the metal detector, he put his shoes, wallet and his watch into the plastic bin and pushed it toward the security scanner. Then he threw his duffle bag on the conveyor belt as well. It was that same tan leather color weekender duffle bag that he received as a Christmas present from the Person Who Smiled at Everybody, and it was ready to make the trip of a lifetime. Granvill pushed his things into the darkness of the scanned space and made a few steps toward the metal detector. Without hesitation, he was moving towards the unknown.

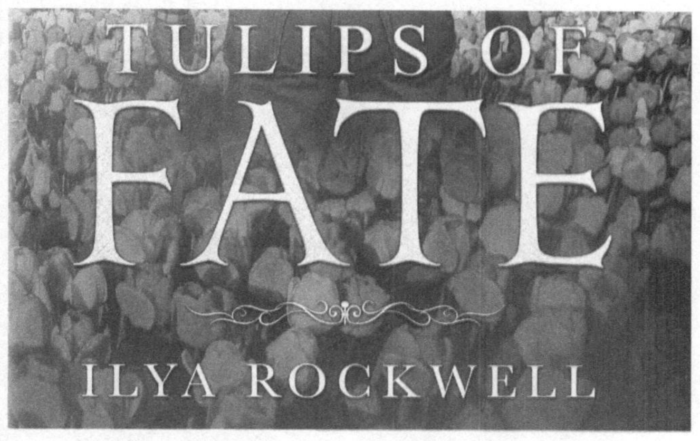

The next book in the "TULIPS OF FATE" series,
"TULIPS OF HOPE", is coming in 2020.

Please visit www.tulipsoffate.com for updates

ABOUT THE AUTHOR

Ilya Rockwell was born and raised in Ahtme, Estonia, a town known for its village-like simplicity and beautiful birch trees. He immigrated to the United States at the age of 21 to find a place to implement his vision. He now lives in Las Vegas, Nevada and gets a chance to try something new every day. He likes to spend his free time watching an inordinate amount of movies and forcing his 15-year-old daughter, Ilana, to listen to his philosophical life speeches. He uses his job as an author to help pass on what he's learned through his life to others.

Instagram @ilyarockwell

www.tulipsoffate.com